LOVELY MOVER

The Harpur & Iles Series

Bill James

LOVELY MOVER

W. W. Norton & Company
New York • London

First published 1998 by Macmillian Publishers Ltd.

Copyright © 1998 by Bill James

First American edition 1999
First published as a Norton paperback 2000

For information about permission to reproduce selections from this book,
write to Permissions, W. W. Norton & Company, Inc.,
500 Fifth Avenue, New York, NY 10110.

Manufacturing by Courier Westford

Library of Congress Cataloging-in-Publication Data

James, Bill, 1929–
      Lovely mover / Bill James. — 1st American ed.
        p. cm.
      ISBN 0-393-04763-6
      I. Title.
      PR6070.U23L6 1999b
      823'.914—dc21

                                        99-11489
                                         CIP

ISBN 0-393-32034-0 pbk.

W. W. Norton & Company, Inc., 500 Fifth Avenue, New York, N.Y. 10110
www.wwnorton.com

W. W. Norton & Company Ltd., 10 Coptic Street, London WC1A 1PU

1 2 3 4 5 6 7 8 9 0

1

The thought sickened him, of course, but he knew he had to kill Eleri ap Vaughan. Although this was an unusual name, he had been told there were plenty like it over in Wales and she would not stand out there at all. That is, her name would not stand out there. Eleri herself would stand out wherever she was. In many, many ways Eleri was a delight – old and thin-legged but a delight all the same, and probably the most skilled pusher of cocaine to the gentry in Britain. If other countries had gentry this flair would have brought her a world title, not just national. He, as wholesaler, supplied Eleri. And Eleri supplied this golden clientele which she, personally, by skill and charm and reliability, had assembled during quite a distinguished period of years, really. In Wales, 'Eleri' probably meant a clear mountain stream or a female peregrine falcon, something entirely lovely.

The site was a problem. Vine did not want to kill her at home. She lived in a flat block, a damn good flat block where soundproofing was sure to be up to the Institute of Bricks, Mortar and Pelmets' highest standard. But the noise of a shot at night would still travel. And it might take more than one, even close up. For God's sake, who would want a fine old lady like Eleri threshing about in throes? There was no such thing as a fully silenced handgun, and people had come to recognize that popping sound through watching so much crime drama on TV.

The trouble with Eleri was treachery – a hellish word, but Keith Vine could not come up with any other. There had been a perfect trade relationship, beautifully profitable to her as well as to Vine and his associates, and then he gets a whisper she is turning away and will take her consignments in future from elsewhere. The first time he heard this and confirmed it as true, he was really hurt. Immediately, he went around to Eleri's place and gave her a bit of a slapping. She had boyfriends off and on, which was part of her wonderful energy and cock-devotion, even so late in life, but none of them was actually living-in at the time and, really, none was so regular that they would come looking for who thumped her.

In any case, the slight battering he gave her was only that, slight, nothing over the top. There had been the noise difficulty to think about then, too. Someone falling or getting knocked against a wall would most likely be heard by neighbours, despite the sound insulation, even someone as lightweight as Eleri. Also, it would have been disgusting to hammer a woman of that age really badly, regardless of what she was doing. Eleri was over sixty, for God's sake, a pensioner. And it would not have made any sense to bang her into a condition where she could not go back to work soon. Wasn't this the whole point of visiting her? Vine had wanted Eleri to continue in her unique role of dealer aboard *The Eton Boating Song,* but dealing only with stuff supplied by him. God, he gave nobody bigger discounts than Eleri, as recognition of her undoubted flair and established list of superb, faithful customers.

For a while after that visit to her place, Eleri seemed to revert to decency and, as soon as she recovered and had some dental work, she went back to her spot in the bar of the *Eton* and resumed selling with at least all previous success, and, of course, using supplies from Keith. This floating restaurant and a big new disco-dance hall not far along the dockside were parts of the marina development. It thrilled Keith. Shipping had declined and the port district with it, but now the good aim was to transform all this decay into a cheery entertainment area. The *Eton*, with its brilliantly loaded and professional regulars, seemed designed especially for Eleri. Keith would call in for a drink now and then to see everything looked fine, and to have a chat with her during quiet spells. He was fond of Eleri, and not just because of the trade aspect.

And then he had a report that she had been making approaches again to outside elements. The stories said a possible London supplier this time. He saw that as damn grave. Vine had heard of something called the domino theory. It said that if one element in an organization went wrong it could bring down all the others, the way a model made with dominoes might collapse because of a single piece toppling. If he did nothing about Eleri, other dealers would drift away to the opposition, too – if the opposition looked as though its terms were better, or if the opposition could terrorize them. You had to get your own terrorism going. It was known as pre-empting, if you were lucky. There were rumour that one of the big London outfits had definitely sent a missionary down to feel out the place lately. Nobody had an identification for him, but apparently he was quite a dresser and of true all-round elegance. Metropolitan. Someone gave him the name Lovely Mover. He'd disappeared for the moment, but he would be back. Perhaps more than one. A trend. For a while now London outfits, Manchester outfits, Liverpool outfits had been looking for other selling grounds they could colonize, because things were getting crowded, hot, or both at home. Eleri was the kind of dealer they would all be trying to woo. One or two might have already. This had to be stopped.

Vine went down to the *Eton* again, just to give Eleri a chance. He would hate to be casual or oppressive. Keith's own girlfriend, Rebecca, would grow as old as this one day, God willing, and he would hate to think of her being ill-treated, never mind how unpresentable she might be by then. If Eleri told him someone had been trying to negotiate but she had turned it down he would be satisfied. That would be honesty, and he certainly did not want to kill a generally pleasant lady of sixty-odd who had come to appreciate late in life that deceit was intolerable.

'Eleri,' he said, 'here's a treat seeing you looking so settled and happy.'

'Yes, like that,' she replied. Eleri gave him a bit of a smile but it was formal. He did not blame her too much for this. She might be nervy if she had negotiations going. And, in any case, it was never going to be totally the same between them again after that punishment afternoon. He thought the teeth were extremely tidy.

'Business bright?' he asked.

'Can't go wrong, Keith.'

'Let's keep it like that,' he said.

'You're right.'

Oh, God, Eleri, confess, confess. Don't force me into it, old love.

'See any new faces?' he asked.

'Not really. Just long-term customers – or friends, I'd prefer to call them.'

'Exactly,' Vine said. *You're fucking dead, Eleri.* He thought he could see how and where to do it.

Apparently, the *Eton* was a one-time China clipper sailing vessel called *Imperial Majesty* in those more triumphant days – you saw a falling-away everywhere. Now, it had been converted to a restaurant and bar and given this new name, which contained a social class aspect, obviously, and a tone of merriment, which Keith was in favour of, if it was going to be a restaurant at all. The vessel was moored at a spot where marina development and the skeletons of old docks buildings lay alongside one another. The ruins would be properly demolished soon and replaced, but they could be handy for him now.

The *Eton* stayed open until 2 or 3 a.m., like real big city nightlife. Customers loved its maritime flavour, with flags of many nations flapping above, and portholes. People could come out on deck after their meal and lean on the rail gazing at the dockside, like a Caribbean cruise. This restaurant had quite a reputation – octopus, nearly raw veg, wine always free from bits of cork – the whole carry-on that would appeal to Eleri's kind of regulars. They could get a good feed and pick up some stuff for afterwards all at the same time. This was the sort of beautiful, honest, all-round money these folk possessed, and they had to be looked after. Eleri's client roll was so good it would be a kind of memorial to her, like the one in that famed film a few years ago, *Schindler's List*.

She had a certain table in a corner of the bar where she always sat with a rum and black in front of her, her sign she was trading – the way priests switched on the light outside a confessional box. The management kept that table for her – it did not matter how busy the place was – because Eleri was recognized as a distinguished feature, and she brought in so many eaters and quality drinkers. The thing was, some of her customers had actually been to that famed college, Eton, or said so, and would be wearing the special tie. They were brought up on that Boating Song, the way Keith was brought up on 'Tom, Tom, the Piper's Son', and 'Eskimo Nell'.

Sometimes Eleri would go home to her own place after work, sometimes to a man friend's. The men must be very understanding if they did not mind her turning up at 3 or 4 a.m. and climbing into bed, her breath full of rum and black. Vine had done a study of her ways. He did this for everyone he had regular business with. Dossiers could turn out crucial. Eleri came and went by taxi. There was a late-night rank on the dockside halfway between the *Eton* and Magenta, the new disco. Eleri would walk to the taxis when she finished.

That took her between what used to be a customs store and the Seamen's Union buildings in the old days. Both were boarded up and roofless now, sad sights, Keith thought, but some of the boarding had been ripped away by weather or vandals and he could wait for her there. He had come armed tonight. In the shoulder pouch which he had made himself he carried a .38 revolver. There was a silencer in his pocket, to be fitted just before. If he could get her into one of the buildings he would move the body afterwards – take her to another abandoned office or workshop on the docks. It would be an error to leave Eleri so close to the *Eton* after he had been seen talking to her there tonight. About these disposal details, he would have liked to consult Detective Chief Superintendent Colin Harpur, a cop paid plump retainers by Vine's firm. Col would know this sort of thing right through, although from the other side, obviously. But there was no time to get round to Harpur's house in Arthur Street. And if Vine telephoned at this hour there would probably be no answer because Harpur would be in bed with that girl student who half lived there since the terrible death of his wife, ears thigh-stopped.

Vine went down the *Eton*'s boarding ramp, walked over to the old customs building and found himself a fair niche in one of the doorways which had no door or boarding. He listened. Although these places were used now and then by winos and/or tarts, he heard no bottle clinks or snoring or gasps. Vine unbuttoned the holster but did not bring the gun out yet. With the silencer on it was too big for the holster or his pocket, and he did not want to hold it while he waited.

That would seem so damn threatening. He found it strange to be lurking here, waiting to finish someone, in what remained of a building that had been for years to do with law and order. Probably, if only you could discover them, this old construction would be the centre of many wonderful historic tales. Someone ought to write a book about a customs house.

At a little before 3 a.m. he saw Eleri coming, that very jaunty, businesslike walk, so terrific for sixty. When he visited her, he had not damaged her legs. He touched the open flap of the holster, then, as she passed, reached out and grabbed Eleri around the chin and mouth so she could not shout. He dragged her into the doorway. It was easy. He had known it would be, she was so light. Possibly the new teeth were still strange to her and she did not even bite him. 'I'm so fucking disappointed in you, Eleri,' he said, his mouth against her ear.

2

For the safety of police officers working undercover inside a criminal firm, a wide, wise set of rules had been evolved, and Harpur broke all of them. So, when now he came to feel he had been targeted, he also came to feel he deserved it. Any colleague would have told him the same. But none could, because none knew his situation. Above all, undercover officers were instructed to keep in secret, continual touch with somebody who could lay on rapid support if needed. This followed one or two bad tragedies. That is, one or two deaths. Harpur kept in touch with nobody. How could he? None of his superiors knew what he was doing. This included Assistant Chief Constable Desmond Iles, the superior who might have organized the fastest and most effective rescue. That is, of course, as long as it suited Iles at the time to rescue him.

When Harpur first thought he might be getting some attention, he was with his two daughters. People wanting to scare you occasionally did it like this: they were giving notice not just that you could be hit yourself, but that those dear to you were known, and could be hit, also. In one sense, it might be good news, meaning that no more than a fright and threats were intended. *Just do it our way and you and yours will not be hurt.*

But perhaps it was only a fluke that this nicely groomed

lad turned up when the children were present. Since the death of his wife, Colin Harpur was a one-parent family, and recognized a duty to spend what was jargonized as 'quality time' with his daughters. Obviously, this pretty well pissed them off, but it meant that anyone doing an approach on Harpur these days – even on Harpur only – was still liable to find him with the two girls.

Now, he discovered he had what might be a sweet, motherly urge to get himself between the children and this stranger, like a lioness or she-rat shielding the litter. Harpur resisted it. That kind of quick, minder-style shift would proclaim he knew what was happening here. Smarter to stay like unaware, at least for now. He glanced at the girls' faces to see whether they had spotted anything. His daughters were sharp. Although, naturally, they loathed having a cop in the family, they were also protective, and sensitive to perils near Harpur. They thought him dim and blasé about dangers. He was not, but allowed Hazel and Jill to believe it. This kept them alert and even caring, and provided two extra pairs of young eyes, two young twitching noses and some good, young antennae. But, apparently, they had seen nothing to upset them now. This watcher, this tail, might be beyond their range. He had the full gleam and hard jauntiness of elite London villainy, and the tailoring.

But it was the graceful economy of his movements that registered first with Harpur. He had seen a great cat burglar pace her remand cell like this. He had seen a congenital security-van raider lope from the dock like this and back to work, case dismissed on a technicality, another technicality.

This lad today emerged suddenly yet smoothly from between long, gently billowing, cream lace curtains. He stood there for half a second, not seeming to look at Harpur or the children, but looking at Harpur and the children, and then moved off left, letting one hand trail lightly down a curtain as he went. The sequence was brief though unhurried, and deeply beautiful. It would have thrilled many to tears. Had he only been a woman, the elegance of this scene might have put you in mind of a superior, soft-sell TV ad for one of the smarter face packs. Had he been a woman, though, he would not have on that lovely grey summer-weight suit, undoubtedly custom built, brilliantly loose cut and balanced, and yet still not quite brilliantly loose cut and balanced enough to hide the mild swell of a shoulder holster in its ideal nesting place, just above the left tit.

'How about this?' Hazel asked.

'Manic,' Jill said.

Harpur and the girls were in Debenham's curtain department, choosing what might match new decoration in their sitting room: there had been big changes since Megan's death. The tail had entered this end of the store through the lace display, which so gorgeously set him off – much better than any dossier mugshot ever would. A happy summer breeze from two half-open windows produced delightful, languid swirlings in the light draperies, and the material had seemed to reach out adoringly, as if yearning to embrace with love such a wondrous suit and its worthy wearer. Harpur, on the other hand, yearned to reach out and remove the weapon, then go through the pockets of the wondrous suit for ammunition, identity, and anything else. When you were unarmed yourself, as was, of course, ordained for British police out shopping with their daughters, you grew jumpy about shoulder holsters.

Hazel, holding up the same sample, said: 'I think this would chime with all the highlights marvellously.'

'Chime! Highlights! Oh, wow, but wow,' Jill replied.

'What do *you* think, Dad? All she does is knock, the little twit.'

Harpur could not see him any longer. Probably if he did return he would use one of the other, less dramatic ways into the department. There were two. He watched them, but did glance at the sample, too. 'Nice. Why do you hate it, Jill? Which one would you prefer?'

'Oh, she doesn't,' Hazel said. 'Nothing constructive. All she can do is criticize. So juvenile.'

3

Harpur could not give as much time as he would have wanted to thinking about this chic visiting gunman. In the evening he had a diaried meeting with what he must call for now his employer, and he did not mean the Police Authority.

Keith Vine said: 'Colin, I want you to come on a little trip with me to look at something ... well, something awkward ... yes awkward. Immediately. We can use your cop skills.'

Harpur said: 'Fine. Time I earned my honorarium.'

It was dark, but Harpur saw a frown imprint Vine's square, big-chinned face. 'Don't talk like that, Col. Just having you in the firm – the fall-back potential of it – is enough to justify the fees.'

'Thanks, Keith,' Harpur replied.

'Definitely. Wonderful to know you might – I say only *might* – I realize what the difficulties are for you, believe me, a serving Detective Chief Super – but you *might* be able to get the pressure off me – off the whole firm, in fact – as to prosecution, or during plea bargaining and so on, should anything ever go wrong. Which it won't, won't ever, don't fret – not as long as Keith Vine's in charge.'

'I'd always try to look after you, Keith.'

This was supposed to be merely a routine, secret business meeting between Vine and his bought detective, but Keith was obviously preoccupied by a sudden crisis. It might have clouded his mind: he spoke of leaving at once, but did not move. He and Harpur had rendezvoused at one of their agreed clandestine spots, the remains of a Second World War anti-aircraft gun emplacement, on a wooded hillside overlooking the town. Vine said: 'Col, what I would never do – and what's been built into this good trade arrangement from the very outset – is involve you in any part of our work where you might be recognized.'

'Thanks, Keith.'

'If that happened, the arrangement would be dead. Your loss, yes, but also the firm's loss, my personal loss. I can't afford it. But that's not going to happen with this specific task tonight.' He sighed. 'Tragic. Anyway, no possibility you'll be seen, let alone seen and recognized, Col.'

'Thanks, Keith.' Harpur would tell him about the lace-draped stalker in Debenham's shortly, but did not want to hinder Keith's flow or disturb him too soon, more than he was already disturbed.

'You're entitled to protection, Col. What I'd like is for you to come with me and just glance at ... well ... at a certain ... at a certain, well, call it *item*, and tell me if there are any mistakes, any give-aways, that's all. The object being total watertightness. As ever.'

'What sort of give-aways?'

'This is Eleri ap Vaughan,' Vine replied.

'I'm known to Eleri from way back, Keith. She *will* recognize me.'

For a moment, Vine did not answer, so Harpur kept quiet also. Then Vine muttered: 'Unavoidable.'

Harpur gazed down at what could be seen of the town. Troops manning the anti-aircraft battery in the early 1940s must have felt they had a whole population in their care. And often when Harpur looked out over the streets and lights from here these nights and days he, too, felt like that: and not much more effective than the guns were against invading Heinkels. Keith would see simply a fine drugs market below, if he could hang on to it. Difficult. There were modern invaders, too.

'Shall I tell you about her, Col?' Vine said. He shouted a bit. It seemed defensive, edgy. Maybe Keith worried he might have overdone things, whatever it was he *had* done to Eleri. Keith Vine did worry sometimes. 'Col, Eleri was an absolutely prime pusher with a very favoured franchise from this firm. Until lately.'

Again Harpur stayed mute, as mute as a funeral mute. Yes.

'Well, I don't have to tell you, Col – I mean, the stature of her habit clientele! People straight out of that Home Office pamphlet – you know the one—'

'*Drugs Misuse Declared.*'

'Oh, misuse, so judgemental. About the sale of stuff to the urban rich. That's Eleri's realm. And then . . .' He gave something between a sob and a snarl. 'Then she deserts me, Col.' He corrected hurriedly: 'I mean, deserts *us.*' Vine stopped talking, held up a hand and gazed left and right anxiously. Harpur listened and also stared about. He heard nothing out of the way, saw nothing. Vine was always jumpy at this meeting place. Perhaps they should drop it from their list, or use it only in winter when nothing grew: Keith Vine hated Nature at full gallop, and especially trees. He saw all this summer greenness as ungovernable, and stupidly indifferent to him. For someone only twenty-five, yet with brilliant crooked business achievements, this was hurtful. Tonight, when he yelled, his voice drifted over the dark oaks and conifers and scrub towards the spread of lights from roads and houses below. They were shrouded and faint and dully yellow, under a lingering film of heat haze from the day. 'Let's go, shall we?' he said. 'This rotten place.' They began to descend the hill towards the cars, Vine occasionally dredging good quantities of angry phlegm to spit at a tree trunk.

4

Eleri ap Vaughan lay pretty well concealed under a lean-to built by Vine against the wall with good-sized pieces of timber. She was in an ancient, now mostly roofless, long-abandoned die-cast works in the docks. The hutch reminded Harpur of a talking donkey's house in some Christopher Robin yarn his younger daughter used to read, before her mind hardened against such stuff at about six-and-a-half. Jill was on to the Orton *Diaries* and a book of boxing journalism now.

Harpur moved the wood, switched on his pencil-beam torch and looked. He thought one shot only, in the back of the head, a classic execution: ask the Nazis. The bullet had exited from just above Eleri's right ear, leaving her face undamaged, though forcing a flat, triangular piece of skull bone out and into view. Anyone who saw her would understand the message Vine wanted to give. Harpur understood it.

'She wasn't killed here?' Harpur said.

'How can you tell?' Vine replied, full of alarm. His words came in a screech, ricocheted off debris and seemed to hang jagged in the air for a second, up near the ruined bits of roof. 'What do you see?' It was as if he had been expecting such quick insights: the detective would glance at this body and know the complete story. It was why he wanted *his* detective to see her before the rest did. 'How can you tell?' he asked again.

'I can't. It was a question,' Harpur said.

'No, not here.'

'So you had to drive up close, then drag her from the car?'

'Yes.'

'Your own car?'

'Yes, but it was night. I wasn't seen, I swear. I could drive right into the building, through that collapsed wall. I put false plates on.'

'Have you searched her?' Harpur said. 'And searched her place?'

'For what?'

'We're taught to keep an open mind.'

'I thought—'

It started as a snarl. Perhaps Vine was going to say, *I thought an open hand.*

Then he drew back, though: 'Thought I'd better leave all the detailed work to you, Col. I might put more pointers down without knowing it.'

Harpur crouched and quickly took all Eleri's clothes off. Her old, very white skin almost gave a glow against the dark filth of the floor. Harpur went carefully through her garments. There was nothing. He turned her over.

'God, this is necessary, Col? Someone so old and bony.'

'She might have hidden that signed, prized Valentine you sent in her knickers. They'd get you for a *crime passionnel*.' He turned Eleri on to her back again, then began to re-dress her. She was in deepest rigor, and this meant difficulties. 'Was there a handbag?' He searched the ground nearby with his flashlight.

'Disposed of.'

'Where?'

'Disposed of. But anything here that could give me away, Col?'

Harpur put the light out. 'Nothing I've seen. It probably comes down to whether your car was spotted. Or whether it's spotted tonight.'

'This hour, nobody's about. Well, you can see.'

'Say maybe. I like the shack.'

'Well, she wasn't a bad old thing, regardless,' Vine replied. 'And I love simple, constructive manual work. Plus almost all handicraft. I made this holster.' He opened his jacket a little. Harpur put the torch on again and lit up Vine with it for a moment. He saw a canvas pouch which might have been fashioned from a holdall. He saw, too, the butt of what could be a Russian automatic: a flood of them around since the Wall went down. Plenty of shoulder holsters about, too. Vine was giving a sweet proof that he went armed. Harpur had better not turn into a full-out cop and try to arrest him for Eleri. 'Suits you, Keith,' he said.

He put the light off again. Vine paced a bit, skirting oil pools and debris and speaking with raw vivacity: 'You're bound to be upset about this, Col. I do see it. But I want you to understand what she did to me.' Again he corrected. 'To *us*. This is *our* firm she treated with such disregard, in fact, contempt. Col, she would have taken that brilliant list of customers with her and bought her supplies from someone else. A supplier from outside.' There was a pause. 'Possibly London.' He more or less howled this, and especially 'London'.

'I'd heard Eleri gave you a problem or two, but thought it was all sorted out,' Harpur said. 'Didn't you bring her back to cooperation and understanding?' Still crouched on the floor, he worked carefully to make Eleri's clothes look as if they were on her as they had been on her when she dressed for work. Iles might be scrutinizing this scene shortly, and Iles saw a lot. Vine had stopped strolling and stood on the other side of Eleri, watching Harpur. 'How about staining of the car when you brought her, Keith? You put her in the boot?'

'It's all right. I had good plastic sheeting. No leaks.'

'Burned since?'

'Of course.'

This was like a formal interrogation, except, of course, that Harpur was on his knees in grime getting Eleri's tights back on her stiff legs, and occasionally looking up towards Vine in the darkness. The questions were those Harpur might have put to a villain, so the answers could be read to a court. But this interrogation was aimed at keeping Vine out of court, for now, at any rate. 'You used that Russian automatic?' Harpur asked.

'No. Christ, do you think I'm some daft kid?'

'So where's the other gun?'

'It's gone.'

'Where?' Harpur asked.

'Gone.' Yes, like an interrogation: Vine must feel this, too, and kept calling up his right to silence, even with a partner. Now and then, seeing Keith's nerves and caginess, Harpur could become fond of him, almost, despite all the violence and greed. Another of the hazards in going undercover: you could get to like, half-like, the people you spied on, and shopping them then became tough. Tough, not impossible.

'Where did the gun you used come from?'

'Not traceable, don't worry.'

'Hired?'

'You don't need to worry, Col.'

'*You* should worry.'

'Why? They're not going to find the bullet to match to a gun, anyway. One reason I moved the body.'

Harpur buttoned Eleri's cerise blouse. 'You don't know what they'll find. Hired from Leyton Harbinger? That's one of the first calls they'll make.'

'Leyton doesn't talk.'

'Jesus, it *was* hired from him?'

'I didn't say that. I said he didn't talk.'

'Everybody talks, if there's enough pressure.'

'Well, go easy on him,' Vine replied in a deliberately slow, spelling-out tone. 'Exactly why you're hired, Col.'

'I might not be questioning him on my own.'

'Make sure you are. You're the boss. *Exactly why you're employed, Col.*' Vine was beginning to grow ratty. 'I don't think you see what a disaster it would have been if Eleri went to some other supplier. Probably the end of us.' He took another pause and then removed some edge from his voice. Instead, he expounded like a lecturer, patiently getting to grips with Harpur's ignorance. 'Her clients are beautifully prosperous. These are people who can finance a really robust habit, yet not let it batter the metabolism so bad it stops them working or makes them useless, meaning the salary dries up and hence purchasing power.' Vine bent forward to bring his mouth nearer to Harpur's ear. 'Col, ever hear about that jazzman, Charlie Parker? He's using stuff all his life, and, when he died at thirty-four, the doctor put his age at late fifties. I mention it only because Eleri's people are so different. These are surgeons, opticians, people who can't have shaky hands, but who still want a regular, quality sensation and are ready to pay for it – pay Eleri, because they trusted her for only the best stuff, mainly coke, naturally. These customers don't have to thieve to buy – thieve and get caught by your boys, and removed as purchasers for a term of years.'

Harpur had almost finished getting her clothes right. He would have liked to close her mouth and end the uncommunicative grin. Her false teeth looked new and pricey and assertive. But he could not move her jaw up.

Vine said: 'You thought difficulties had been resolved between us. So did I. Slackness on my part. Look, I considered we were giving her a fine deal – but, Christ, I *knew* we were.' He bellowed that, and his voice clanged about the bare building again. He bent and peered at Eleri. 'Isn't it finished, yet?'

'Clothes can tell a dangerous tale,' Harpur said.

Vine straightened. 'There were two or three of them like

Eleri, getting high-grade stuff from us – well, Col, we were letting them have it ten, fifteen per cent below what we asked from other street pushers – our profit margin right down. But, OK, not charity. Eleri brought us clients that, for example, Ralphy Ember and his lot would never even get near. Can you see Eleri's patrons happy with Ralphy or his crude crew, Foster and that spiel-king, Gerry Reid? Eleri had an entitlement from us and she was still a bargain.'

'My mother always used to say you get what you pay for.'

'There are all kinds of mothers. But it was more than just the customers. We had to have Eleri as well, on account of this reverence they gave her. Ember had nothing to touch that.'

Harpur stood and began to brush himself down. Vine helped. 'I'm grateful for what you've done tonight, Col.' He nodded three or four times. 'And then, suddenly, Col, I hear Eleri is thinking of operating for someone else, regardless.' He shook his head in sorrow and disbelief.

Harpur put the torch on once more and, moving away from Eleri, began to look very thoroughly around the floor. Vine walked with him, still talking: 'I was easy with her, Col. To do her serious injury would be the kind of loutishness Ember might have slipped into in the circumstances – or more likely he would have put Harry Foster on to it. Moderation. And it seemed to work, Col. But . . .' He left it at that.

They came back to the body. Harpur had found nothing

give-away in his search. He lit up some oil patches on the knees of his trousers with the torch.

'Just bill me for a new suit,' Vine said, 'and for fuck's sake get something smarter. You're a businessman.'

'I wasn't thinking of that. You'll have it on your shoes, now and when you brought her. If you've been walking it around your house and car—'

'Forensic?'

'Now and then a jury will still believe them,' Harpur replied.

'I'll get rid of the shoes,' Vine said.

'Both pairs, if you had others on first time. Burn. Likewise car mats. Have a good look about the house. Any black marks, get to work with petrol. Did you return the hire gun to Leyton or get rid of it?'

Vine said: 'All these points you're making, Col – this is why I wanted you to look, you see. Exactly why you're employed – I keep saying "employed", but I mean made a partner.'

'If you got rid of the gun, go and pay Leyton for it. I mean, not just the hire cost. Do a backdate purchase. Otherwise, he's liable to grow nasty and he can drop hints to us.'

'Us?'

'The other us. Police.'

'Leyton would never talk.'

'Leyton runs a business,' Harpur replied. 'Leyton thinks survival.'

They stood looking at Eleri and Vine bent down and brushed back some hair that had fallen on to her forehead.

'Listen, Col, I don't want you thinking I'm heartless. I know this is no place and no condition for an old lady. But it was not just another ordinary betrayal – not just going over, say, to Ember. This is at a graver level altogether. Vile. Something beyond what a beating could take care of.'

'Yes?'

'We should get out of here,' Vine replied. But just as at the gun emplacement he seemed transfixed by doubts and anxieties. 'I thought you would ditch me, too, tonight, you know, Col. Didn't believe you'd follow. Obviously, you guessed what we'd find here and I was afraid you'd decide you didn't want any more of Keith Vine if Keith Vine was someone who killed old ladies – even if the old lady was a foul disloyal bitch.'

'I came,' Harpur said.

They had arrived for their hillside meeting in separate cars. Then, Vine had led the way to dockland in his Escort. Now, he put a comradely hand very briefly on Harpur's arm. Vine was young and brassy and bright enough. He could do a boyish, impish smile to soften some of his more brutal moments, and he called one up, just visible in the darkness: 'I would have hated it if you'd let me down – fucked off when you were supposed to be behind me. I regard this with Eleri . . . I regard it not as a test, Col . . . I hate that word between equals. But I do see it as important.'

'I came,' Harpur said. Vine was telling him that if he had failed to help, the partnership would have died. And possibly worse than that. Oh, yes, worse. Vine talked comradeship – and thought and acted business tactics. He had a cop as colleague, wanted to trust him, but was nowhere near so stupid as to believe he could in full. Trust him half? Maybe. Harpur still needed to convince Keith. To date Harpur had nothing like enough on him and the rest to make a workable, safe case that would eliminate major drug trading in the city, for a while. This was the mission. With luck, there could be information on the side via Vine about Ralph Ember, too, and his little competing confederacy with Foster and Reid. The prospect was enough – was it, was it? – enough to justify staying quiet about a murder and a murderer temporarily.

'I do believe in you, Col – that you'll stick with me,' Vine said. He gave another grand, mate-to-mate smile. Psychopaths did fine smiles. Vine and Harpur began caringly to rebuild Eleri's little wooden mausoleum. It was clear Vine took pride in the work.

Harpur said: 'This is not a good spot, Keith. Surveyors and such are busy around here most days now.' Some time, all these buildings would be demolished in the jolly marina development when it spread this far, and when there were funds to replace them with something chic.

'As long as she's not found immediately, Col.'

Probably, he had it right, and Eleri would lie undiscovered for a day or two. There would be nobody to report her missing. Vine would certainly want her found eventually, though. How could her death issue a general warning otherwise?

Altogether, this was a subtle situation, one proving Vine capable of brilliantly calculated thought. The boy had a fine future, unless Harpur could fuck it up. Vine needed Eleri to be discovered, yes, but not before Harpur had checked that her corpse and where it lay gave no leads. And although Vine would like it widely and instructively known among pushers that he, Keith Vine, had punished her for disloyalty, he would not like this provably known to the police – except, of course, to Harpur, who was implicated police, tame police, probably.

The hut looked cosy again, and Eleri was hidden. Vine said: 'I had to bring her here. It wasn't like just beating her up. I could do that on her own property, because I knew she'd never fuss. How could she bleat to your lads? They'd want to know why she got slapped, and right off all her business is out on display. Well, the Drugs Squad know about her business, obviously, but not in an evidential way. If she once made a complaint they'd dig, and find the provable lot.'

'Shall we go, then?' Harpur asked. 'It's not clever to hang about.'

But Vine still seemed stuck. 'So, you accept this was inevitable, Col? I'm glad. Your opinion really does count for me. Listen, you won't know this.' His voice grew plump, the voice of leadership: 'I mean, the wider, strategic aspect – my responsibility, personally. I'd like to keep you informed, though, Col. What's happened is London crews eventually picked up a whiff of trafficking chances on offer here. It's wide open now, isn't it?'

Vine must be talking about the death a few months ago of Oliphant Kenward Knapp, a supreme dealer, whose glorious crack and coke empire had become suddenly available to anyone who could take it and hold it. That meant visitors. Iles had forecast this would happen. To stop it, and to prevent a dangerous vacuum, he had proposed that a couple of local big-time drug dealers should be tolerated. Let them keep control of the scene. They would be manageable. People from London or Manchester might not be. Yardies certainly would not be. But the Chief in his purist way had turned down this plan – *I will not connive at dealing from any quarter, Desmond* – and, in any case, no home-patch firms seemed strong enough to achieve Kenward's kind of dominance and peace.

Harpur said: 'Yes, I thought London might be trying for a spot.'

Vine was startled. He had begun to walk towards the collapsed wall which was now the way in and out. He stopped and turned. His voice had sharpened, weakened. '*Why* did you think it? How could you know that, Col? Jesus, you're telling me your drugs people have spotted this so soon? These London sods only started poking around a couple of weeks ago. Your boys and girls are on to it?'

'No. I saw it myself – smelt the metropolis.'

'You *what*? You *saw* it? Saw what? Where?'

'Debenham's.'

'What's that mean? Stop fucking about, Col. This is—'

'And Eleri had fixed to go over to one of them for whole-sale supplies?' Harpur asked.

'How do you mean, you saw it?'

'A tail.'

Vine put that grip on Harpur's arm again, but this time

not in a try at friendliness but from terror. 'The London crew have you marked?'

'How it seemed.'

In a brief spell of moonlight through what had been a window, Harpur now saw quivers of confusion touch Vine's blunt face. Then he grew reflective. 'Yes, they wanted Eleri and she was ready to go. A plum. How could I allow this, Col – London people, strong, vicious? If Eleri went – someone with such glossy prestige in the trade – how many others follow? You see what I mean – why it had to be made plain through her?' He pointed towards her corpse and gave a respectful nod. 'Cautionary.' Then Vine glanced about urgently, as he had up the hill. 'And they've got you noted? Jesus, this is hazard.'

'Nobody with me tonight,' Harpur said.

'You can't be sure.'

'No. But I was careful.' Harpur himself took a long look around. And he had studied his driving mirror all night.

Vine said: 'Bloody smart London bastards. Of course, they'd want to knock you over first. A working senior cop. They'd spot you as my firm's top strength . . . well, one of.'

'Thanks, Keith.'

'They'd see you as a real danger. So, you're carrying something?'

'Perhaps I will.'

'I'll provide.'

'No. I'll do it.'

'How? You can't draw a police weapon. What explanation would you give?'

'This will be from elsewhere.'

'What elsewhere?'

'Elsewhere.'

'Let me get it for you, Col. Frankly, Keith Vine would be proud to.'

'I'll deal with it. All the armourers you use are on file, Keith. Especially Leyton.'

They walked together and paused at the exit. Vine said: 'Jesus, London people at work already. They might look for me as well.'

'Of course,' Harpur said.

'As a principal.'

'Of course. Now tell me, Keith, is that Russian job from Harbinger?'

Once more Vine became defensive. 'Leyton can be slack, yes, but this is brand new. Never been fired, not even by me – no tracing. But *you* – you must get equipped, Col. To be frank, I consider you an investment and liable to damage – but also a good friend, I trust.' He played with this phrase. 'Yes, a good friend that I trust.'

They had parked at a distance from the works and at a distance from each other. Harpur said: 'Do all the cleaning and incendiarizing we spoke of, Keith.' He turned away and made for his car, walking fast. Of course, Vine was right to have feared Harpur might not stay with him tonight – might have dodged out of visiting Eleri. There were dark hazards. One day, Harpur would probably have to tell a court what he knew about Keith Vine's business. And then the customary danger: a defence lawyer would wonder repeatedly and in the jury's hearing whether Harpur had been in it for himself, and only turned true cop again because of some unexpected twist – say, a dispute with other partners over money, or a woman, or both, the standard troubles. Two hellish hazards dogged all undercover work. First – and worst – the gang you've infiltrated might find out and finish you. Second, close behind, was this chill likelihood that a smart QC could upend the prosecution so that suddenly all the shit was hitting *you*, not the accused. Juries and judges did not understand these operations, though they thought they did: that was the peril. They loathed grey areas – hated police acting all-out crooked in order to be accepted as all-out crooked by crooks – in order finally to act all-out right. It enraged and sickened them to hear a detective had been living far above his salary, and, to look convincing to Vine, Harpur did. If the defence could make an undercover officer appear self-interested and not much else, his/her evidence was trash. And, if it could also be shown that Harpur was somehow implicated in a drugs war killing, all the jury's traditional, in-built wish to believe the worst of police would shove the case against Vine's firm into the bin. Harpur's future would go with it, naturally. His freedom might not be assured, either. You could find yourself locked up for ever with vengeful people you had helped lock up for ever. Of course, when it came to the reveal-all moment Harpur would have to reveal all he knew about the murder of Eleri. He liked to think – was entitled to think, wasn't he? – liked to think he was only a *temporary* accessory after the fact. He intended to tell what he knew, when the undercover job finished. But wasn't some belligerent lawyer likely to say then that Harpur had only chosen to disclose – to disclose so late in the course of things – because of fear he might be accused as a partner in the death?

Harpur saw Vine realized all this. He had genuinely wanted Harpur's help tonight but this was not the whole scheme. Suck the cop further in. Keith Vine meant to ensure his investment and trusty friend could never risk going fink. These boys had learned how to enmesh people, get them tarnished. These boys had come to realize the courts were very playable. All they needed to do was read the Press and watch TV to discover that. On the drive to dockland Harpur had wondered, and wondered more, about the wisdom of what he was doing. As usual, he was unarmed. Even before he saw the holstered Russian automatic he had known Vine would be tooled up. Par for the Keith Vine course. Was it intelligent to follow him into such a remote and deserted spot at night? This was someone who would be showing him evidence of a murder he had done. That had been clear almost as soon as Vine spoke of Eleri ap Vaughan up the hill. Might he have second thoughts – begin to doubt that even this bought cop would, could, keep his mouth shut about such a killing? Harpur had asked himself as they drove to Eleri whether it was *necessary* to go with him. It certainly was not *intelligent* to go. But he had decided, yes, it *was* necessary. And it looked as if he had come out of it intact: was almost at his old banger and away. The short-term threats were over. He had only all the rest of them to disturb him now. Before unlocking the car, he turned and glanced back. Vine was still standing at the gap in the shattered wall, watching him. Harpur did not wave and neither did Vine. Weren't they strangers?

5

So, Harpur would be off to that scruffy place of his in Arthur
Street where the two children were probably asleep by now,
and where Harpur's young bird, Denise, might be waiting to
offer a bit more nice comfort in his widowhood. Vine could
not return home himself yet. He had responsibilities. This
was it – the thing about running a good company – demands
came non-stop and you could never relax. Keith did not
mind. Balls to did not mind! He loved it – loved responsibility, pressure – thrived on stress, needed it. He'd heard
Margaret Thatcher was like this. Some grew sick from stress,
but not Keith – because stress was what he was born to
handle. Although he felt sure Becky, his live-in partner, knew
she had been lucky to meet him, sometimes he wondered
if she knew *how* lucky. But this was not a point to keep on
at her about, it would be arrogant, and he hated anything
like that.

Vine watched Harpur turn his car and drive off. Then he
went back into the die-works for his last look at where Eleri
lay – just a second check that nothing of her was visible.
Thoroughness was another requirement in his position. It
was right that Harpur should have gone first. What it was,
was – if there *was* extra risk to be faced by staying longer
with Eleri, he, Keith Vine, had to be who faced it – another
way obligations should be accepted by the one in charge,

34

and gladly. There was quite a well-known phrase for this, *noblesse oblige*, meaning when Supremo you did have these obligations.

But, also, he had not wanted Harpur left alone with Eleri, obviously. Harpur was great, and probably well purchased by now, but Harpur was cop still, too. Look at the eyes and listen to that questioning – oh, sure, supposed to be to help Vine get no trouble, but information lasted a long time and could be used for all sorts. And then again, if Harpur had been left by himself here he could have taken something from the body which might come in useful for him one day. For instance, Eleri had a couple of decent rings on, distinctive, even valuable – probably real sapphires in one – which Keith would never have stolen – but Harpur might take them off and next time he was in Keith Vine's car, so easy to hide them there, jammed down behind the seat. Consequently, if the big court case came some time, a nice little inspired search of the vehicle would occur, and Keith Vine was then beautifully tied to dead Eleri, and a lot of the background would be in Harpur's notebook. Vine had to trust Harpur – of course he had to trust him – he *did* trust him – didn't Keith Vine on his own say-so bring him into the business, partner status? – yes, certainly trust him, but not trust him to crazy lengths, such as fully, for God's sake.

Even inside with her, Vine could hear that vehicle of Harpur's coughing its way slowly out of dockland for what must have been nearly five minutes. The car was an Ital, one of those ancient near-wrecks from his headquarters pool that Harpur thought made him look unpolice – like all would mistake this thug-hulk driving for a nun, off to give midnight succour. Through its wooden protective cover, Vine said goodbye to the body and prepared to leave. 'I know you'd see the thinking behind this action, Eleri. There has to be order or where are we?' He considered it disgusting the way Harpur took her clothes off, a really ageing lady. Previously ageing.

Vine drove to the other side of the docks and the *Eton*. Keith did not sit down at Eleri's place, because of the fuss from management sure to come if it looked like he had taken this seat from ignorance. He could not tell them he knew she would not be along tonight – in fact eternally. But he waited in the bar nearby, drinking a rum and black, and watched to see if people showed who looked like clients. You could always tell – the cheerful little smile and shortage of breath. These joyful symptoms came from a fraction of the high they got just by imagining the *total* high they would be into shortly. Customer-contact was not something he usually handled personally, but with an emergency you adapted. He had five wrapped grams with him, all good stuff – well, obviously, the kind of stuff Eleri would have had from him to retail. These people, the punters, would not know he was the wholesaler, of course, and would not recognize him, so they would probably want some quality testing – especially the Eton College people, believing the whole universe meant to screw them, due to their privileges and noise. This had been the wonderful asset Eleri brought – confidence all round, the two-timing old doll, and it had to be admitted she was in the best place for her now.

Well, a lad comes in in due course who is definitely not Eton, and probably not a user, but obviously looking for Eleri, really circling that table – a fine mover, maybe ballet-trained or burgling. And such a suit – grey lightweight, even silk, and cut with a real sense of what the human body could say, but still a bit close around the left shoulder and – if you could read a message – signalling better than Morse code he had a heavy piece of mischief hammocked. Of course, all of this – the swagger, the suit, the gun – could still have been Eton, very much so, but the face badly lacked that golden-road, know-all, prime-grade-beef look, and the voice, when he came over to Vine and spoke, was totally non-old-money or masterful, most probably London East End.

'You local, mate?'

'In a way,' Vine replied.

'That rum and black?'

'Well, yes.'

He went to the bar and bought himself vodka, and Vine another rum and black. 'I've got a friend who always drinks rum and black,' he said.

'Thanks,' Vine replied. 'Here's to you, then.'

'I thought this friend might be here tonight.'

'This place – a lot of change and change-about,' Vine said. 'Some rum and black, some you name it.'

'You local?'

'As I said, in a way.'

'This table – usually, she sat at this table.' He pointed.

'Who?' Vine said.

'This friend.'

'This friend is a woman?'

'The one who drinks rum and black. If you're local, maybe you've seen her here.'

'Rum and black?' Vine replied. 'It's one of those drinks – men *and* women go for it these days. I've known many.'

'She could be helpful.'

'I like women like that,' Vine said.

'Do you know the one I mean?'

'I think I've seen a woman sitting there some nights. Not young, but they can't all be or where's motherhood?'

'This one of her nights?' he asked.

'When you say helpful?' Vine replied.

'If you were short of something.'

'She might be in later,' Vine replied.

'You pissing me about, cunt?' he said. 'I mean, you drinking rum and black – her sign. You here instead of her? I mean, if something's happened to her.'

'What?' Vine said. 'You local?'

'I had a look in the restaurant.'

'Does she go in there?' Vine asked. 'Likes her grub?'

'Full. The restaurant full of great big eager nostrils. This kind of night – she would be here. She's missing business.'

'What? You've got some business to talk? Look, I could let her know, if I see her. Bit of a gourmet, is she? Likes a platter? That's the least I can do for you, inform her, after you supplied the rum and black and having travelled. Just you wanted to buy something from her? Or is it to make some offer?'

'What offer? Who said any offer?'

'I see her sometimes getting offers,' Vine replied. 'Well, it could be – could be – I'm guessing – could be wholesalers wanting to supply her with some product. Wanting to be her only supplier. She has popularity. She gets bids. From what are known as syndicates, as I understand it. I've overheard such offers. You here with a bid? You're not local, are you? I'd say the metropolis – real scope about you. Wonderful.'

'You know her?'

Vine said: 'I see her at that table now and then. When I come in.'

'You pissing me about? You're in touch with her, are you? Her assistant, on nights off?'

'If I bumped into her, I could say an offer,' Vine replied. 'Where does she reach you?'

'Did she send you?' he asked. 'She knows I'm around and keeps clear? Are you her agent, handle her deals? That's all right. I've heard of protocol.'

'You're not local, are you?' Vine said.

'What? Did I ought to know who you are? The only one I know is some big cop with kids. He's into things, as I hear it.'

'Which one is that?'

'You pissing me about? You in the trade?'

'Me? I just drop in for a drink once in a while,' Vine replied. 'But if she wanted to get in touch. How?'

'You mean everything's got to go through you? Christ, this town.' He moved away. 'Look out for me,' he said.

Vine stayed on, and after a while a few customers came in and dealt. They all took the rum and black message. There was no trouble. He explained that Eleri had been called away, but promised them this was the same stuff she would have brought, and none argued or wanted to analyse. That was the kind of lovely reputation she had – all you needed was mention her name and people trusted you – like a new ambassador arriving abroad with a letter of introduction from the Foreign Secretary. And especially they'd trust you if they were desperate for a ration, and had friends to impress with the package. Even that London visitor – oh, definitely Lovely Mover – even Lovely Mover and his London associates had heard of Eleri and wanted to enrol her. It had been such a bright thought to make her unavailable. Next job was to find someone who would come in in her place – run this list and cherish it. He did not mind some personal business with clients once in a while, but only once in a while. It was a poor use of his time. He had other, heavier work to look after.

Tonight, he sold cheap – to keep these folk content and get them to tell their friends. You had to or someone would definitely sniff the absence and try to get in here, they would love it. Doing the deals, he murmured that Eleri could be away a while and to watch for a new rum and black presence at the table – but quality guaranteed, very much so. These customers seemed happy. Keith Vine thought that if he wanted to turn pusher himself, he would be fine – he had the friendly talk and a manner the public could believe in. That was little folks' work, though – even with Eleri's clients. Anyway, it was natural these bloody customers looked completely content – weren't they getting coke at

Lovely Mover

£40 a gram tonight, a charming discount as memorial to Eleri? No time ago, good coke – which was what this was – no big mix-in of glucose or baby powder – no time ago this would be £80 the gram. It was glutting a bit now because of industrial improvements in Colombia, but £40 was still a snip.

6

Harpur was back with Eleri three days later. Marina planners, down to look at the site for new developments, had found her and reported it. The Chief and Iles arrived soon after Harpur, ahead of the Scene of Crime crew. A uniformed woman constable stood guard. It was day, and plenty of light entered through the ex-windows and what had been the roof. Inside, the old works had a sunny, desolate dignity now, and seemed more suitable. Iles bent low and stuck his head into the little hut, and the other two crouched with him. 'Oh, Eleri, Eleri,' the Assistant Chief murmured, 'this is no way to finish a fine, dirty career, love. What's the place going to be without you?'

'You knew her?' the Chief asked.

'You'd have adored Eleri, sir,' Iles replied. 'Even if not actually buying for a habit – which goes without saying, of course – you'd still have recognized grace, quality, and fervour. Wouldn't you agree, Col?'

The ACC liked replies to his questions. Harpur said: 'Our drugs people were never able to get ap Vaughan when actually trading or with stuff on her or in her house.'

Still with his head in the hut, Iles said back over his shoulder to Mark Lane: 'That might seem no fucking answer at all, sir, to what I asked, and yet in a devious way it is, and, obviously, one is never going to get anything direct from Harpur. What he's saying, Chief, is Eleri was such a splendid lady that nobody could bear the idea of planting commodity on her for a conviction, although her pushing was famous and, on the face of it, she was ripe for noble-cause framing. Some sod's had all her clothes off and then put them back. She'd have enjoyed the first part when alive, supposing a bloke with gentle fingers. This was a woman who began her working days as egg grader with a packing firm, but quietly fought her way to eminence, Chief, entirely self-made like Marks and Spencer.'

Lane edged his head into the hut alongside the ACC's. The Chief was in uniform today for some function later, but without his cap. 'She was stripped? Why?'

'This would be after death, I should think,' Iles said. 'Nothing sexual. Body search. Someone very thorough, and almost clever enough to get the clothes back on right. What do you say, Col?'

Harpur had straightened up and their voices reached him muffled through the rotten wood of the lean-to. 'I can't believe she was trading in this kind of setting,' he replied towards the timber. 'Not right for her or her clients.'

Lane stood and looked about the wreckage of the place, then back at the hut. He did not say anything, but Harpur knew the Chief would be in agonizing touch with symbolism now. A murdered, old, balding, villain-woman in this aban-doned place would scream to him of the decay he saw everywhere. This dump was civilization on the slide. And he would blame himself for being unable to stop it. The obligations of leadership tortured Lane. It was when he felt a crime might have such big overtones that he insisted on visiting the site himself. These days, at his rank, he dealt very much in overtones, heavy metaphor and trends. There had been a time when he was a fine nose-to-the-ground detective on the neighbouring patch, and Harpur had sometimes worked with him then, and seen his worth. Promotion into the realm of large thoughts had half destroyed him. Iles might destroy the other half, given the time: say a year or two. One.

The ACC straightened and lifted away a couple of beams at each end of the hut, putting her head and feet on view. 'These teeth,' Iles stated. 'Probably she's been doing pretty well, but, even so.'

'What, Desmond?' Lane asked.

'They look like exceptional profits to me. Possibly she was allowed big discounts. I don't recall these teeth last time she gave me one of her lovely smiles in the street, so Celtic and disarming. This could be very lately, sir. How do you see it, Col?'

Harpur said: 'I know a lot of people in the trade were telling her to retire. She should have enough put by.'

Iles gazed at Eleri's smart cream flat-heeled shoes. He himself was in red wellington boots and a brilliant, lightweight navy suit. He had managed to keep oil off the trousers while crouched near her. He said: 'Well she could have taken a corrective thump in the mouth awhile previously and had some rebuilding. These people live with constant business pressures. What I'd say we see here, sir, is a grand girl who had begun to think very constructively about when she would give up work, and who started looking around for better terms in the final months, to make herself really secure. Understandably, she wished to capitalize on a wonderful, lifelong business reputation. Of course, whoever she had been dealing with up to now would fight against losing her. So, repercussions. Then the compensation and dentistry, and finally this, when she persisted in her ambitions. Is that how you'd see it, Col?'

'I—'

'Oh, such a sweet, wholesome operator, and all that jolly Welshery in her name,' Iles sobbed. He went to the other end of the hut where her head was and, bending low again, kissed Eleri twice on the forehead. 'Goodbye, darling. Tell the Judgement Seat you never sold a wonky gram, and feel free to mention my name. Oh, I hate to visualize some bastard getting her decent garments off when dead here, don't you, Chief? I think of her vest dragged up over that patchy grey hair. So insolent.'

'Perhaps you should replace the timber, for the Scene of Crime photographer, Desmond,' Lane said.

'As a matter of fact, "ap" means child of,' Iles replied. 'In Welsh. She's a child of someone, sir. It's a reminder that any of us might produce a gifted career pusher who could nevertheless get laid bare as a corpse in her maturity. We all have daughters.'

'Shoes,' Lane said.

Iles went ostentatiously silent, gazing rapt at the Chief as at an oracle or barometer.

'Her shoes are oil-free,' the Chief said.

'Ah,' Iles replied. 'Ah!'

'Yet this floor – oil covered.'

'Ah,' Iles replied.

'She has not been walking about in here. She was brought, perhaps carried from a car. Killed elsewhere,' Lane said.

Iles crouched again and stared at Eleri's shoes. He shook his head slowly for a while over them, in wonderment at Lane's acuteness. This kind of act he often put on when the Chief offered detection. 'Unquestionably oilless,' he declared. 'Would you could always make these sorties to the sharp end, sir, and set us right. Harpur, think shoes.'

'Rigor's completely gone, so she's probably been there at least forty-eight hours,' Harpur replied.

Iles straightened again. 'Meant to deter,' he said. 'There's been non-stop jostling among our pushers since Kenward Knapp went, leaving a fine inviting field. We've watched it for months, haven't we, sir? Now some foul big-city elements could be finally moving in, and trying to buy up native talent. Eleri's death will have been locally organized and is meant to warn others in the trade not to join the outsiders.'

The Chief struck ferociously with both fists in turn at the air. 'My God, alien gangs?' he cried, and his words bounced and cavorted as Vine's had in here. 'This must not be, Desmond. I will not have it.'

'Well, I share your horror, sir,' Iles said. 'We were spoiled by that grand stability under Kenward. But then Keithy and Beau Derek came to seem very acceptable successors. Some basic nastiness, naturally, but nothing preposterous. Same

with darling Ralphy and his two, Foster and Reid. Or Mansel.
All of them more or less bearable, more or less reasonable.
But now – well, yes, invaders. Unknowns. Savages. They'd
woo Eleri, of course. A prize,' Iles replied. 'Smell London,
Col?'

'It's remote here,' Harpur replied, 'and I'd imagine the
body was brought at night. We probably won't get any
witness sightings of the vehicle.'

Lane left them, picking his way slowly over the rubble
towards the collapsed wall and wharf. Iles murmured con-
siderately: 'He wants escape, Col, the dear suzerain. Our
Chief will gaze at the sea and think of God who made it on
the right day. He'll gaze at ships and know the captain's
on the bridge. Anything to tell him there's still order, a
system. Eleri murdered tells him the fucking opposite,
breathes new spirit into all his dreads. You and I don't need
a corpse to prove chaos has come again, but Lane still nurses
the unconquerable hope. You got her clothes off and back
on? I don't mean today. You'd be in a mess. But some previous visit, Col?'

'Right,' Harpur replied.

Now and then, this kind of thing did happen to Harpur:
he would suddenly decide it was wrong to hide matters from
Iles. Harpur could never tell when he might be struck like
this, nor why. Perhaps it was the shared sorrow at seeing
someone as old and local and venerably crooked as Eleri
stretched out, broken, on this historic floor between them.
Sad affection for her bound them, and it would have seemed
cheap now to go on fooling the ACC. Occasionally moments

would come when Harpur felt he was not complete without Iles. They needed a sound alliance, to carry not just their own work but most of Mark Lane's, too. At these times, Harpur would grow sick about blanketing out the ACC, say like answering his questions without answering them – as Iles had just mentioned. It went beyond normal police stealth, and probably even beyond what Iles deserved. Of course, the Assistant Chief did have monstrously evil aspects, or he would not be in his job; but these were only rarely exercised against Harpur, and in a police force this must rate as virtual friendship.

'When were you here before?' Iles asked.

'Three nights ago.'

'You wanted to see if she was carrying something? What?'

'Anything,' Harpur replied.

'Do you mean anything that might incriminate someone?'

'I'm working with one of the firms,' Harpur replied. 'Inside.'

'Well, yes, obviously, Col, I knew that.'

Harpur stepped towards him, accidentally knocking one of the hut timbers down on to Eleri. He had put his fists up, as the Chief had just now, but Harpur's had been aimed at Iles. Now, horrified, he bent quickly to lift the baulk off Eleri's throat. Crouched, he yelled at the ACC: 'You fucking liar, Iles. You can never admit ignorance of something, can you?'

'I've thought all along it was a wise move, Col,' the ACC replied. 'You'll be on the spot to see the whole impact of the London incursion.' He stuck out a thumb towards Eleri. 'This was Keithy Vine, was it? That's the outfit you're with? Not Ralphy. Ralphy would spot any deceit you tried. There's a foolish, tender side to Vine. He'd do Eleri as painlessly as possible, despite that earlier thing with the teeth. You'll want to let your operation run and grow for a while yet, without arrests or other crudity, and I'm sure you're right. You'll be safe enough from him and his, don't you think? Oh, yes. Is Keith Vine going to kill you, for Heaven's sake, no matter what he might suspect about your ultimate intentions? Keith Vine kill Colin Harpur? He lacks the class.'

'Thank you, sir.'

'And then these London people: they also might want to knock you over. I mean, if they think you're helping one of the syndicates. But how *could* they know?'

'Quite, sir.'

'Oh, they do, do they? You've noticed someone?'

The Chief returned, looking no better. 'Desmond,' he said, 'have you thought how this body was found?'

'Marina pricks in their yellow helmets.'

'Yes, the marina. What does this say to you?'

Iles said: 'I—'

'It says the future,' Lane declared. 'The bright, hopeful, constructive future, yet it's already tainted by sordid tragedy, don't you see? My God! I watch people outside going happily about their usual lives on what will be the marina – shops, houses, offices – but I know that, nearby, within these miserable walls lies a sign, another sign, that we have lost.'

'Lost what, sir?' Iles asked.

'Control. I look at those folk and wonder, *Can I guard*

them, can I guarantee the quiet enjoyment of their lives hence-forward? Oh, but when I say "I" I clearly mean not merely I but I, you, Harpur, indeed the whole of the Force. One simply represents the general body.'

'Harpur and I are tickled to be incorporated in yourself, sir.'

7

Naturally, Ralph Ember had to see his partners pretty often about the business, but he did not like them coming to the club for meetings. It was too obvious, like a conspiracy, that grim word. Foster and Reid were members of The Monty, of course, and entitled to drift in and out when they wished. Ember did not mind that – something casual. But planned get-togethers around a table with him were not on. He had made that clear. Probably the Ember–Foster–Reid syndicate was unofficially known about, but just the same he did not want things placarded, did he?

Now and then those two bullying cops, Iles and Harpur, looked in here, no warning: supposed to be a licensing check. An assistant chief and detective chief superintendent doing such a chicken-feed job? They were nosing and terror-izing, that was all, and collecting free drinks. It would be such a mistake to get caught by those two in heavy talks with Harry and Reid. Ember wanted to think he was gradu-ally guiding The Monty back towards the noble reputation of decades ago when it was a club favoured by genuine professional people – solicitors, chartered accountants, company directors, dentists. He had kept a lot of the mahogany and brass fittings for the sake of that atmosphere, and trade talks with such a pair as Harry and Reid could never seem right. God, that brushed-back, piled-up Kray brothers hairstyle Foster had.

When they came in tonight he could see they were after a business conversation. It enraged him sometimes, the way they would ignore his orders. They had Deloraine with them now, though, which perhaps they thought gave the visit some cover, making it seem just a night out. So he did not show rage. Always he had fancied the look and odour of Deloraine. Usually she made quite a fuss of Ember, referring often to his famed resemblance to Charlton Heston – when Chuck was younger, of course. Now and then Foster turned ratty about this special friendliness, but Ralph was used to seeing men worried at the way their girls went for him, and he always stayed reserved. She certainly made their visits to the club more pleasant. He knew a savage yokel like Harry Foster could never do enough for her.

Ember put Kressmann Armagnac on the bar in a good welcoming gesture and said: 'How great to see you lads and lass! Suddenly, everything's aglow.' At least it was better than those two sods turning up at his house. He had forced himself to let them in there once or twice for negotiaions. In those days, he had been trying to persuade them to come in on the syndicate and needed to show the kind of property and stature he had, including the exposed beams and paddock. That was a while ago, and he would not want people like this regularly using his home furniture and possibly running into Margaret or one of his daughters. You had to fix barriers.

Deloraine said: 'I've got orders, Mr Heston, dear.' She was

leaning over the bar, increasing her nearness to him as she
often did, and which would sometimes bring a gross remark
about her body from Foster. When she was in this kind of
attitude Ember could breathe the great warm smell of her
womanliness and fervour.

'Oh?' Ember replied.

'Yes, I've got to go and play the one-armed bandit while
these two big operators talk to you in confidence.'

'That seems a pity, Del,' he said, and meant it. He knew
what Foster and Reid would want. This was going to be
about Eleri ap Vaughan, reported dead in the media. These
two would long to get in there and collect her trade. They
were great lads but too primitive to see the difficulties,
especially Harry.

'Not at once, not disappear at once,' Deloraine said.
'You're allowed to give me some chat for a little while.'

'Grand,' Ember replied. He poured drinks but stayed
behind the bar. It would be a mistake to come out and take
a table with them, even when Deloraine was present. The
club was crowded and all sorts would be watching. Harpur
and Iles were not here, but he had to worry about more than
police. A good syndicate made people envious, keen to get
in on it, liable to turn threatening.

Deloraine ran her hand slowly over the mahogany of the
bar: 'This is a real class spot you've made here, Ralph.'

'Thanks. It's coming along.'

'When Harry says a saunter to The Monty, first thing I
always think is, have I got something smart enough?'

'You're looking really elegant,' Ember replied. She had on

a yellowy, silk-style suit that kept the womanliness in view but nothing pushy or raw. 'Doesn't she, lads?' Such a mistake to corner the conversation with a girl like Del when her man was present. It could bring trouble and get a clamp put on, making good private contact later tricky, particularly for a full night.

Reid said: 'Well, you too, your good self, looking fine, Ralph. I always get the impression not just of a prestige place, but of a presence when I come here. And that presence is you, Ralph. I don't mean the Chuck Heston thing. Not as definable as that. You're Aura Man.'

'And you're Soft Soap Man – but it's very acceptable, Gerry,' Ember said. Reid spieled, almost always.

'To me, Ralph Ember looks like the future. Wouldn't you say, Harry?'

'To me he looks like a future with a very interesting past,' Deloraine replied. 'I'm going to get you to tell me some of that one of these days. Or would I die of jealousy?'

'How's your wife, Ralph?' Foster said.

'Terrific.'

'Margaret, a gem of a woman,' Reid cried. 'Dignity. Insight.'

'Thanks, Gerry,' Ember replied.

'I've never even met her,' Deloraine said. 'Does she come to the club?'

'Oh, yes,' Ember said.

'He tries to keep her clear of our sort, don't you, Ralphy?' Foster said.

'Whose sort?' Deloraine asked.

'Yours, love,' Foster replied. 'Here's a handful of coins. Go and play with yourself now, will you?'

'Already?'

'We won't be long. You can come and sweet talk him again in a minute.'

'I love the scar on your jaw, Ralph,' she said. 'That's what I mean, the past.'

'Cut himself on his Horlicks glass,' Foster replied.

When Deloraine had gone to the machine, Reid said: 'Do forgive us, Ralph. I know how you abhor business on these fine premises. But Harry and I, well, we both thought, without consultation – we both came up with an idea, and it does entail a little urgency.'

'Oh?' Ember replied. 'Sounds interesting, but mysterious.'

'Don't fuck about, Ralphy,' Foster said. 'This is ap Vaughan.'

'I read of that.'

'Really?' Foster replied.

You had to manage Harry, and, yes indeed, sometimes Ember wondered whether it was worth the trouble, even with the prospect of Deloraine. 'We should be in there,' Foster said.

Ember poured some more.

Reid said: 'That *Eton Boating Song* work station, Ralph. It's fairly priceless. Such custom! And what I thought was you'd know how to get one of our pushers in there, nobody better. This would be where your club experience comes in so beautifully. All right, the *Eton* is just some phoney, floating gimmick, nothing like the sound heritage of The Monty, but a club's a club and who understands them better than Ralph Ember?'

'This was Vine did her, no question – a little gesture,' Foster said. 'Now he'll be frantic to get a replacement working.'

'The ap Vaughan situation did strike me as interesting,' Ember replied.

'It's a race,' Foster said.

'The Queen is dead, long live the successor,' Reid remarked. 'How we see it, Ralph.' He was in a denim waistcoat and jeans. The whole outfit would be worth £2.

'Look, why don't we talk at a table, Ralphy?' Foster said. 'Blurting things here. Easy to be overheard.' He nodded towards the big table near a blow-up picture of members on that messy Monty outing to Paris a few years ago.

'Call me Ralph, call me Ember, but not Ralphy,' Ember replied. Of course, he had told Foster this fifty times before. Foster did it to bring him down, make him sound like someone's half-daft cousin kept upstairs. Foster wanted the primacy in this firm, you could feel it all the time. He was a next-to-nothing who didn't even have the brain to know he was next to nothing. This was why he would get so off-key and ratty: he was trying to pull Ember down, yet his girl so obviously thought Ember an entirely fuckable prize. She had just hit a jackpot and the money rushed and rattled and rattled for her. She beamed across at Ember like foreplay. He ignored the table suggestion. 'I don't fancy being stampeded into a commitment on ap Vaughan, Harry,' he said. 'That's not how a good business runs.'

'So, how does it run? Like a dead march?' Foster replied.

'We've got no street trader who would fit that spot in the *Eton*,' Ember said. 'This is a specialized role. If we put someone in there and they make a muck of it the rot could set in right through our operation.'

'I don't see it,' Foster said.

'Maybe you don't,' Ember replied.

Reid said: 'Ralph means once you get the stink of a failure in one part of your activity the stink spreads. I can see that.'

'What about the stink of failure that comes if we don't even contest?' Foster asked. 'This is a stink like gutlessness or tiredness or age. This is a stink like famous fucking Panicking Ralphy.' He had forgotten the possibility of being overheard. His voice was right up.

'Oh, now Harry, this is a reasonable discussion, surely, surely. Ralph is entitled to bring all his experience to a problem, all his maturity. That's how I would prefer to think of it – not age, maturity.'

'I thought about it and decided against,' Ember stated. 'We don't want trouble with Vine. We don't want any degree of overlap with Vine.'

'No?' Foster replied. Deloraine came back, cradling a mass of coins in two hands against her stomach. 'Would you like to run your fingers through my bonny assets, Ralph?' she cried.

Foster grabbed her arm and the money hit the floor and rolled. She screamed and bent to recover the pound pieces. Foster tugged her away: 'We're going,' he said. 'There's nothing here.'

She began to cry: 'But, Harry, I—'
He dragged her towards the door.
Ember called: 'I'll pick it all up and keep it for you, Del.
'Yes, keep something for me, Ralph,' she replied.

8

Now and then and not always when he was expecting it Keith Vine would get a complete re-run in his head of that business in the old customs house with Eleri ap Vaughan. This was a thing about him, sensitivity. Sometimes he thought he could have done without it. What agonizing memories like this made him determined on, though, was that her fine work at the *Eton* should be maintained, and by someone with a suitable gift – obviously not as brilliant a gift as her own, but real flair, all the same.

He had not kept his hand over her mouth for very long when he dragged her into the customs house ruin. Unnecessary. This was a huge place and voices did not have much chance of getting out, not even screams. Anyway, the thing about screams – suppose they *were* heard – the thing about screams was you would get all sorts of yells and dins from in here – drunks, whores, junkies – and nobody from outside was going to come looking. There was a din of taxis not far off, as people left from the disco and the *Eton*. It would drown Eleri, even if she did screech. He thought she was probably not like that. She had dignity.

She was struggling a bit when he pulled her in. It was nothing, she was so old and feeble. But then he realized she was not trying to break out of his grip and save herself like that but wanted to reach her handbag. He thought maybe a pistol and let his hand slip down from her neck and mouth and knocked the bag out of her grip and on to the ground. She said: 'Cash in there, Keith. It's yours. Take it.'

God, like a bribe. Or maybe it really was his money. Did she owe him for a consignment? That would be in the books. If she thought he would attack her just for loot it was damn hurtful. 'This is deep, Eleri, love,' he replied.

'Let me get it for you.' Her voice was tiny, so scared. He hated the situation. '*Can* I get it for you, Keith?'

He was holding her with only one arm now and he slackened this so she could bend for the bag. 'Don't open it,' he said. 'Just pick it up and hand it to me.' He had not even unholstered his own gun yet.

She crouched down towards the bag. For her duty at the *Eton* she always dressed in tip-top gear, and a bit of moonlight glinted on sequins as she moved. She could have been such a worthwhile lady. 'This is four or five hundred, Keith,' she said, her face turned up to him, very pale, very skintight in the half dark.

'Been skimming,' he said.

'This is more than just tonight's.' She did not pick up the bag but suddenly ran from him, still crouched, as though to stay below his reach. Oh, God, it was sad – ugly, really, the way she moved, like an old crab in sequins. The ground floor was a great big empty stretch, except for paper and cans and the remains of a sleeping bag and bricks and broken glass. It was the past.

'You'll fall, Eleri,' he called and went after her. Now she did begin to cry out, though it was not a scream, a sound more like a dog howling, but very high and very weak – she did not have much breath at that age. You could not let something like this put you off. Their feet crunched the muck and now and then there was the crack of snapped glass. On the far side was a doorway, the door and boarding gone from here, too, and she was scuttling towards that. The moon made it a silver rectangle, something hopeful. She might have beaten him to it and got out and been safe but then she did trip and fall, as he had warned. She seemed a little dazed and did not get up, lying face down, one arm up around her head, an attempt to protect herself – a bright attempt, as though she knew already where the damage would come. This was a woman who realized what the world was like. Vine put his foot on her back, keeping her there. 'I wanted this all much simpler and easier, Eleri,' he said. He brought out the gun from his holster and fitted the silencer. 'I don't think you should have done that to me – abandoned my firm,' he said.

'I'm free,' she said into the filthy floor, not loud but defiant, he thought. She said: 'I can go to whom I pick.'

'But it wasn't necessary. I'm going to try to manage this with one bullet, Eleri. And afterwards I'll take you somewhere not quite so grim. That's the least I can do. Plus making sure your achievements at the *Eton* are not forgotten or allowed to waste away. The funeral will be damn decent, rest assured of that, and I'll attend because of real affection and respect, as well as the policy side.' He bent down and put the gun to the back of her head on the left and fired. Even in the poor light he could see the skin above her right ear torn open as the bullet exited. It reminded him of a rabbit he had seen once bolt from a hole because the ferret was down there. Probably there would be no real destruction to her face, though he did not turn her over immediately to look. For a few moments he stayed with Eleri, his foot still on her back, waiting to make sure the little movements and breathing did stop soon. He hoped he could keep his word and would not have to fire again. He did dread throes. It looked useless and fairly tragic for her have her arm and hand up to protect her head, so he brought it down to lie at her side.

He left her for a while and went to pick up the handbag. He opened it, but only to push a piece of scrap metal from the floor in among the rolls of money. He took nothing out. He closed the bag on its clasp and also bound it with the strap to keep it shut. The far door gave on to the dockside and he walked over there and outside and dropped the bag into the water.

Although it was going to be tricky getting her body away, he had promised her, and in any case, he still thought it would be stupid to leave her close to the *Eton*. There was not much he could do until the *Eton* and Magenta shut and the last taxis went. He must not sit anywhere in here because of the possible staining to his clothes, and he made do with leaning against a wall for a couple of hours. Through most of this time he thought only of the succession deserved by Eleri.

Just before dawn he went and lifted her and brought her near to the door they had entered by. Perhaps he could have sat down after all because, obviously, he would have to get rid of the suit he was wearing. He could have dragged her over the floor to the doorway by her hair or ankles, but this would have been disgraceful. He walked to his car and brought it to the customs house door, quickly loading her into the boot. He had prepared it for Eleri.

*

This murky vision from the past he had again today on his way to see Simon Pilgrim. Vine said: 'The kind of business to really suit you, Simon.'

'Take over all her people, just like that? Keith, I really don't know, old son.'

'This is a superb business.'

'I worry. Damn it, of course I worry. I'm bound to look at what happened to her, Keith. Wild forces around. If I'm frank, I have to say I even worry about coming out to your place like this. Sorry, Keith, but, well, some people could be targets, the way things look now. If they wanted Eleri done they might want others done.'

'We're fine here. People know better not try anything rough on Keith Vine.'

Pilgrim said: 'Yes, but Keith, listen—'

Vine waved a hand. He was bored by Pilgrim's little anxieties and the fluty, frightened voice. He was almost bored enough to tell Pilgrim to piss off. Did Vine really want someone so feeble and ugly handling Eleri's prime list? Were things sinking, and was Vine adding more weights? Who else was there, though? 'We needed a meeting, Si, because I don't see someone of Simon Pilgrim's calibre trading for ever down back lanes and in dives.'

Pilgrim stretched out his tiny legs, trying for relaxation. 'Thanks, Keith, of course, but I do get a decent life, you know. It's steady. Ah!' He smiled, a truly human smile. The baby had started crying in the other room. 'This is what comes of being a dad, yes? Are Becky and the child well?'

'Great.' Vine could hear Becky moving about in there. The footsteps sounded a bit hurried and urgent. Sometimes she would get nervy when the baby yelled. Vine was never rough with her about that. You had to be understanding, and that baby was very much a joint matter, obviously. He said: 'To me – I can tell you now – to me, Si, you've always seemed just right for the higher area of trade. Poise. Unplastic shoes. Tasteful ties. This is the way quality will just naturally come to the top when there is an opportunity, like Winston Churchill in 1940. A pity Eleri had cornered all that upper-echelon custom. But now this sudden change. Yes, opportunity. I know what you're thinking, Si – can you handle it? But would I ask if I didn't sense you'd be all right? Believe me, Keith Vine can pick personnel. And this is real money, Si.'

'I appreciate it, but—'

Vine gave a small, man-to-man laugh. 'Folk think because of that "ap" in her name, plus the extra Welsh touch – I mean, "Eleri", the strangeness of that name – they think she walked straight into business with select clientele – like she had lineage to some ancient tribal princess in Celtland, giving her the entrée to a modern, quality set as of right.

But it wasn't like that. Eleri had to win those contacts, collect them, hold them, Simon, and I know you could do it, too.'

'She crossed someone, Keith.' He said it like this was some kind of discovery.

Vine said: 'Well, of course she did. I could give you a hint or two on that later, maybe.'

'She crossed someone very big, Keith.' Pilgrim stared around the flat, like he expected enemies to shoulder in the three-ply front door and blast him. 'And anyone they thought might be going after her business they would—'

'Yes, someone big took against her, that's true,' Vine said. 'The kind you're always liable to run into at that level.' He touched his ragged little lips a few times.

Vine poured a couple of whiskies. Jesus, but it was grubby labour. 'Look, Si, there are people I'd never offer this type of business to. Could Luke Malthouse or Slow Victor handle Eleri's list? Fine in their way, but would the *Eton* let either of those buggers sit at work in the bar – I mean sit in the best bar, scaring customers with their clothes and features?'

Pilgrim had a slabby little face, with not much nose or brow, like he'd had some terrible wall impact when very young, or a fall from the Ferris wheel, but he knew how to get what there was of him to look anxious. 'Keith, the tale is people from outside did her. Everyone knows London is on the way into this scene. Or Manchester. They take her out, wanting her trade. This is big menace, Keith.'

Rage tore at Vine. Christ, you kill someone first class like Eleri especially to give a brilliant lesson to people, and the fools read it upside down. She had to go because the greedy cow was creeping towards a London connection. Instead, the fucking half-baked buzz says it was London killed her! This could easily turn out a criminal waste of a good life.

'I don't want to run against outfits like that, Keith. I really couldn't cope. I'm thirty-three, yes, honestly, thirty-three, half retired. You're still young. I want to settle for something peaceful. My asthma. Sorry.'

'You don't look anything like thirty-three.' No. Stick twenty years on. Vine heard Becky call him from the other room, a sort of big, scared whisper, and very urgent. He ignored it – no time to act Daddy just now. He had to bend Pilgrim. In a way, Si was right, and it had probably been a mistake to bring him to the flat – not because of danger, for God's sake – what danger? – but because the place did not look like success. It was untriumphal. Glue was the sideboard's lifeblood. Pilgrim would be saying to himself in that cocktail-party accent, *What's this fucker know about career momentum?* Nobody could make decent promises or threats in such a place.

'We stay on here because when I move I want it to be a real move, Si. Currently, I'm looking at Kenward Knapp's property, as was – The Pines.'

This did get to Pilgrim . . . well of course it did. 'Kenward's? That's true money, Keith. The Pines? This is a home with wide grounds, a gallery.' Pilgrim took a sip of the Scotch. About enough to wet a stamp.

Vine said: 'I don't want to be messing about – moving to somewhere only a bit better than this, but not what we really want, then having to shift again. Draws attention. We hang on, getting the price together. Maybe three hundred grand. And in our trade it's got to be all cash, no mortgage – so, delay. I mean, how do you tell the building society where it's coming from and convince them it will keep on coming, although it will?' He bellowed: 'Shut that bloody kid up, Beck, will you, and stop marching about in there, like Trooping the Colour . . . And that's the thing, Si, you could be doing nearly as good as me yourself – you take this chance, keep on developing the list, nurse it. Eleri did wonders, but this doesn't mean nobody could follow her.' Vine's voice took on rhapsody. 'Look at this city as we advance to greet the millennium – marinas, international capital pouring in – European Community aid – there's going to be such disposable wealth here, Si. Some of it on tap already. I see this list developing the way the city itself will develop, a fine, productive relationship.'

'You always could manage the long view, Keith.'

'Anyone can see it,' Vine replied. 'Basic business flair. This town's going to be fat with grand incomes, even capital, and wanting only the sweetest, purest stuff. Think of the spread of lawyers – all this land-buying. Professional people who like to work hard, clean up, snort hard, Si, even mainline, some. Then there's bound to be super-pimps looking to spend. Plus all the building side – architects, surveyors, engineers, accountants – company chairmen themselves, visiting to see how the work's coming along and on fabulous expense accounts. A wondrously positive scene for us. These are people entitled to relax after big decisions, and they'll need our products as well as girls and boys. They'll need *you*. You, personally, Si, because you're one of the rare people with the instinct how to cater for them.'

Becky came in, holding the baby. Although this was fucking intrusion at a sensitive point Vine kept his rage concealed. The baby was quiet now, staring about that bloody useless way they had, head flopping, but this was all right – you could not expect too much yet. He didn't have to wear a busby.

'I thought I saw someone in the street, Keith,' she said. 'You should come and look. Didn't you hear me call?'

'Who in the street?'

'Watching the flat, pretending not to.'

'Christ,' Pilgrim said, and stood. His legs shook but he stayed just about upright. 'These people have you marked, Keith. I knew we—'

'How it looks to me, anyway,' Becky said. 'Maybe more than one car. I've been getting glimpses from the two windows, dodging between. Don't worry, I was behind the curtain.'

'Christ,' Pilgrim said, and took one step, then stopped. He was wondering, how did he get out if they were waiting? The voice went flutier. You would expect Battle of Britain bravery from someone with such a la-di-da squeak, but Pilgrim was different. 'It's predictable,' he moaned. 'They take out Eleri and now—'

'Come through to the other room. Have a peep, Keith,' Becky said.

The kid seemed to pick up the tension and started to yell again. 'Oh, shut that bugger up,' Pilgrim said.

Vine heard movement on the stairs outside, two, maybe three, people bounding up, some training shoes. He was in his shirtsleeves and wearing no holster – that would be so showy with a guest – and, of course, Pilgrim would not have anything with him, being one for stressless, asthmatic days at the bottom. The doorbell went.

'Don't answer,' Pilgrim said. 'Play it as if nobody here.'

The baby was screaming like a massacre.

'Keithy?' someone called through the door. 'Open up, dear. It's only Piers Seabourne and friends.'

Vine went out into the passage and let them in.

'And Si here, too. This is really nice. Then Becky and young . . .? What did you call him after all, Keith? Not Piers, was it, in token of our fine times?'

'Charles Louis,' Vine said.

'Are this lot police?' Becky asked. 'They move in a mob, take possession, so must be.'

'Only a word with Keith about this and that,' Seabourne said. 'Well, and Si, as he's here.'

Immediately Vine saw this as a bit of a comfort. If they were interested in talking to Pilgrim as well, it meant they knew nothing, were just random trawling, trying for whatever might come up on Eleri.

'What do you mean, "this and that?"' Becky said. It was like her – going at things rough and head-on, her way. But sometimes with police, especially middle-rank police such as Seabourne and these others, you ought to handle things roundabout, get diplomatic. Just the same, there was something really brave and lovely about how Becky took matters direct, if only the mouthy bitch could keep quiet now and then. 'You need three of you for a chat?' she asked.

'In case Charles gets rough,' Seabourne said. The baby had gone quiet again.

So, did Harpur know this lot were going to call? Did the bastard *send* them? If you had a big officer in your firm, one reason was to stop this sort of swarm. Or at least get a little phone warning to you.

'The ap Vaughan inquiry – wheels within wheels,' Seabourne said.

'And what's that mean?' Becky blurted.

'Do you know Jane Bish – Sergeant Jane Bish?' Seabourne replied, as introduction. 'And Wayne Timberlake, of Drugs these days.' He put on a grief look. 'What is it then, Si, Keith, some wake for Eleri? We won't keep you long.'

Becky, standing there, with the baby in her arms, looked grand – so fierce and full of hate, like an artist's picture of Motherhood Fights Back. Vine adored her, the way her jaw came out and a patch of sweat on her forehead – everything so genuine. She obviously felt his proud eyes on her and turned towards him for a moment, so he was able to give her the small intimate sign to keep her fucking trap shut from now on. The trouble with Beck was she saw things simple.

Seabourne said: 'We thought we'd better come in once you'd spotted us. The face at the window.'

The point about Becky was not just getting observed when she thought she was so careful, but a deeper error. She believed everything was like it seemed. For instance, how could you know what this inquiry was really about? There's a murder in the Press and Seabourne mentions Eleri, so you might think it's that – if you were half daft. What did police care if some shag-around old lady trader got shot and dumped in a ruin? This little visit could be about Harpur, really, with Eleri the excuse. Were there tales around the nick about Harpur in a syndicate? Or maybe by some bad luck he was spotted walking near the death site the other night, so many knew him. Any chance to nail Harpur would really interest all his friends and foes in headquarters – and, of course, the thing about police was that friends and foes were the same, especially in high ranks. Like the Shadow Cabinet or cricket.

'Keithy, Si, could we arrange things for a brief chat, then?' Seabourne asked – this sod's way of telling Becky and the kid to get lost, she was too bright and tough. But then Becky did something Vine thought was really so grand. She sat down suddenly on the settee, opened her shirt and started to feed Charles. The creamy flesh and bonny slurping just took over the whole flat. Seabourne did not know what to do. This was a real statement they were a family, and Vine loved it. Tits were sexual in some respects, but were obviously also the future. Becky was telling all of them, including Si, that this family would go on, regardless.

They had to wait. It was terrific. Vine gazed with ample fondness at the mother and child and had time for a think. When Seabourne said *wheels within wheels* you had to wonder what he was telling you. So, was this visit definitely a move against Harpur? Col had greatness, but what Vine did not want was to be sunk with him if missiles flew.

To keep his eyes off the breast, Seabourne stared about, the way Pilgrim had here. Of course, embarrassed or not, Seabourne would diagnose poverty. Vine had bought most of this furniture from second-hand shops at different times. A general bright gingerness gave a pretty good colour match, yet he certainly was not satisfied – felt the items failed to look like a planned scheme as in catalogues.

The other officers gazed around, too. This girl, Jane Bish – as hard as hard despite herself being a mother, and maybe even cleverer than Becky. And then Wayne, up and coming. Harpur might be head of CID, but perhaps he did not even realize this crew were on a mission, because they had been sent secretly by someone longing to see Harpur ashed – some fine colleague with power and loathing and a set of little-known facts. Or what could be turned into facts by a good prosecuting lawyer.

Becky took Charles out to put him in his cot for a while. Seabourne closed the door after her. 'This life after Eleri?' Bish asked. 'Is Si taking over the custom? He's got the aura.'

These police knew a lot, but there was such a useful difference between what they knew and what they could prove, and they should not talk about the business like this unless they had proper evidence – a matter of politeness.

'Eleri – so well loved,' Pilgrim replied. 'Who could wish her ill? Appalled, one read of her death in the Press and could scarcely believe it.'

'It happened,' Jane Bish replied. 'Want to see the body

pics?' She had a briefcase alongside the chair she'd sat down in without being asked, and bent towards it.

Pilgrim held up a hand. 'I just meant that she—'

'You fancied her noble list?' Bish asked. 'And did you find a way to get it, Si?' Vine saw the fright and agony light up again on what Pilgrim used for a face. By coming here to talk trade and the succession he had put himself in the frame.

'Did you hear someone stripped her?' Timberlake asked.

'Oh, my God – disgraceful,' Pilgrim replied. Perhaps he really had not heard. His voice almost left him.

'For a search, not gratification,' Bish said. 'Professional.'

'I'm sorry, I don't understand,' Pilgrim replied.

'Someone who had been trained to go over a corpse,' Bish replied.

'Trained? Who's trained for that, except morticians?' Pilgrim asked.

'When did you last see her?' Bish replied. She was staring at Pilgrim in that crude style she had.

'I'd have to—'

'No, I meant Keith. She was one of your string, wasn't she? You stocked her, at discount?'

'Strings? Lists?' Vine said. 'What *is* this?'

'When?' Bish replied.

'Eleri? This is a tough one,' Vine replied. 'I might bump into her here and there. But when? That's—I'd see her sometimes in that restaurant, you know, the vessel in the marina, *The Eton Boating Song,* when I dropped in for a drink.'

'That would really get you ratty, wouldn't it, Keithy, if

you heard she was moving over to some London invader? She'd been given a fine hammering not very long ago. What seems to have been a reproach. Was it a last warning ignored, Keith?'

Vine turned to Seabourne: 'Listen, Piers, do I have to put up with—?'

Bish said: 'If she went, who might follow her to a new supplier? Stampede. Suddenly, where's Keithy's business disappeared to, and him with a lady's milky chest to keep nourished and a dynasty to found?'

Vine saw Pilgrim was getting revelations here. Great. There was so little nose to him that his eyes seemed like one pale blue pool, and all of it full of belief in what Bish said. Perhaps the jerk would get some gratitude now – realize how this list came to be available to him, how Eleri had been shifted to the side. And not *by* London. *Because of* London.

'But could you get some dead old lady's clothes off, Mr Vine, and then back on more or less right, as I hear it?' Timberlake asked. 'You've got that kind of thoroughness, patience?' He had a black beard, but was still a boy – big, bony, awkward hands. They had brought him into town from some village or field, which meant he still might not know the scene here – but it could also mean he was bright, or they would have left him.

'Yes, it's wheels within wheels,' Seabourne said.

'This could be a big wheel,' Bish replied.

Seabourne stood: 'You two lads, give it a thought, will you? See if you can recollect when you last saw her. The details. The Chief's keen to create some local cleanliness. Obviously, we're interested above all in who was with her or around.'

'She trusted you, I expect, Keith,' Bish said.

'We'd always have a nice old yarn when we ran into each other,' Vine replied.

The three police left then. 'Our best to the babe,' Bish said. 'I'm sure he'll be a credit to you when he grows up, Keith. Hope you live to see it.'

Pilgrim stayed on. He seemed livelier now. 'Keith, I hadn't any idea of the picture, you know. The way the situation had been . . . I suppose "fashioned" is the word. Impressive.'

'They've saved me some explaining.'

Pilgrim almost chortled. 'I like the feel of this. I admire the decisive management, sense of commitment to the firm.'

Probably with Bish's help Si did understand the full, recent business manoeuvring now. As he said, he might be genuinely impressed, or possibly the jittery sod was terrified he could be next, if he came to look as disloyal as Eleri. Vine felt certain Pilgrim would take her list now. You often came across this with people – they suddenly realized that what they thought was a hell-hole was really their full future, because it had fine concealed advantages, or because they had no choice. Pilgrim would do, at least for a week or two. One tale said he had been to a famed school – not Eton, maybe, but probably with its own boating song or chess team chant and high fees. He should get on with some of those charmers. In commerce, it was known as 'horses for courses'. If he fucked up on Eleri's list, or failed to expand it, he could easily be removed. This was a short-term thing – to make sure that what Eleri had so lovingly put together did not disintegrate now or get snatched by Ralphy or outsiders.

9

Iles said that if London people were moving in to take Oliphant Kenward Knapp's late realm, they would probably soon discover Harpur had been bought by one of the local teams, and therefore he and his daughters were in peril. The ACC suggested Hazel and Jill should go to stay with him and his wife for a while at their house in Rougement Place. Harpur did not tell him that a London outrider had probably already done the sniffing around, unearthed what seemed to be Harpur's involvement and located him and the two girls. That would only have made Iles's invitation seem wiser, and Harpur was not keen on it, though the ACC conceivably meant well: this could certainly happen now and then with Iles.

The ACC said: 'These people – London, Manchester gangs – they're very good on information, Col. You might think you've got it all buttoned up, but consider Keithy Vine for a moment. Is this someone who can sit on secrets? Isn't he going to boast to other partners that he's landed you? Debris like Vine might regard you as something quite worthwhile.'

'Thank you, sir.'

'And then these partners take the trumpeting a bit further, to street pushers. It would encourage and comfort some of the nervy ones to think you'd been bought. This is publicity, Harpur.'

'I'll be more careful at home – get some decent locks and tell the girls to check who's at the door before opening.'

They were using Harpur's room at headquarters, Iles in shirtsleeves, immensely clean and debonair, and apparently nagged by benevolence. Kindness did not fit his face, yet he had good impulses now and then. 'You might – might – be able to look after yourself, Col, but your daughters will be very vulnerable. Our armoury can't issue you with a weapon. What reason could you give? Lane personally examines the register. Guns fret him. Well, anything frets him now, the weary one.'

'I might get something from elsewhere.'

Iles did a combined giggle and shrug, then passed a hand slowly over his longish, quiffed grey hair. He seemed to have given up the *en brosse* style, adopted for a time after a local season of Jean Gabin films. These reactions were meant to signal something or other, perhaps anxiety, more likely contempt. 'You'll go to Leyton Harbinger? Oh, fine. Why not? I mean, what's wrong in a senior officer buying guns from a dealer who kits every armed villain south of the Tyne?'

'Not guns, sir, a gun.'

'You won't be able to call for aid, Col, will you?'

'I could call *you*.'

Iles threw out his arms. It reminded Harpur of Sunday School pictures of the Good Shepherd about to rescue and cuddle that lost, hundredth sheep. 'Well, how I hope you would, Col! Sometimes I feel you are too proud to ask help from me. But am I always at home?'

'If they come, it's likely to be late at night, sir.'

'But am I always at home? Col, I've commitments, one way and the other, yes, even late at night. I'm allowed out in the dark. You're worried about your daughters if they were at my house, are you?'

'Probably only the older one, sir. As yet.'

'Hazel?'

'Some uneasiness if you were close to her in a host role, yes, sir. But you must not worry, I'll be able to look after them.'

'Hazel's a lovely girl and—'

'She's still not sixteen, sir.'

'Exactly. I can recognize a child, you know. This is your ACC speaking, Harpur. Am I going to try anything on with the underage daughter of a fine subordinate, for God's sake?'

As always with Iles, an answer was needed. Harpur, seated at his desk, lounged back, eyes closed, and grew reflective. 'I think I should come out from under cover now, earlier than I'd hoped, and use what material I have for prosecution. It might work.'

Iles paced the room in splendidly caring style, and his voice grew subtly soothing and musical: 'Col, I can sympathize with your wanting to chicken like that, you feeble fucking bastard.'

'Thank you, sir.'

'I certainly don't see why you should feel you have to complete properly something you arrogantly took it on yourself to start.'

'Thank you, sir.'

The ACC's pacing seemed to brisk up his brain. His

thoughts came flying at Harpur from different angles, like a revolving lawn spray, sometimes head-on, sometimes from over Iles's slim shoulder. 'But, possibly, Col, for once we have to consider rather more than preservation of your tripey skin. If you come out now and sink one or more of the local firms through prosecution, what happens?'

Again Iles would want a reply, and Harpur said: 'I don't say it's all one-way, sir. I've certainly heard Hazel call you "a greasy old lech", but I think you also exercise a half-genuine, sleazy fascination.'

'Thanks, Harpur.'

'Kids of that age are so easily taken in by prancing and wordage. So, you see, I'd be scared to let—'

Iles beamed and came to rest alongside Harpur's Crimes Against The Person graph on the wall. That seemed fair enough. 'She's such a bright kid!' the ACC cried. 'Oh, no, you can't come out now, Harpur, because to destroy local syndicates in the courts would leave a hole. People like Charlie Misto, Silver and Manse Shale have already quit the battle. Just what these London gangs want. They could speed their invasion, fill the space immediately. By removing all possible resistance, you'd be doing their work for them. They colonize whole police areas faster than the plague. Think what it would do to someone in the Chief's condition. Has that crossed your turbid mind? One breakdown already, the gibbering saint. This high-flying scruff, Mark Lane, is a lovely relic of a gentler time, Col. His sort grow scarce and must be conserved. I might be able to smuggle out a .38 for you, or even something fatter. But not a Heckler and Koch submachine job. How would I get that safely down the front of my trousers?'

'Thanks, sir.'

Iles lowered himself slowly but very emphatically into an armchair. 'Absolutely no strings, you know, Col. I'm certainly not saying, I'll get you a gun if you let Hazel ... if you let the girls come to Idylls.'

'Thanks, sir. I did hear once where you got that poncy name for your house. But the mind's a self-preserving thing and keeps blotting out what I was told.'

'Well, it's from a substantial, renowned poem, Harpur. No reason why you should have heard of it, coming up the way you did. The full title is *Idylls of the King*. With anyone even marginally educated there's no need to spell that out. They get the point. Do you think you might let the girls come, Harpur?'

'No. I have to protect them. Her.'

Iles offered something between another giggle and a larger sound, possibly a chuckle. 'Of course. Isn't that why I'm offering to shelter them?'

'It's typical selflessness, sir.'

'It might take a while to get the .38.'

'I'll be patient.'

He digested this for a time. 'You know, Harpur, I've met others like you.'

'What happened to them, sir?'

'They—'

Harpur's intercom cut across the reply. The apparatus was switched to voice box, and they could both listen. The Chief said: 'Colin, the hutment over her body. I feel this was not meant as concealment, since the construction was liable itself to draw attention. No, a tenderness in the killer. He would execute ap Vaughan, yet wished also, as it were, to protect her. We should be looking for someone ruthless, yet not without soul.'

Iles leaned forward and spoke into the machine. 'I'm writing that down, sir.'

'Desmond, you're there?'

'Harpur and I were discussing things, and felt pretty near despair. But now this. *Ruthless, yet not without soul.* I'll personally get the computer to give us a shortlist of the likelies.'

Lane closed the call, as if pushed off balance by hearing Iles instead of Harpur.

'It's not a bad guess, sir,' Harpur said.

'Perhaps not. These little insights do come to him now and then. But we can't wait for them, Col. While he's thinking, we'd lose the realm.'

10

Keith Vine thought he should be at *The Eton Boating Song* when Si Pilgrim did his first trading session there – though, obviously, there was no duty on Keith to nurse the big-talk bugger, no duty at all. Pilgrim was not a member of the firm, he was a pusher, that's all – buying his supplies just like he always had, but now – post Eleri – buying to retail them mainly at the *Eton*. But the *Eton* was bound to be a tricky spot to get accepted in, even for someone who told the world he had been at a good school. Vine did not believe in the kind of business where you just made the deal, then forgot the buyer. Shortsighted. He wanted a good and lasting relationship with his customers, something steady and long-term, not just casual. If you lost an operative like Eleri through no real fault of your own – considering the disloyal way she behaved, the thoughtless old darling – you had to coach along the replacement.

Tonight, Vine stood at the bar alone and just watched Si work. They did not speak or even do eye messages, but Pilgrim would know he had support plus, of course, super-vision. He did not look too bad in Eleri's special place. It still gave Vine a tremor now and then, though, when he had turned away for a while and then glanced back and saw Si there. Pilgrim had the famed rum and black in front of him as open-for-trade sign, but he also had his personal face, and, so far, it seemed wrong for him to be where Eleri had always been, lately so full of those clever teeth. A wonderful era was gone, like the end of steam trains.

Si was a jumpy one – well, Vine had seen that when the police came – and seemed definitely short on brassiness, which made you wonder if he had really been at a top school. But he would get used to things pretty fast, probably – especially if there was no bad trouble here in the first few weeks. Why Vine had come – to make sure there was no bad trouble. Obviously, he had the automatic aboard. Vine watched Si do a few good sales – everything quick and friendly, with a subtle passing of the money and the item. That was vital. Although the *Eton* owners were good as gold and appreciated the drawing power of a nice trading corner, they would object to blatant business. This place had all kinds of patrons, quite a few not into coke, and these might feel offended if they saw commerce. One of the *Eton*'s aims was to be a spot you could bring well-off, elderly, utterly non-snort ladies for a pleasant evening, and Vine considered this quite permissible, really. He believed in tolerance, up to quite a point.

Obviously, above all he kept an eye for that London path-finder who came wanting Eleri last time. Another reason to be with Si tonight. What Vine planned was locate this explorer and get behind him when he left – find out where he was living, who he was, whether there were others, the whole dirty ensemble. Knock over one or two of them early and it might stop the rest coming, though Vine did not really believe it – too much on offer here, if it could be taken. He had to make sure it never *was* taken. Defence of territory was a deep, noble impulse in animals and Man. Think of the polar bear. But you had to get beyond defence. Keith Vine was not one to just hang about waiting for an enemy to come and get him. He was the kind who went after the enemy instead.

The London lad did not appear until about half an hour before the *Eton* was due to shut. Vine had come out from the bar by then and was on a little tour of the boat, looking for him – in case he was around and doing something subtle and secret, like spying on Keith Vine and Si. That would be simple. This boat had genuine maritime portholes everywhere. Vine recognized the walk first – oh, such a nimble mover. He was coming up the gangplank, alone again, and not in the suit this time but a khaki or beige jacket with jeans. Vine might have missed him but for that bouncy lope. His hair was dark and pretty ordinary and he had no height, so he was easy not to recognize.

Vine turned away quickly and walked up to the bow, passing the door to the bar. From behind the fat foremast he could watch without being seen, he hoped. This boy came along the deck and also passed the door to the bar, and for a moment Vine thought he had been spotted. Then he realized the visitor was giving the bar a good squint through the door and a porthole – casing as he walked. He stopped after a couple more paces, turned, strolled back, and went in.

Of course, he would be playing it cagey. Eleri's body had been all over local media, and even national. This was a hot death and nobody would want to get linked. The lad in the jacket was not here for a meeting this time, but to size up the aftermath – trying to work out what was new. He had been sent here with a job, which was to talk to Eleri. The job had disappeared before he even arrived, so he was bound to feel lost. Vine could almost feel sorry for him.

Keith walked back along the deck and paused for a few moments at the same porthole. Many of the *Eton's* customers had gone home now and he had a good view across the bar to where the khaki jacket was making a buy from Pilgrim. That would be mainly to get contact close up. There seemed to be no talk beyond the basic for a purchase – that same swift handover as with earlier customers. The Jacket would be getting a long, memorizing stare at Si, of course, and probably he would also be looking around for a sight of Vine at the bar. It had been smart to move out, lucky smart. The khaki coat stayed buttoned and might be off the peg – nothing like as special as the grey suit – a very loose loose fit, and not showing any holster contours. No, but then you had to think, why did he have a jacket like that except for concealment? Maybe it was his sort made the fashion world move from tight styles.

Si gave him a nice, businesslike smile, meant to say, *I trust we can do business on many future occasions, friend*, and if he had been bothered by the dregs London accent never showed it. Si had true flair, under all the weakness. As Vine had said lately, one of his own most brilliant flairs was personnel selection. He stepped back a bit, not to be visible. This turned the porthole into a kind of picture frame, one of those fancy round ones they did for weddings, and it held the lad's face there for a few moments, on its own, like a pose, something to be studied. What you had to be careful of when you were looking hard at a face like this, reading it, was that you did not bring the ideas you already had about this person and say you could discover it all in the face. That was not discovering, that was back to front. He was about Vine's age, mid-twenties, and the same sort of big neck and shoulders. This kid could be mistaken for wholesome, that was the point. He had a fresh look to him, or even what was known as gauche. It was hard to think of him hunting Harpur, and maybe Harpur's daughters and woman. Yes, this boy could have been the hopeful bridegroom, lit up like that with the circle around him and giving the smile back to Si. Bright, friendly eyes, unstoked up by anything yet tonight, and decent skin, not a scar on it that Vine could see, and the nose still neat. This was a good employee for someone, probably on an accelerated promotion track. He would be able to act harmlessness when needed, a true asset. Vine had not really noticed all this first time, probably because as soon as the visitor began talking in his rough-house voice you could guess the sort who sent him, and you concentrated on that. Vine would never forgive anyone who called him a cunt. That word was beyond. And yet, why? This was such a delicious thing, and where would the twenty-first century be without?

The face moved out of the frame. He might be leaving. Vine moved quickly back to his cover behind the mast. The Jacket did not come out though, and, after a couple of minutes, Vine went back along the deck and carefully looked through the porthole again, close up to it once more now, so he had a wide view of the bar. Si downed the last of his rum and black and had obviously decided business was over for the night. The Jacket was alone at a table with his back to Vine. He might be watching Si, perhaps still trying to sort out what had happened. He could not have found out much here tonight, only that Eleri had a successor. Most likely he would be wondering whether Si had all her list wrapped up – whether this replacement guy was worth the offer that had been meant for Eleri. He might even be wondering whether Si had knocked over Eleri, to take her customers. But could he really think Si Pilgrim was up to that, for God's sake, the mouthy, fading nobody? Briefly, Vine felt a real pang, in case Pilgrim or anyone else should get the credit.

When the Jacket came out on to the deck, Vine stayed for a good while behind the mast. There was hardly anyone about now and a close tail would be obvious. He waited until this jaunty lad was halfway down the gangplank before moving out and following. If the Jacket had a hire car here, Vine would probably lose him. By the time he reached his own vehicle it would be too late. But, no, the visitor kept walking, up past the public phone booth, towards the docks exit and the Valencia Esplanade district. Perhaps he had a room in one of the crumbling big old villas there, nearly all of them cheap lodging houses these days or flats. Or he might be looking for a girl. If he was alone in the town, perhaps he wanted buyable company for the night, someone to share his expensive little parcel and so on.

Dring Place, off the Valencia, was one of the great streets if you needed something like that. Vine let him stay far ahead while they were still on the docks. Until the Valencia, they were the only two walking, and he still felt very exposed. There were some bits of cover along the docks road, such as scrap-metal heaps, Portakabins, an occasional ruined lifeboat or cruiser dumped far from the water – but on long stretches he had to make the best of it in the open. The lighting was good down here now, too bloody good – part of the thoughtful marina developments, meant to convince people on their first trip to *The Eton Boating Song* they were not driving into some pit.

As they approached the Valencia he shortened the distance. There were people about here and it would be easy to lose him. Vine liked this area. It was rough and falling to pieces so fast, but you could always find activity, and it had history – going right back to when the port really was a port, not some phoney home for a boat-restaurant. They said this Valencia Esplanade earned its name from all the grand vessels that used to trade with Spain in that previous time. Now a word like Esplanade was too gorgeous for such a shagged-out district, and people usually just called it Valencia or the Valencia. It had a lot of clubs and late-night bars, and it had the girls – not completely top-of-the-range girls, but a few all right.

Somebody must have told the Jacket about Dring Place, because he went straight there, really springy, as ever, and eager. He was staring about, looking for something he fancied, and Vine went up even nearer, to keep him in sight.

The Jacket started talking to a very smart, very young, very smiley black girl in leathers and seemed to be making quite a commitment, when suddenly he turned around and came fast towards Vine.

It was still that walk, so bright with push and flexibility, like one of those tall ants Vine had seen in the Middle East when he worked there. The Jacket was smiling at him, a smile with so much kindness in it – the way a mother might look at a feeble-minded kid. 'I love it when you're behind me like that, right from the boat,' he told Vine. 'Then I know where you are, don't I?'

'I *thought* it might be you,' Vine replied, and gave a good, friendly smile back. Match this sort of bastard. 'I saw you walking ahead, as a matter of fact.' A nice bit of casualness.

'Did you have a message? Did you see the lady I wanted to meet?'

'Well, no. As a matter of fact.'

'No, I don't suppose so. So why you so keen to be with me, sweetheart? Who, as a matter of fucking fact, are you?'

That echo, the mockery in it – *as a matter of fucking fact* – scared Keith Vine. Now and then, he would run into people who made him feel he was not clever enough or big enough to run a family on this career. Or much worse than that – he would feel he was not clever enough or big enough to stay alive in it. None of this happened very often. How would he be so far on in business if it did? But this now – this Jacket – was one of those times.

'You're in business?' he asked Vine. 'If you say so. But – well, I look at you at the boat and now and I consider those clothes and the general demeanour. Demeanour. You OK with that word? Am I leaving you behind?'

Suddenly, this boy had a tongue, a cockney flow. Yes, the accent was still there, but he could do like speeches.

'When I say demeanour I mean your fucking hopelessness,' he went on. 'You're in business? For instance, who tails like that, so obvious? Not intending the slightest offence, but who? All right, I'm in a town I don't know. Things could be different here, and I've got to be ready for new sights. You're definitely one. And, for example, I look at that quiet tradesman in the boat and wonder. It might be good material he sells. I'll let you know. Or maybe you already know. You're this sweetheart's wholesaler, are you? If you tell me that, I'll believe it, make no harmful comment at all.'

'You've lost *your* sweetheart, sweetheart,' Vine replied.

The young black tart had seemed to be waiting for Lovely Mover to return, but now she waved to someone in a big Rover that had just stopped across the street. She looked so pleased, and made for this car in a rush – not just a tarty rush, with no feeling, like scared another girl would get there first. This was such real eagerness, the way a fiancée might welcome her lover back from war. The passenger door was pushed open and the girl did not wait, no arguing about price, but just entered the car at once. Now it was as though she was a wife being picked up from the shopping. She pulled the door shut after her and seemed to lean across to kiss the driver on the cheek. The Rover moved off and turned right, giving Vine a fair view of the man behind the wheel, sideface. He thought it might be that difficult cop, Assistant Chief Desmond Iles.

'What the fuck?' the Jacket said, and started to return to the girl, still a fine movement, though hurried, but it was too late and the car went out of sight. Through the rear window, Vine could see the tart did not look back. She would take Ilesy back to her own place now for something meaningful, not just a scramble in the back of the car.

This incident really helped Vine, sweetly convalesced him. The black girl did not think London was so great, then. She would prefer something good and local that she already knew and even revered. Tonight, Vine could think of Iles as a sort of ally. Obviously, he was not an actual mate or business partner – not like Harpur – but he lived in this city, and he would want to keep the London people out, just as Vine did. And wasn't it brilliant that, although this girl had already been talking to the Jacket and setting something up, Iles could arrive and she longed to be with him instead, screwing him – yes, for good money, clearly, but also because she wanted it, as a preference? This was community.

Vine felt so strong again. Sometimes, when he was not sure he could really make it in business, he would consider getting out – right out – start something new and safe away from here. That was how he had felt when the Jacket suddenly turned it all around by coming at him, smiling. But Iles, cavalrying in like that, full of local salary and appeal, put everything right again. Vine had been thinking of going home and saying to Becky they would leave, even go to France – which she had wanted for ages. She would still be pleased to do it, he knew that. Iles had changed this, and Vine felt ashamed he had been going to chuck everything. He decided he had been a bit slack, that was all, not tailing the Jacket properly. It was still important he knew where he was staying and how many in the unit, and whether it would be easy to take him out, them out, when necessary. You did not wait to be stalked, you stalked.

So, now, Lovely Mover had to find a replacement and Vine knew this second girl he picked and where her place was. She would have to take him there, not because she wanted it to be special, but because he had no vehicle and was most likely not the kind for wasteground or the floor of a derelict house. Vine pretended to leave, like it was over, a defeat for him – just a doomed outing against the big, metro-politan champ. But he went around right away by a different couple of streets to the road on the edge of the Valencia where she had a room and soon saw them go in. He waited. That smart shit would not see him this time. Tailing, buying, research, selling, personnel selection – Keith Vine could do them all. It was these that qualified him not just for business but for fatherhood. Oh, yes, he saw work and family as very connected. He hated all narrowness, such as the idea that one side of you was trade, while looking after those at home was something else. Your life was one broad, wonderful thing. Did this intruder believe that if Vine really could not run an operation properly he would have taken on a woman and now a child also to support? Christ, it was obvious Lovely Mover had not done research, or he would know Vine had mighty commitments, irresistible incentives.

Keith found a fine spot for viewing the girl's rooms from behind a couple of good big car wrecks, a Granada and an Ambassador. You could have thought they had been dumped there just for someone who wanted to wait hidden from a man leaving after dalliance, as some called it. But the point about a great tail was he could make his own cover from anything – even on that dock road if Vine had been concentrating right. This Jacket was the sort who would have a ton of London money on him and a macho need to prove sex stamina, so he might be here all night. A great tail always had the patience, especially when with responsibilities to breadwin. And then, also, this responsibility to Iles. Eventually, the Assistant Chief might hear that a London visitor had met with a death not too far away, and he would probably know this was brought off by someone local and very gifted. Vine considered he owed Iles something along those lines for snatching the Jacket's fine, friendly, ethnic girl from right underneath his nose.

11

Jill said: 'A shadow moved on the grass – only a moment.'

'But, of course, *she* spotted it,' Hazel said. 'I didn't see anything.'

In the big sitting room, Harpur had been arguing with his daughters about new security arrangements which he wanted applied immediately.

Jill, near the window, said someone was in the garden and trying to stay hidden behind a couple of rhododendron bushes. Harpur did not turn at once to look. He wondered whether he had made Jill jumpy. Usually, she was pretty cool. Both girls had seemed to be listening calmly enough when he spoke of the new deadlocks and an alarm, and only really grew disturbed when he said he would take them to and from school whenever he could. They hated being seen with him by their friends. They said everything about him screamed *Cop, Cop, Cop*, even when he was driving an old, unmarked vehicle.

Now, he did turn slowly and stared into the garden, but saw nobody and only leafy shadows. 'What kind of movement, Jill? Very swift? Very graceful? A youngish man?'

'Graceful? How do I know?'

'It's nothing,' Hazel said. 'So, what's this all about, Dad – the fortress stuff?'

'And if I'm not here, check who's at the front door before opening,' he replied.

'Check how?' Hazel asked.

'Ask.'

Jill said: 'If Iles found out about this peril, I bet he'd offer for Hazel to live up there. Even me – so she'd go.'

'Cow-child,' Hazel replied.

'I wouldn't think so,' Harpur said.

'He's already offered, has he, Mr Harpur?' Hazel's boy-friend, Scott, was lying on the sofa watching a big, impassioned political interview on television, the sound turned off. 'My mother says police such as you with their name and address in the phone book – crazy. Is this some drugs gang thing? My mother says they're taking over.'

'Your mother's got second sight,' Hazel replied.

'*There. Now,* Dad,' Jill said.

'Yes, I see it.' A bit of wind shifted some of the rhododendron branches for a moment. Harpur saw in shadow-shape on the garden path half or less of a head. He tried to relate it to that lovely mover in the curtain department, but couldn't relate it to anyone. On Christmas Day last year, Jill had spotted Mark Lane lurking at that spot in the garden and wanting a secret word with Harpur, but he did not think this was a repeat visit by the Chief.

Harpur told the two girls and Scott to leave the sitting room unhurriedly and go upstairs.

'Then?' Hazel asked.

'Well . . . I'll make certain,' Harpur replied.

'Of what?' Hazel said.

'Well . . . the nature of it,' Harpur replied.

'Of what?' Hazel said.

'Well . . . the visit,' Harpur replied.

'Is that what it is?' Hazel said.

'Know a better word?' Jill asked. Gazing into the garden again, she said: 'I think it's a woman, Dad.'

'Why?' Hazel asked. 'How?' She peered, too. 'Oh, God, is this someone you've been playing around with and ditched, Dad? We're not heartbreak house again, are we?'

'Just go upstairs now, will you?' Harpur replied. It was as Iles had said: he could not ask for help. If he did, it would brilliantly make the ACC's case for moving Hazel and Jill into his unreliable premises. But possibly Jill had it right and this was not the London trailblazer.

'Hazel, you're so rude to your father,' Scott said. 'Yes, he's police, but why talk to him like that?'

'Thanks, Scott,' Harpur said. His daughters and the boy left then. Harpur was about to open the French windows and go down the garden when he saw that Jill *was* right. A woman in her late twenties appeared from behind the bushes and began to walk quickly up towards the house. She saw him watching and gave a small wave, but no smile. He did not know her. She had on an ankle-length, billowing dark skirt in cotton, a slate-grey shirt and grey cotton waistcoat. Harpur opened the windows.

'My mother said to come to you if . . . if the worst happened. But she said to come direct, you know? Not via the nick.' The voice was Midlands.

'Come in.' Harpur stood aside. 'Your mother?'

'So, the worst *has* happened, hasn't it?'

'You're Eleri ap Vaughan's daughter?'

'I saw it on the *News*. Am I supposed to identify? And then, who runs the funeral, and so on?'

'We tried to locate relatives.'

'I expect so. Only me. And I'd hardly go by that folksy, neon surname, would I? In fact, I'm damned glad I don't – such a death. She never expected anything of this sort, you know? Mother thought she'd worked herself into safety and distinction: *The Eton Boating Song*, well-placed friends and clients, the whole panoply. All right, she did not talk of *you* as a friend, Harpur – I know that would be quite wrong – but she seemed to half trust you.'

'Some do. All sorts thought very well of Eleri.' He looked for grief in her and did see a down-slant to her mouth and pain in the eyes. Mainly, though, he was aware of toughness, and competence.

'She felt she couldn't lose. It was always a tonic to visit Mum,' she said.

'Yet she . . .'

'You're right: she said get to you, you personally, if things went bad, so she did realize that they might, yes. That was only recent. The new stresses. And then there was a beating, of course.'

'You saw her pretty often?' Harpur replied. Occasionally, he would run up against this kind of tricky development. Someone from outside the domain would arrive, seeming to know a little of how things operated here, but almost certain to be crudely wrong about one or more of the essentials. He tried to size up from this woman's face what she understood and what she thought she understood. Her features did not remind him of Eleri's but of his own children's: that similar eager-eyed insolence which in the same moment gave an impression of girlish openness and terrible distance. Harpur would have liked to know how to deal with it but had no time for a parenthood course.

He cleared an armchair of newspapers and a Pepsi can for her and took a seat himself on the sofa. The positioning put them not quite head-on to each other, which was how Harpur preferred things, but she moved the chair on its castors so she was directly opposite him, like a pupil to a teacher: a teacher this pupil possibly did not think much of, yet the only one on offer. He still had not seen her smile. Of course, she would be in mourning, if she really was Eleri's daughter and as close as she said. Her russet hair was done in a good up-to-date jumble of go-anywhere tight spirals. Harpur felt she had too much watchful poise for any coiffure to bring even a hint of frenzy. 'My mother always spoke of you as "Harpur", Harpur.'

'OK.'

'I don't mind if you call me Louise. And there was another officer, named Iles. My mother said, failing you, see him. She said he could seem vicious and ungovernable but had very occasional pluses.'

'Well, fewer than that. He thought a lot of your mother – her discretion. Mr Iles values discretion in others.'

Louise glanced around at the new decor and seemed to approve: she gave a small nod. 'Probably you know who killed her, do you, Harpur? But there'd obviously be local politics.'

'The kind of life she led makes it difficult to trace all her contacts quickly.'

'Sure. I'll buy that. I thought maybe this egomaniac youngster, Vine? Psychopath? As I hear it, he'd be able to manage the beating. Mother said she was looking for a juicier discount with some London people, and Vine hated it.'

'She seems to have talked very openly to—'

'You saw her where she was found? But of course you did. Aren't you the top detective? Some dump of a place, wasn't it, where Mother would never have gone, except forced or dead? You'll show me the spot?'

'If you think you—'

'And were you the first to see her? I mean, the first except for the man who found her?'

'They'd notify me first.'

'I suppose they would,' she replied.

Years ago Harpur had come to realize he must be the sort of detective who was interrogated as much as he interrogated. When he got questioned there were no protective rules, though.

Harpur's daughters and Scott returned and he introduced them. The girls considered that anyone who came to the house on business had to be given the impression of a happy family setting, and they always offered questions, conversation, and refreshment. 'Look, if it's private police matters, we'll get lost,' Hazel said. 'Naturally.'

'Yes, it's private police matters,' Harpur replied. The girls and Scott found seats.

Jill said: 'When people come in through the garden, it's *usually* something confidential. We've seen a lot of that.'

'Yes.' Harpur wondered whether Louise spotted the harsh resemblance between herself and these two.

'I'm here for a funeral,' Louise said.

'Oh, well, if you've come a distance you should have a meal,' Hazel replied. 'We had a funeral for my mother. It's a while ago. Bad, bad, but I don't mind talking about it now.'

'This is *my* mother's.'

'He thought you were something pretty rough, down behind the bushes,' Hazel said. 'Dad's expecting interference. That's part of his job.'

'Louise wants some advice now, kids,' Harpur replied. 'One to one.'

'He's not just saying this, is he, Louise, because you're some girl he's wronged?' Hazel asked. 'He's a great wronger.'

Louise said: 'I don't know if he's wronged me.'

'Oh, you'd know,' Hazel replied.

'What do you mean, Louise?' Jill asked. 'To do with your mother's death?'

'Look, is your mother . . . I mean, was she, Eleri ap Vaughan – the one in the media?' Hazel said.

'Of course she is, dumbo,' Jill replied. 'So I suppose you're here to find who did it. And the funeral's not the total story.'

'Dad might help you,' Hazel said. 'But there are some very . . . well, *quiet* sides to policing here.'

'Have you got a father, Louise?' Jill asked. 'That's

important. Dad's been useful. He got rid of nearly all Mum's books, so we could begin a new life. But he let them stay a short time, while everything was still sad. Like I said, looking at him, plus knowing he's in the police, you might not believe he's a carer, but now and then, yes. Parents like to do whatever they want. Dad soon had a girlfriend after Mum's death. Or probably before. They were both like that, Mum and Dad. A bit free. We'd speak to them about it, but they kept on.'

'God,' Scott said.

'Or Iles – he might help you,' Hazel said. 'He's mad, but he knows quite a bit.'

'She's soft on Iles, Louise,' Jill said. 'He's madder than just mad. Iles has this menacing side. Dad's the best for you.'

'I don't know what it would be like to have a mother who was a brilliant pusher,' Scott said.

Hazel said: 'Dad probably knows who killed your mother, but that doesn't mean he'll definitely help you. You'll run into some strangenesses here. Do you know that phrase "wheels within wheels", Louise? This city's main industry.'

'We'll make you some sandwiches and tea, Louise – that kind of thing – so you can have more talk with Dad on an intimate basis.'

When the three of them had gone to the kitchen, Louise said: 'My mother thought you might know Keith Vine.'

'Of course,' Harpur replied. 'Most detectives know Vine, or of him.'

'No, I meant, *really* know him.'

'Your mother talked to you about her work in detail?'

'Her work, your work. She was very open. Your word. At the end, she was wide open, wasn't she?'

Louise seemed the sort of girl Iles would love to attempt, despite her age: he went for younger ones mostly. Those bleak eyes and her remoteness would call out to him, and Iles answered such calls. Because her soul was so guarded, the ACC would be sure it waited tenderly and specifically for him. Iles believed in soul contact and was convinced that anyone who could reach his would gain marvellous riches. Possibly some of the young tarts at the Valenica could reach it. Possibly, his wife, Sarah, did now and then. Possibly he believed Hazel might, but Harpur would stop that. There was room in Iles's soul for so many women and girls, and he would have no trouble accommodating Louise. She held her head like a cormorant on a rock measuring the sea and listening for fish: this would make Iles weep internally with awe. Harpur admired it, also. As anyone might have expected, Eleri had bred a noble child. Lineage.

Louise said: 'I looked in at the *Eton* last night. There's someone else in her spot now, trading as if he'd been there for ever. I suppose this would be a prized workstation. Myself, I didn't buy. Couldn't bring myself to it. This creep even displayed Mother's rum and black.' For half a second her voice was flecked with sadness. Then she asked: 'You blind-eye this, Harpur?'

The children came back carrying trays of food, the biggest teapot, and crockery. Jill said: 'As a matter of fact, people think Dad blind-eyes all sorts, but eventually they find out different.'

'I think I trust your dad, on the whole,' Louise said.

People visiting the realm in a search for information about relatives who had suffered in some way – injury, death – sometimes brought with them a fine, aggressive clarity. Think of this woman nominating Vine like that as her mother's killer. Yet these intruders could not understand, and could not be expected to understand, that policing here contained some special sides. Hazel had spoken of it. There was a mystical aspect. Home Office investigators sent down to examine how things worked also generally failed to grasp this and would have to be brought gradually into line by Iles, or not so gradually.

In any case, Louise's clarity was fallible. She seemed to suspect that if it was not Vine it must be Si Pilgrim, as if Si had it in him to kill, the shaky also-ran. This girl's wonderful hard eyes saw a great deal, and some of it was as it was, but only some of it. Harpur would always be civil to her, though, and as kindly as possible.

12

Becky was a very sensitive and bright kid, and Vine saw that she had picked up there were new problems, the interfering bitch. Women did not always spot the intricacies, especially when they were mothers. All they could think of was the safety of the child, which undoubtedly had importance, but did not mean you had to run because there was a mere difficulty or two. That way, would Britain ever have won the Empire? He considered the baby as much as she did – even more – but he had to think of the entire future for Charles – a career plan. She just thought of now, and maybe tomorrow – the immediate perils – perils as *she* saw things. It had happened before. When she was pregnant, she had actually tried to leave him, even leave the country. Luckily, he was able to catch her looking for a lift on the link road – his girl, full of his child, thumbing cars, the fool! Yes, he was luckily able to bring her back and get her into a good pre-motherly state again. She had a lot of strength and Keith Vine knew how to persuade her to use it, eventually. He loved her for this strength and knew he probably needed her more than she needed him. Himself, he would never think of leaving her. She had a mind, education. He had mentioned the London aspect of present matters to her, the intruder at the *Eton*. Communication covering most issues between partners he believed in to the limit, but, Christ, on this topic it had been such a mistake.

'London?' she replied. 'Heavies from London trying to move in?'

'It will be fine, Beck. He can be dealt with. Keith Vine's got him located.' Eventually, it had been simple to follow him from the girl's flat to his base. And Vine was sure he stayed unobserved this time.

'London gangs? They don't pussyfoot.'

She had had a weakness about names of places, as if the name itself contained life and magic – so, for example, everyone from London was unbeatable, hell-folk. And it would be no good trying to show her this was mad by saying the Archbishop of Canterbury lived in London, or the Queen Mother. Besides London, there was another name that always got her – France. To Becky France was eternally wonderful, spoken very wide and warm – *Frawnce*. All sunshine and friendly peasants, with the red tiles and slow, slow rivers, and azaleas so plentiful and aglint. Now and then she wanted the three of them, Vine, herself and the child, to quit the business here and get to 'Frawnce'. No, not now and then. Now.

Although she had not said it yet today, he could feel fucking 'Frawnce' was coming. 'We've made a decent little bit, haven't we, Keith? Do you know what I fancy, really fancy, from everyone's point of view, but especially Charles's?'

Well, of course he knew what she fancied, but it should be 'fawncied'. 'One or two roughish moments here, admittedly,'

Vine replied. 'But it's all sorted now. The great thing in business, Beck, is to turn problems into assets. This is Keith Vine's special skill.'

'Frawnce,' she said. 'The kindly *chaleur*, and plenty of fruit. We could live so cheaply.'

'Beck, I . . .'

'Police calling here, leaning hard, clearly trying to frame you for Eleri. They want a victim. So crude and malevolent, and, yes, frightening.'

'That's all they can do, try. And bully. We mustn't collapse.'

'Keith, I really thought you had some understanding with the police now.'

Yes. 'That visit meant nothing – for show and the record, that's all.'

'Persecution. Do we want Charles Louis brought up with incidents like that, police bursting in?'

She had Charles in her arms, trying to rock him to sleep. Vine loathed it when she stood like this – the two of them, his girl and his child, in this wonderful, meaningful pose, but with the drab flat as background – the insulting furniture and so-called decor. He went out then, before she could set her full, smart mind on him like a ratting dog. He drove to Ralph Ember's club, The Monty.

An alliance. This was the idea his mind had begun to play with lately. If you had possible trouble from outside, the obvious way to handle it was get together with someone else local, who might also be worried. Usually, of course, Ralphy Ember was the competition. But Vine had heard a saying, *My enemy's enemy is my friend*. Ember would see that the London lad was his enemy, too.

It was early evening, and Ralph usually did a stint himself in The Monty at this time. He liked to open up the place and then leave it to staff until he came back around closing. There should be an hour or so for talks. Ralphy you needed to go so cagey with. He saw a lot and had riches that dated right back, even five, six years – what was called 'old money' in the trade. The club did not look like class, though Ember thought so, and Ralph did not always look like class himself, because of jumpiness in his face and a thick scar along the jaw-line. Yet in a way he *was* class. Many women thought he resembled Charlton Heston when younger, and he did brilliantly for offers. People called him 'Panicking Ralph', following disasters at armoured van occasions and even a bank. Keith Vine considered it unnecessary and very poor business to call him 'Panicking' face-to-face. In any case, the thing about Ember was he always seemed to come out of these panic situations with good gains, regardless – no matter what happened to the other people on the operation with him, like jail or injury, or even death.

'You're looking great, Ralph,' Vine said. 'The perfect whiteness of that shirt sets you off. You've got a missus who really takes care of you, and why not? I thought a business talk – supposing it's convenient, obviously.'

Ember did not reply. He brought out a black bottle of Kressmann Armagnac, though, and a couple of glasses, and Kressmann was usually a good sign. There were not many members in the club this early. Around midnight was

The Monty's high period, unless there had been a good Crown Court acquittal of a member or close family, when the party might start at any hour.

'Keithy, I had an idea you might show. You're thinking merger?'

How it was with Ember. He could panic, but he could also do fierce insights. 'Merger? Merger?' Vine replied, chuckling rather. 'This is rushing things a bit, Ralph.'

They went to a table near the wall and Ember poured drinks. He wet his lips with his. 'You've had trouble, Keith, I know, and I thought it might be more than you can manage solo.'

This was it – the knocking had started. 'Oh, no, not like that at all, Ralph,' Vine said. 'Much more positive. Lately, I came to think a merger had to be the only thing, but from, yes, an entirely positive aspect, not on account of trouble.' He had another chuckle and a further one. He made a series of it. 'I mean, *what* trouble?'

'Eleri getting killed like that. And then I heard police at your bijou spot, including the savage girl cop, Biss, Bish, Fish, Dish? Who wants to be lined up for something like that death, Keith? Plus, much more important, this London cohort. They come wanting Eleri and find she's been snuffed. This will lead to you, Keithy. I mean, who else is it going to lead to? All in all, you do need friends. I accept that.'

It was always the thing with this bastard, you would come feeling strong and helpful, and he would turn it around and make you believe it was *you* needing *him*, not the other way.

'We could both do with friends, Ralph. Who's going to

fight London on his own?' He sounded like Becky, for God's sake.

'And now I hear Pilgrim's in Eleri's corner! Really, Keith, what kind of an outfit is that? Si Pilgrim!'

'Obviously not permanent, Ralph. Just it was vital for continuity.'

Ember behaved amazed. 'Get rid of him? That says further trouble. Once he has the feel and knows the easy earnings, is Si going to give it up?'

'Si could be thoroughly advised.'

'That's what I said – trouble. Si dead or hurt after Eleri and the police would have to consider real action, even here, Keith. It would be plural deaths then. Two deads are a lot more than twice as much as one. This is carnage. There'd be media interest. The Press knows how to spell gun-law.'

They were sitting at the usual negotiation table in the club. It gave you some distance and privacy, but not in a dark corner of the place, like a plot. This table was under a blow-up photograph of The Monty outing to Paris a few years ago when a French whore was kidnapped by some members for more than thirty-six hours, and two pimps given grievous bodily harm when they came looking. It was well known Ralphy wanted to think of this place like one of those London clubs such as The Carlton, full of heavy conversation and great wines, but he had definitely not managed it yet, and you could get tired of all his daft dignity.

'I've run into some bother at home, Ralph. Oh, Becky – indecisive? You know what it does to them, breastfeeding.

Why I'm here now. Coming to offer like this – it's a big step for me, Ralph. Keith Vine is not usually one to look for aid.'

'You've advanced fast, Keith. I don't say too fast, but this kind of work is like building a structure, creating a fabric. Perhaps it does need time.'

'Well, sure, Ralph.' Vine stared around the club. 'You've built a structure, no question, and developed a fabric.' You buttered the bugger. 'But some of us have to go this other route, like more casual.'

'Becky wants out?'

'Look, Ralph, she's got full trust in me, never a doubt.'

'I can understand that.'

'But, yes, when they've got a kid their judgement is— They're different people then, Ralph. As, of course, you know. Margaret's given you two lovely children.'

'Margaret is indeed marvellous. She's the only woman I would ever consider being close to.'

'Wonderful.'

'Oh, I may bump into other girls around from time to time, obviously. A man has to. This kind of life. But real closeness, I mean.'

'Wonderful, Ralph.'

Ember hit the table with the knuckle side of his spread hand. It might be something he saw in a film – supposed to say they had reached the important bit of the discussion. He was taking charge. 'So, are you really talking merger or sell-out, Keith?'

'Sell-out?' Vine had a full, long, but unhostile laugh at

this, far advanced on a chuckle. 'Keith Vine does not sell out, Ralph.'

'You and Becky want Provence or whatever? Me buy your street pusher list? I don't know, really don't know, Keith. I'm pretty well at optimum already. And now you've lost Eleri. Do I want dealings with Si Pilgrim?'

Vine spoke gently, very seriously: 'The list's unavailable, Ralph. Unavailable on the terms you speak of. That's not my purpose.'

'This is what Becky would want.'

'Beck's so great, but she can't see the whole picture, can she, Ralph, the moody dear?'

Ember had to go back to the bar and serve. A new group had come in and were asking for Scotch. There were two blacks with them. Vine loved this. He thought it so right they could also be members. They had to have a role in life. Ember stayed at the bar, talking to them all for a few minutes, smiling and getting the profile going. There were a couple of white girls in the group, decent looking in their way, and Vine had definitely seen rougher, especially in The Monty. Sometimes Ralphy's profile was Charlton Heston and sometimes Cardew the Cad, that tall, gawky idiot comic, all chin, who used to be on TV.

When Ember returned to the table, he said: 'I greatly respect women like those two. Beautifully manicured, both, and a sort of happy, unassailable innocence all through them, yet I hear their blood whistling to me.' He filled up the glasses again.

Vine said: 'Ralph, the point is I'd be able to hold Becky

here if I was able to buy Kenward Knapp's old place, The Pines.'

'That's certainly a property.'

'She'd see the point of it all then. Playroom for Charles, grounds, a pony when he's a bit older. She could not mistake this for anything but a true style of life. I know that ever since childhood she's fancied a gallery.'

'Money?' Ember replied. 'You're looking for money? The Pines is, say, three hundred grand, even in a problematical market.'

'About that. I thought . . . I thought some Mid-East or South American bank might do it – a bank that's used to risk for high interest. I could put down, say, fifty grand.' No way of knowing whether Ember would think that good or pathetic. Probably pathetic.

Ember nodded, but not to show he agreed with anything. It would be because he suddenly saw the direction: 'You want my recommendation and guarantee, do you?'

'Obviously, the house itself, repossessable, that's a guarantee. But I know some of these off-Broadway banks ask more than that. You're a figure, Ralph, weight – and deservedly. There's this marvellous club, your residence, Low Pastures.'

Ember nodded some more and seemed to drift. 'Keith, I was taking a university degree you know, mature student, very.'

'Another thing to your credit.'

'In suspension because of the way business raced ahead. I feared I wouldn't do myself justice in the finals. But, look, there was a bit of English Literature and other general stuff for mature students first year, to fill in their gaps. I have to tell you all sorts of big novels last century are about someone in a mess because they guaranteed a loan. I expect you saw *Middlemarch* on TV.'

'Such a viewing experience,' Vine replied, 'the properties and gavottes. This would be a short-term advance, Ralph – the way the money's coming in now.'

Ember stood and went to the blow-up picture of the outing. He began pointing to various faces, including the ones who snatched that Frog whore, speaking all the names with heavy respect: 'This membership here, Keith, looks to me for the occasional sensible example, and for mild, thoughtful guidance.'

'I know it. Everyone does.'

'Keith, I wonder what they'd say, and what they'd think of me, if I put Ralph W. Ember's name on a bond so Keith Vine can keep his bird and child with him, despite acute business perils.'

'Confidential, Ralph. In any case, many might see the advantages. It could be a fine commercial move.'

'What are you offering?' Ember asked. He resumed his chair. Vine could not be sure which of the women at the bar Ralph watched most. But Vine had an idea that both of them, when they glanced over this way, looked at him, more than at Ember. Although this would be so natural, Keith did not respond to either. It would be stupid to turn Ember evil just now. Crucial to keep Ralphy content, soothed by the happy lust calls he thought he heard, the sad old jerk.

'You ask what I can offer,' Vine said, and gave it a good, ringing, almost amused tone.

'What was your best asset is due to be torched at the crem the day after tomorrow,' Ember replied.

This was a bargaining situation, so you had to expect brisk tactics, but all the same Vine was shocked by that – the crudity, the callousness. There had been through-and-through sweetness in Eleri, everyone said it, plus occasional integrity even, and there was no need to speak of her like that. To get dominance, Ralphy would blot out all decency. Maybe his experience told him to behave like that, but Vine hoped no quantity of experience would ever make him, personally, so inhuman. Eleri had been a treacherous, gifted Welsh sow who deserved everything that came to her, but some respect could be offered, surely, especially about an event like cremation.

Ember said: 'Keith, I've got a very sweet little business. One of its strengths is its cohesiveness. Myself and two accomplished partners. Our list is solid. I've a fine supplier and The Monty and so on as an impeccable business front. What's in it for me, Keith, to open up the operation to a damaged outfit like yours, and put myself in hock because your girl wants a big house?'

Keith began to get angry, though he did not show it, not right away. It sickened him to hear women he felt so much for spoken of without any regard. 'Besides my list, Ralph, what I can offer is crucial facts about this London invasion. I've done research – what I mean when I say together we can triumph over the bastard colonizers.'

'Oh, research,' Ember replied. He flapped a hand, like brushing a nothing word away.

'I tailed him from a whore.'

'Of course you did,' Ember replied.

Vine did not understand what this meant – whether Ember believed him, or thought it was the kind of useless thing Vine would do, or already knew Vine had done this.

'And, of course, he never spotted you,' Ember said.

'We could pre-empt, Ralph,' Vine replied. 'Knock them before they even start.'

Ember stood again, and this time picked up the bottle and glasses. 'A few things to do now, Keithy. The Monty doesn't run itself. London? I don't imagine I'll be fretting about that. I've seen off far worse.'

Vine gave up. He said with a full snarl to Ember's back: 'I'm stupid, stupid. Why should you want to help me stay in Britain? I'm the competition, aren't I, Ralph?'

'Stay or go, Keith. You don't trouble me.'

When Vine came here he had meant to make his offer to Ember in three parts. To sweeten the merger, he would have put in his list, obviously, and, then, secondly, all he knew about the London visitors. Finally, and most important, he was going to tell him he had Harpur well and truly bought and would bring him usefully into the combined firm. But now, fuck Ember. The lordly twat in his dim palace did not deserve such treasure, not even to persuade him to an agreement. Vine stood, too: 'You're on your own then, Panicking,' he said, and left.

13

Harpur was sleeping the sleep of the just legal, a jumpy, interesting, blame-splintered sleep, when he suddenly realized that Denise was out of bed naked and gazing down at the street around the edge of the curtains, a hand up to her mouth, as if afraid she might scream. She was young, heard more than Harpur even when blotto. Did he need alarms if she was here? But she was not always here, yet. So, yes, probably he did. Any time now he would get them installed. He would have to pay for the buggers himself, though: could not put in an expenses claim to Lane saying he was in particular danger because he had improperly gone undercover.

Denise stepped back, possibly scared she had been spotted. For a few seconds, she stayed almost completely still, except that her breathing was heavy and anxious. Then she moved forward to her post again. He loved her back: the length and narrowness of it and the sheen, even in the dark. He loved the delicacy of her shoulders.

There had been other times at night when she alerted Harpur, thinking they had intruders. Those crises had turned out to be nothing – usually Vine making a secret business visit by tapping the kitchen window – but they might have been peril. Really, in general, he must wake up. He reclosed his eyes, hoping for more of his last dream: at a thoughtful meeting of the Trinity, he was admitted to heaven on a split vote, despite what the Holy Ghost termed 'several laughably slight besmirchments of professional police standards', before giving a casting nod for Harpur. God Himself had been against – some grunts about 'corner-cutting at the very least' and a finicky reference to 'illegal hetero anal sex'. Lately, Harpur often had dreams of Judgement Day, and they did not always turn out as favourable.

He opened his eyes a little and watched Denise. Turning from the window, she quickly pulled on some clothes, then moved towards the door, evidently meaning to deal with whatever it was down there on her own: no useless fuss this time. She might be dressed now, but his mind held on to the memory of her naked back and arse as she stood at the window, glorious and destructible, and as ever he grieved to imagine her skin at risk. He jumped out of bed and grabbed her hand to stop her going from the room. She waited while he dressed.

'Two men, I think,' she whispered. 'Twenties.'

Christ, and she would have taken them on without telling him. This was madness and love – it had to be love, surely, no matter what she said viciously now and then about his being a cop.

'Maybe the two are not together, Col. That was my impression.'

'How do you mean?'

'What I said. Not together.'

'But *here* together. I don't understand,' he said. 'What did you hear?'

'Possibly glass breaking. Not much.'

But enough. His daughters might have heard that, too. Their ears would be at least as sharp as Denise's. They might be downstairs, probing. Jesus.

'You stay here,' he said.

'No.'

He thought he would get out fast and lock her in. She might forgive that, in due course. 'All right,' he said. 'Give me a minute, then follow.'

'No. We go together.'

He disliked that wording, like a suicide pact. 'Right,' he replied. He would have to be fast – give her a shove back as he opened the door, then lock it before she recovered. No, perhaps, she would never forgive that: kids of her age and poise expected to go on living as a right, and resented forcible care. Just the same, she was going to get some.

His hand was on the doorknob, and he was about to half turn his body and push her away from him when he heard one muted sound from below, almost certainly a silenced shot. For a second, he could not move. Gunfire would do that to Harpur sometimes, especially when unexpected – not a good quality in a detective. His only coherent thought was that he should get to the bedside phone and ring Iles. Jesus, what dependence! There was not time to call the ACC, and no certainty he would be at home, and definitely no certainty he would come if he were. A door slammed shut below. Harpur pulled the bedroom door open and was about to sidle onto the landing when there were rushed footsteps up the stairs. This time his only coherent thought was where to find a weapon, any weapon. To this there was no coherent answer: the best and sole and nearest was the lavatory brush. 'Stay,' he said over his shoulder to Denise, like instructing a dog, and again he half turned and would have grabbed her fine shoulder to propel her back into the room, but she seemed to foresee the move, and kept to the side of him, out of reach. When he looked back along the landing a man had appeared in the shadows at the top of the stairs. He was holding what looked like an automatic pistol.

Vine said: 'Thank God, you're all right, Mr Harpur. And with the young friend in tonight. You're definitely entitled. I've been following him, researching.'

'Who?'

'London. Lovely Mover. He would have seen you off, Mr Harpur. And anyone close, if I may so describe your friend. Denise, isn't it? That's one of his assignments, I should think – finish you.'

'You shot him?' Harpur said.

'Would I fire in your home, Mr Harpur? Children possibly about. Plus your friend. And this weapon is not silenced.'

'Him firing?'

'If I fired, wouldn't he be dead, Mr Harpur?'

'Where is he?'

'He's nimble, I'll give him that. He ran. I could have chased. But I needed to know you and yours were all right. He'd been in the house awhile. Anything might have happened to you in that time.'

'All right, I think.'

'I see it as an outrage, breaking into the head of CID's house while he's asleep and cohabiting,' Vine replied. 'This is what things are coming to here. It's the foul ways of the States moving in on us – if – I definitely say *if* – *if* we will allow it, Mr Harpur.'

The Chief often spoke like this. He and Vine should get together and write letters to the Press.

'We must *not* allow it,' Vine said . . . 'The children?'

Harpur moved quickly along the landing and opened the doors of his daughters' rooms. Both appeared to be sleeping undisturbed. Vine, Denise and he went downstairs and switched on the lights. One of the small, ornamental panes of glass was out in the front door. In the sitting room a book had been knocked from the shelf by a bullet and lay on the settee with a ragged hole right through the top right-hand corner. It was Jill's collection of boxing essays, *The Sweet Science*. She had insisted on keeping this, along with *The Orton Diaries*, when Megan's library was disposed of. Harpur brought out some drinks and they sat down.

'Of course, we've met before,' Vine said to Denise. He had holstered the automatic now.

'Of course we have. Here,' she said. 'You say following him – following "London". I mean, why? Who's London?'

'This is business research,' Vine replied.

Harpur saw Keith was being careful – could not tell how much Denise knew or suspected. Harpur himself could not tell. This girl was getting some rapid introductions to a rough life. Vine had called him Mr Harpur throughout, never the familiarity of Colin or Col, as would suit a supposed partner.

'Well, my God, research!' Denise said. 'A break-in and

then shooting. You waving a pistol. I bet they don't cater for that in Harvard Business School.'

'You've seen some education, have you, love?' Vine replied. 'Anyone could tell. I admire all that. Gives a person outlook. I'll be getting Charles – that's my son – young yet – but I'll be getting Charles a real education, as a priority. This will be so crucial in the twenty-first century.'

'But why does he come here, this "London"?' Denise asked.

'It's not friendliness. Mr Harpur's a crux figure, in many respects,' Vine replied.

'What's that mean?' Denise asked.

'Oh, yes, crux,' Vine replied.

Harpur saw she expected no proper answers. She had accepted a long time ago that about wide areas of his work she would never be told anything direct. This would include people running loose in the house with guns. It did not stop her guessing, nosing, intuiting, suspecting, asking, remembering. 'So what do you do now, Col?' she asked. 'Someone's broken into your house, fired a gun. Serious?'

'Oh, *eventually* Mr Harpur is sure to do something. These are offences, like you said. Can they be simply forgotten? Hardly.' He went into a short, comfortable laugh.

'You could call people right away, couldn't you, *shouldn't* you, Col, to look for him?'

'There's more than one way of playing these situations,' Harpur replied.

'Timing,' Vine said.

Denise finished her drink and said she would go back upstairs.

Vine stood. 'I won't keep Mr Harpur long, rely on it. I, too, hate a lonely bed, believe me, Denise.'

When she had gone, Vine said: 'Thank God I was right on that lad's tail, Col. I can't afford to lose you, not in the present state of things.'

'Thanks, Keith.'

'Tailing's an art, Col. When he puts his mind to it – really puts his mind to it – there's nobody can equal Keith Vine.'

Harpur wondered about that. He'd only ever known one real tail, Erogenous Jones, dead now. 'Well, he might have seen you, all the same, Keith. He'd want to lead you here, knock you over in my sitting room, leave me millstoned with the body. That's two people taken out of his way at once.'

Vine began to growl: 'Of course he didn't see Keith Vine. What am I, some lout, some novice? Well, he has to go, Col. He can't hit something moving in the dark, and not many can, but someone happily asleep with his lady, or sitting peacefully here on the settee, or with his head framed in the car window in daylight – that would be so much easier. You'd be a prize for them. I've got to look after you. You never carry anything.'

'Thanks, Keith.'

'Will you be secure now, do you think?' He rose to leave. 'Please, Col, let me get you something for self-defence, only that.'

'Perhaps later.'

It seemed almost an insult to the rest of Denise's body – to all the more recognised sexual regions – that when Harpur returned to bed he wanted to caress her back, run his hand slowly down its smooth length time and again, broadening out to her shoulders and tops of her arms now and then, but essentially just the line of her back, and not even as far as the lovely curve of her bottom. She lay prone, arms down at her side, her face turned away from him on the pillow. 'Sometimes, Col, I think you really value me.'

'A bit.'

'Sometimes, Col, I think it's probably bullshit that I'm ever going to drift into a marriage with some coeval and keep you on the side, the way we agreed. Don't argue. We did. There are decent precedents. It's like Cathy planned to keep Heathcliff on the side when married to Edgar Linton.'

'Who? Who? *Who?* Anyway, *you* agreed. Not me. You're never going to find anyone else who'll revere your back. Coevals are not bred to it. Oh, especially not coevals.'

'You rub your knuckles along the bumpy bone system that holds me together and you wonder if because of you and your bed and your connections someone's going to knock it to bits one day or night, don't you? Morbid of you, Col. And then your daughters. Are they all right here? Isn't there somewhere you could send them until things quieten down?'

'Where, for Heaven's sake?' he asked. 'No. This was just a one-off.'

'Yes?' Her voice sank into exasperation and weariness. 'You're undercovering in Vine's firm after all, are you?' she asked. He saw she had come to suspect this a long while ago.

'He helped us tonight.'

'Of course. Because you helped him first. Mates.'

She had noted the late-night visits by Vine, the bullshit excuses. And there had been other evidence she found, too. She used to ask and ask Harpur about it all, but seemed to have given that up lately. He thought he had convinced her the idea was dead. Yes, thought he had. Now this.

He said: 'Well, I've done the full homage to your back. You could turn over. I'd like to see your face.'

She did not move at once, sulking. 'I'd like to see yours,' she said. 'The true one.'

14

Ralph Ember had a summons down to see his supplier. That's what it was, a summons. Ember always grew evil over these sudden calls from Barney. And he always went. The last guess Ember heard said Barney earned half a million a year from imports, and he had the irresistibility that suited this. Perhaps by now he made more.

Barney would sound wonderfully spontaneous and ample when he phoned, so much easy power, like talking to a waterfall. *How about tomorrow then, Ralphy? That fit your diary?* Meaning, *Get here.* This was a half-day's journey each way. Barney loved boating and lived on a river in Hampshire where big yachts clustered just outside his window, ready for Cowes and sunny, far seas. Ember saw a different money league when he called on Barney, and felt small. He was meant to. He hated these visits. That classy sound of rigging rapping masts in the breeze gave him colic. Barney himself would never travel to see Ember, of course. Ralph was glad. He did not want Barney in The Monty, getting a grand giggle from the clientele, their clothes and shoes and radiant jailbird slipperiness.

Something else about these orders from Barney angered Ember as well. Always, he demanded that not only Ralph came but all the other what he termed 'principals' in the business, as if the sod did not know who really ran the outfit, or as if he did not trust Ember. So he had to take Harry Foster and Gerry Reid. Barney would explain really so very fucking hearteningly that he liked to see the other two in case Ember was knifed or shot in an inevitable business fight one day, or locked up if the police turned to victimizing even him. Then it would be important that Barney knew personally and well those who would continue the firm, and important that Foster and Reid were familiar with how Barney ran his operation. 'Guarantee succession,' he would say. 'Crucial in all great businesses. Look at the Royals, so far.' But this was not how Ember liked to manage an enterprise. Although Harry and Gerry Reid were tip-top lads and brilliant at their rock-bottom level, that's only where they *were* tip-top, at rock-bottom. Talking of Royals, you did not let the sentries run Buck House. Foster and Reid knew how to marshal street pushers, sell to them and collect. They were never going to be boardroom, and Ralph considered it a deep kindness not to burden them with the syndicate's accounting and strategy. It was damned hurtful insolence for Barney to behave as though Ralph, Harry and Gerry Reid were on a par. Christ, Mouth-Mouth Reid and the dump where he lived!

'I get unpleasant whispers from your realm, lads,' Barney said. He was in some sort of beige smock today, possibly related to yachting, though Ember would have thought more rural, shepherdy or village idiot. 'I have to wonder whether you boys are sufficiently alert to the menace from outside there. If you're exposed through slackness, I'm exposed, too.' When he really got going, Barney could sound like a brigadier, a hard, now-hear-this, apportion-the-blame voice. 'One thing I hate – as you know, Ralph – one thing I hate is dealing with a region of potential turmoil. That can spread so destructively.' He waved his hand, to mean the house at risk and his boat, his cars, his dreary women in those Margate Sands dresses. 'What everybody forecast after Kenward went like that, and what you said could not happen, Ralph, is, it seems to me – and to those who advise me – under way. That's my impression. I mean London spotting a vacuum, moving in. I have to tell you that, as a basic policy matter, I do not run against London or Manchester teams. Those people believe they can't lose, so generally they don't.'

'Vacuum? We're no fucking vacuum,' Harry Foster replied. He twitched his shoulders to show he had bulk to fill any space. That was like him. He looked for insults all the time when they came to Barney's place, and you had to admit there were plenty. But Harry did not know how to use gradualness and skill.

Reid said: 'Well, I'm entirely sure Barney knows that. He would hardly be dealing with us, would he, if he thought we were nothing?' That mild Irish accent helped when Reid was theorizing.

Barney smiled at Gerry for his efforts and ignored Foster. This was how people like Barney behaved, a kind of aristocratic touch. They just sailed on regardless, imitating Nelson. 'These invading gangs aim to colonize, always that. They know if they don't grow they die.'

'Let's help them fucking die, then,' Foster replied.

Barney shrugged. It might mean *Too true*. Or it might mean *Can you handle it?* Or it might mean he had been using a figure of speech and was not asking for real violence and death. People up there at Barney's level could be blunt and they could be roundabout – now and then leaving a vagueness, so they could say they had been misunderstood if things went wrong. Last time they visited him they talked in what he had called the Games Room, where there was a dartboard. Today, he had taken them to a different first-floor room which he said he used for meditation and prayer. It was unfurnished, but had a scatter of Turkish-style mats on the board floor, and they sat on these. The walls and ceiling were painted brilliant white. A couple of large birdcages stood at one end of the room, unoccupied now except by ancient droppings. Near them was a gymnasium vaulting horse. A chimney-sweeping brush and its poles had been propped against this. Barney said he came to this room as often as he could in a busy, frequently nautical life to be in touch with that selfhood which all of us needed to find and cherish. Ember saw that this room, like the rest of the house, produced confusion and rage in Harry Foster. He did not understand how Barney could buy such a wondrous place and then equip it like a junkyard. Gerry Reid, though, was different. He always tried to fit in and had said as they entered and he excitedly sat on his mat: 'Barney, let this not be deemed presumptuous, but I feel I have reached a haven. Here is empathy, here is the unconstrained.' Reid was a born placator, though could now and then turn hard.

'I'd regret having to end the arrangement with you

people, but that's the way I'm thinking,' Barney replied. 'Simply, you don't look big enough to confront this incursion – even incursions.'

'What's that mean, incursions?' Foster asked.

'I cannot, *cannot*, be linked to disaster, Ralphy. Weakness is progressive.' He lifted his eyes a bit mystically towards the sweep's brush. 'I have to tell you I like the sound of this boy Vine, the other local team.'

'Keithy?' Foster replied. 'Keithy's just a dim, jumped-up kid.'

Gerry Reid said: 'Well, we must allow *some* strengths to him, Harry. A kid moving with some speed.'

'I refer to the killing of Eleri ap Vaughan,' Barney replied.

'Such a dear old lady,' Reid said.

Barney's broad, small-nosed, ungenial face glinted with admiration: 'This must have been such a terrible moral and business dilemma for Keith Vine,' he said. 'I'd like to hear some Oxford philosopher sort out the deep intricacies of that situation. It required real mental strength to deal with: to slaughter one's star in order to prove resolution and combativeness. That act was so fine, boys. This was somebody saying, "If I can't have Eleri, London will not have her either." Such a message! At her funeral, Keith Vine will be able to gaze about the church with warrantable pride, knowing that pusher colleagues of Eleri will understand what is being said via that coffin, and decide it's best to stick with Keith. This is the one blow against London I've heard of. I get nothing firm that says you think of defending yourselves. To me it looks depressingly as if only Vine and his associates are capable of taking on this outside challenge, or challenges, and beating it/them.'

So where did the exhaustive information come from? Sometimes, Ember wondered whether Barney supplied Vine as well, and talked to him. That would be just like Barney, too: people floating up there in their riches might deal with one business and deal with its prime rival, as well, to make sure that if one of them collapsed Barney would still be happy.

'Keith Vine will bring genuine grief to the funeral, for someone esteemed and, yes, loved. If he did not grieve, his message to pushers would be weaker. His presence will declare: *I cherished this lady, yet had to knock her over for the sake of general business.* This is maturity, Ralph, Harry, Gerry.' He had a light, quick, skimming voice, like a superior yacht over waves, which seemed to say on top of what it did say that he had no time to dawdle with such people as Ember.

Ember said: 'I'm thinking urgently of a merger with Keith, as a matter of fact, Barney. I've long recognized his exceptional worth.'

Barney gave another of those shrugs.

'You what?' Harry asked.

'Oh, yes,' Ember said. 'Keith approached me. Obviously, I played cautious, at that early, as it were, feeling-out stage. But I've come to see the sense.' Yes, he had come to see an alliance with that little jerk might be wise since he heard Barney threaten severance of supplies, and heard the rhapsodies over Vine. This was how business thinking at the summit functioned: it was swift, it was incisive, it took account of new factors. Perhaps Barney already knew Vine had made the proposal. Perhaps Barney had told him to make it. Perhaps that was why Ember had been called down here today. 'I'll be in contact with him, soonest,' Ember said.

'Me, work with Keith Vine?' Foster said.

'Keith's the sort who would have charted in full this London intrusion,' Barney said. 'With Keith in charge, it's perfectly possible the threat or threats will be negatived. My aim.'

'In fucking *charge*?' Foster howled.

Reid said: 'Within the large framework of combined firms, partners will have areas of specialization, that's plain. Keith's, perhaps, will be countering this invasion. He'd be *in charge* of that aspect. This is what Barney means, Harry. We would all have our own particular fields, like the Cabinet.'

'Talking to Vine without informing the rest of the partnership, Ralphy?' Foster said. 'I don't—'

The door of the meditation room opened. 'Ah, here are Maud and Camilla now,' Barney cried. 'They are going to sing for us, before we sit down to the health meal they've provided. We are rediscovering home entertainment. Such a treat to escape television now and then, isn't it, gals?' Both women were in their fifties and dressed like a senior citizens' day centre. Whenever Ember saw them it badly upset him to think of Barney finding gratification there, either singly or as a pair. They sang 'Drake's Drum' now, unaccompanied, and, because of Reid's applause, 'Shipmates o' Mine' as an encore. Their voices were thin, high, unseaworthy.

'How do you see these three, Camilla, Maud, dears?' Barney asked, when they had finished and taken some bows. 'Do I persist with them, or are they going to land me up to my eyebrows in the kacky?'

'They do have a waft of catastrophe to them, especially this one,' Maud replied, pointing at Ember.

'Now, I don't want you to imagine I put Maud up to that,' Barney said.

'What the fuck does she know about anything, anyway?' Foster asked.

'Myself, I see her reply as something of a light-hearted leg-pull, nothing more,' Reid said. 'What's referred to as a joshing – yes, funny word – joshing of Ralph.'

15

Harpur was having an argument with his children about Eleri ap Vaughan's funeral when the phone rang and Jill went to answer. He was glad of the break. Because they now knew Eleri's daughter, the girls insisted they should take a day off school and attend the service. 'Louise has been to our home, Dad,' Hazel had said. 'Important that. She's in strange territory and needs support. Why she sought us out via the garden, like some small, troubled animal.'

'Oh, my,' Jill said.

'She sought *me* out,' Harpur said, 'because her mother told her to.'

'Right,' Hazel replied. 'Her mother had spoken well of you.'

'Sometimes you go to funerals of murder victims yourself, Dad,' Jill said. 'Or often.'

'As a gesture of commiseration, we go to funerals of the innocent, not of murder victims who were full-out, prospering crooks,' Harpur said.

'Only a cop could speak like that,' Hazel replied. 'Death is death. It makes everyone equal, like the paths of glory leading but to the grave in that poem in school.'

'Oh, my,' Jill said.

'I *am* a cop,' Harpur said.

'Yes,' Hazel said.

'I'm not sure it's safe,' Harpur replied.

'What, at a *funeral*?' Jill said.

'So, is that why *you're* not going?' Hazel asked.

'I mean not safe for *you*,' Harpur replied.

This was when the phone rang. Jill came back almost immediately. 'Sounds like a bought voice, Dad. No name, lots of urgency.' She went into a super-deferential sing-song: *Might I speak to Detective Chief Superintendent Harpur, please, should he perchance be at home?*

When Harpur picked up the receiver, Jack Lamb said: 'Which of them was that, Col?'

'Jill.'

'Ah, they grow apace, become old and colder and colder. They learned from Mummy to despise informants? But they're good kids – never ask who's calling.'

'What is it, Jack?'

'We ought to meet.'

Harpur remained silent, which was consent, or eagerness, or whatever Jack wished to make of it, though not refusal, of course. When someone of Lamb's eminence as a tipster offered to see you, you let him say what suited. It was *his* skin, and with Jack there was a lot of it.

'Rendezvous 3?' Jack suggested.

He adored codes and almost all the hygiene of secrecy. 'Right,' Harpur replied.

'We'd need a note for school,' Jill said, when Harpur returned. 'You could say a funeral of some close friend of the family.'

'Oh, I don't fancy that,' Harpur said. 'Teacher will know

whose funeral is the day after tomorrow. Eleri's famous. How do I describe some gnarled pusher as a special friend of a police family?'

'You've got all sorts as special friends, haven't you?' Jill said. 'Think of Iles.'

'Or whoever just phoned,' Hazel said. 'Do you know *De mortuis nil nisi bonum*, Dad? Genuine Latin – what's known as a maxim. Meaning, speak only good of the dead. In school they teach famous classical phrases, so later we can pretend we were not at a comp. It's like potted Harrow.'

'No point giving him Latin,' Jill replied. 'Stop bringing school home. That will only turn him more against. He hates education, not having one.'

'Why a note, anyway?' Harpur replied.

'It's regulations,' Hazel said.

'What happens if I don't?' Harpur asked.

'You'll have the school attendance officer here, badgering,' Jill said.

'That's all right,' Harpur replied. 'I'll explain you were at a funeral.'

'Well, then, why can't you do it in advance, as laid down?' Hazel asked.

'Because I don't think you should go,' Harpur replied.

'People could slag off many things about you, Dad – I mean your clothes and hair and dirty corner-cutting and sex – but never that you were heartless. Not until now,' Hazel said. 'That was a lovely side of you, despite everything.'

'I don't want you to go,' Harpur replied.

'We'd wear something dark and respectful,' Jill said. 'Not like at Mum's.'

'So, why for this one?' Harpur asked.

'Because she *was* crooked, of course. We have to let Louise know that in death this does not matter to us, regardless of our father.'

'But you're still invited, too, Dad,' Jill said, 'regardless.'

*

Rendezvous 3 was Jack's favourite, and occasionally Harpur thought they used it too often. He even had the notion that criminals might also come here for their secret meetings – planning sessions or share-outs. Absurd and typical: when law and order moved out after its confidential exchanges, criminality moved in for some of its own. But this place reached Jack's soul, because of its military connections. He was keen on all things Army. A Second World War concrete blockhouse on the foreshore, it was built half a century ago to throw back invaders. Likewise, Rendezvous 1, where Jack also felt very happy, was the hillside anti-aircraft battery – that site Harpur had used for a meeting with Keith Vine. It might be unwise to go there in future with Lamb.

It was dark, but inside the blockhouse Harpur could just make out Jack move urgently to one of the observation slits, like suddenly alerted troops. Crouched, he stared out across mudflats to the sea, as if intently seeking Hitler's invasion fleet. Lamb loved to imagine himself in times of war, fighting to secure a free and wholesome Britain in which his shady art business and serious grassing could thrive. Quite often at these meetings Jack would turn up wearing items of uniform bought with dash at army surplus shops. To Harpur, they looked wildly conspicuous, especially on someone as huge as Jack: seemed to wipe out the purpose in meeting at remote spots. It did not trouble Lamb.

'This defence post was put here to repel intruders – like the gun-site, Col. Now there are other intruders in the realm.'

'Yes?'

'How will they be stemmed?'

Harpur waited to be told.

'Oh, you'll know some of them,' Lamb said.

'Yes?'

'But perhaps not the principal one, the most ambitious and dangerous. You've been misled.'

'Oh?' He wanted to ask whether this intruder might be a lovely London mover in a fine suit that failed to conceal his intentions. But let Jack milk his moment. He liked to release information slowly, to be savoured. He had on a high-necked khaki sweater, with button-down epaulettes. On his left shoulder was the discreet rank insignia of possibly a general or even a field marshal. The Badge and Stripes Shop might have had only the one set. Better half a general than none.

'It worries me to think of you, Desmond Iles and the Chief being simply shattered by the pace of what is happening. I have to take the overview, Col.' He half turned his head away from the slit and spoke to Harpur across the decorated epaulette, the grave voice of a commander. 'I'm selective about what I bring to you as insights. I hope you'd agree with that. I wouldn't drop anyone in it who has done me no harm.'

'Ever your grassing gospel, Jack.'

'Col, you're the kind to imagine he sees what's what and yet all the time is looking in the wrong direction. And especially now.'

'Thanks, Jack.'

Lamb began to lilt. 'There was a peaceable quality to this whole patch, a sophistication. Folk as varied as yourself, myself, Iles, Mark Lane, could lie down together in comparative contentment, like the wolf and the lamb in, I think, Scripture. When I say lamb, I don't mean I see myself in that role necessarily, Lamb equals lamb, not at all. It's a general point.'

Jack Lamb could lie down in contentment because he slept with a beautiful young former punk girlfriend, Helen Surtees, friend of Denise, in his fine manor house called Darien – and because he had an established, sparkling, probably criminal art dealership to finance both. Could you call an art business 'grey-area'? Jack's was. Many of the paintings he handled featured a clever use of cloud – obscuring where they came from. It was part of *quid pro quo* decencies between Harpur and him that questions about his trade were not pressed. Lamb said: 'Someone comes slinking into town, foregrounding himself at the *Eton* and with "Pathfinder" written all over him – this is bound to get your attention. I mean, you're a senior cop and sure to notice the obvious.'

'Thanks, Jack.'

'And he's interested in you, too? Is there a tale around

that you're consultant to one of the syndicates? I could never believe it, Col, but this would make you a target, clearly.'

'These rumours, Jack!'

'This gent's called Lincoln W. Lincoln from London – as you may have discovered, of course. I should think conceivably he'd even want to try something rough at your house, Col. He has? Of course. He's young, but he's done a lot of this sort of preparatory work elsewhere. So I'm advised. His type feel out a place, clear away troubles and make it comfortable for the main men who follow. And when there's somebody giving you and your prized ones this kind of savage attention, it's bound to focus all your mind on him, isn't it? Mistake. Obviously, you can't ignore him totally, Col, and yet he's a distraction from the real peril.' Lamb began to pace the width of the blockhouse, his huge frame and head sometimes pretty clear in the little light from the observation slits, and sometimes as vague and shadowy and intimidating as a liner in fog. 'You need guidance, Col.'

'I can believe it.' Well, *whatever* Lamb said you had better believe. No informant came anywhere near him for quality, but he failed to fit into the tight body of rules laid down for the running of tipsters. One of those rules said that an informant belonged to the police service, never to an individual officer. Harpur disagreed. Jack was his.

'Start from Eleri's death,' Lamb said.

'This is still a mystery.'

'Well, maybe. You dawdle for your due reasons, and you're entitled. Who did it is not so crucial. It's who comes after that counts, isn't it?'

'Well, I heard Si Pilgrim sits in at the *Eton* and looks the part.'

Lamb straightened violently from the wall, brushed himself down and made towards the blockhouse door, as though suddenly offended by the pitiable level of talk. But then he paused and the spasm of anger seemed to die. Lamb did not leave. He stood in front of Harpur and glared at him. Harpur was big enough, but Jack had to bend forward to meet his eyes. 'I said succession, Col, not some temping by a sad little dreamer in quality shoes. Si Pilgrim is the future, you think?'

Harpur considered. 'You mean family?'

'Of course family.'

'Eleri has relatives?' Harpur asked.

'There's a daughter.'

'Yes?'

'Already a towering eminence in the drugs trade, but elsewhere. She has friends to suit. I'm advised she and they will be looking for a way in here, once the tender observances of mourning have been wrapped up the day after tomorrow.'

'Who advises you, Jack?' Of course, no informant of Lamb's quality ever answered such questions. Harpur asked them only to irritate and get a word in.

Lamb said: 'She and the troupe she runs with make Lincoln W. Lincoln insignificant.'

'And where have she and her group operated until now?'

'Her name's Louise,' Lamb replied. 'Louise des Moines. It's a place in the States. I understand she was shacked up for a week or ten days with some lad from there and must have felt this gave her a right to the name. Perhaps she was fed up with the ap Vaughan label, but still wanted a double barrel. I hear she's around already and will certainly be at Mummy's funeral. Clearly, she has vengeance intentions, but, beyond all that, comes a calculated, professional interest to use her mother's former trading corner as the start place for a takeover.'

'Where does this information come from, Jack?'

'We're not talking simply of a spot at *The Eton Boating Song*, Col. They'll go for that first, but it's a start point only. Naturally, she'd been briefed up to the eyebrows by Eleri on the gaping situation here post Kenward, the richness of the chances. They'll march in, all prepared, like Adolf into France, Col – just roll the opposition over: you, Iles, Lane and all the hopeful local syndicates and freelances like Vine and Ralphy and Shale, if Shale's still reckonable, and Les Tranter – as well as L.W.L.'

'God, imagine Eleri with a working daughter!' Harpur mused.

'Oh,' Lamb said, squinting at him in the dark, trying to read his face: 'You've met her already, have you, you deceptive sod?'

16

On the way home in the car after seeing Barney and eating and drinking with him and the two women into the night, Ralph Ember felt the warm muzzle of a handgun, probably a 9mm automatic, gently nudge the back of his neck. They were approaching the turn-off for Winchester at the time and Gerry Reid, driving, had begun to speak enthusiastically of the well-known traditions of scholarship and wholesome living represented by the public school there. Gerry said it was late for a visit to the school now, but he would have loved to see the fine old buildings. Although Irish, Gerry prized such famed, historic elements in England's heritage, and always said a little or more about the six-hundred-year-old college when they passed the signs on these trips to and from Barney's place. Ember had never liked being in the passenger seat with Harry Foster behind. Restraint Harry despised, and he carried so many grievances and ambitions. Ember once saw a film called *The Friends of Eddie Coyle*, when Mitchum in this spot was neatly executed from the rear as the car drove on. Foster always travelled armed. It was how he saw himself: unendingly heavy and on duty. This had its uses, as long as you were not at the wrong end. Of course he would not know whether Ember had something, too, and Harry might be jumpy. Unweaponed, Ember felt middle-aged, smug and feeble.

'Pull off, Gerry,' Foster said.

'What? You want to see the school even in the dark? I'm sure it's *so* impressive and bracing,' Gerry said. 'Many of the great went there – maybe Gaitskell.' Reid's eyes were ahead on the road and he had not noticed the automatic yet.

'Find somewhere secluded, leafy – a bit of forest,' Foster replied.

His voice crackled, like orders, and Gerry must have realized something. Ember saw his eyes move for a second onto the gun. In a few minutes he took the exit to Winchester. Foster was sitting well forward behind Ember, probably hiding the automatic with his body. It was night, but the gun might be suddenly lit up by headlights and seen from other vehicles.

For fear of frightening Foster into haste, Ember did not turn but said over his shoulder: 'What, Harry – first peeved about Eleri and now re the negotiations with Keith Vine just mentioned? That's understandable. But, look, it wasn't like I told Barney. Just damn necessary at the time.' Ember was pleased to find his voice not too bad, almost steady and boardroom, although he felt one of his panics about to welcome him in.

'I'm sorry about this, Gerry,' Foster said.

'It doesn't seem decent behaviour, no, not in the circumstances,' Reid replied. 'Christ, Harry, I talk about the ethic of a place like Winchester College and then this.'

'I'm acting for you as well as myself,' Foster said.

'That so? Did I miss the vote?'

'Shall I tell you how I see things?' Foster asked.

'However you see things, I don't consider it enough for a big loaded gun in Ralph's neck after a communal day out. A friend and colleague.' He kept driving, but with no speed. If he put his foot down it might help by bringing the police.

'I watch Ralphy turn down every idea but his own – such as not trying for Eleri's,' Foster said, 'and then he goes big-wheel negotiating – no place for us, Gerry. This is Ralphy in nod-and-wink talks with Barney, and Ralphy in secret talks with Keith Vine. *With Keith Vine.* Keith Vine is the fucking opposition. The bare and outright fucking opposition, who killed Eleri. Here's our friend and colleague doing deals with him, and won't try to get in where Eleri used to be. Where are we, Gerry? I don't tolerate that.' He jabbed with the gun and Ember's head was shoved forward.

God, Ember saw Foster could never put this right. He would have to take it the whole way now. How did Ralph ever team with a madman?

'I'd want to know the full picture before I went in for behaviour,' Reid replied.

'You think you'd ever get the full picture from him? Go off here.'

This was some very minor road that looked full of trees and shitty seclusion, created by the Almighty for finales. Oh, Jesus, for a piece. A Baby Browning would do.

'You're not going to see the college from here, even if it's lit up,' Reid said.

'I do want to see it, if it means so much to you,' Foster said. 'These things are important. I don't look down on heritage. But later. At more leisure.'

He sounded almost mild and reasonable and Ember thought there might be a chance, after all. 'Gerry's so right,' he said. 'You haven't got the full picture, Harry.' Now, his voice would hardly do it, though. He was forcing the words through. Panic symptoms galloped: first, always, a disabling ache across his shoulders and terrible sweating. Then he might suffer double or triple vision and, as the foul culmination, he would come to suspect that the ancient scar along his jaw had opened up and was trailing unholy liquid and nerve-ends. Of course, it never did, but in a full-out panic, he always thought it had, and thinking was as bad as if it had.

They drove on unmadeup tracks in what seemed a genuine wood, and eventually Gerry stopped. The surroundings put Ember in mind of somewhere, and of an undefined but terrible, long-drawn-out experience. His brain struggled to place it, and to reject the memory. In a few seconds, though, he had it: this was just the kind of setting where he had had to deep bury a one-time colleague, Caring Oliver, not long ago, after a little shooting accident in the car. That had been near Cheltenham, but the chaotic greenery and indifferent chattering of trees as he dug the grave there was identical. Nobody ever found Caring. This was the plus and the rottenness of countryside. Some thought Nature bad right through and to be avoided. Ember was not extreme like that, but he did find it damned remote and engulfing, especially at night.

Foster leaned over and opened the passenger door. Then he opened his own door on that side. He was going to keep the gun to Ember's neck as they left the car, except for that one half-second when the door pillar intervened. The devotion was like giving plasma to a moving stretcher patient. This bucked Ember up. It meant Foster was scared of him, recognized that Ember could be heavy, too. Jesus, would his legs work and could he keep the fright sweat from blinding him? Could he manage something in that moment when the contact was broken?

'Get out, Ralphy,' Foster said. 'Slow, gentle movements.'

'What about me?' Reid asked.

'Well, you do what you like, Gerry, naturally,' Foster said. 'None of this is aimed against you. I told you, it's *for* you, as much as for me. This fucker would sell the both of us. Can't you see it? Well, we can do without him.'

Ember saw nothing reachable in the car to make him a weapon. Outside on the ground he could make out some fat bits of broken-off branch, but they looked past it.

'I don't know whether I go along with all this,' Reid said. He had a round, boyish face, apparently angry now. 'It seems to be you acting impromptu, Harry – which can certainly be one of your strengths, but then there's another side.' He stayed behind the wheel, illuminated by the courtesy light.

'This is me putting a point of view, that's all,' Foster said. 'So far. Discussion on Eleri, Vine et cetera.'

'I don't regard it like that, not proper discussion when you've got a weighty piece against someone's neck,' Reid replied. 'Naive to talk like that.'

'Get out now, Ralphy,' Foster said. 'Now.' He yelled this, which might signify nerves, but you never knew if nerves were good or bad when someone had their finger on a trigger. Foster's voice climbed and bounced about among the black branches. Ember did what he was told, and found he could stand. Foster came out very fast alongside him and put the muzzle of the automatic back, but this time pressed under Ember's chin and pointing up. If that chance with the door pillar in between them had existed, it was gone. Using his spare hand, Foster gave Ember a careful frisk.

'Would I come armed on a business outing with colleagues?' Ember asked. There were moments in that search, too, when he knew he should have risked it, and the risk would have been reasonable. But this was the way with Ember: there would be these important seconds when he did not act fast enough, because panic nulled him. And then the seconds had gone, and a new stage of disaster started. Ember's enemies claimed he always collapsed when the tension went high. They even said former mates were in prison or wheelchairs or dead due to these failures on old cash-van jobs or banks. Because of such lies his cruelly unjust nickname stuck, Panicking Ralph, he knew that, too.

Now, as Foster worked, Ember could have come up with his knee, or twisted his head away hard from the gun and tried a punch into that oblong face. It had been necessary, no question: Harry was going to kill him, and could not get out of killing him. Impossible ever to restore the normal. Foster was at a stretch and sure to have been unbalanced as he reached around Ember's body. Oh, yes, the chance was there . . . and then not. Soon Harry stood square again, in front of Ember, face close to face, and the automatic prodding up, sure Ember had no defence. Ember saw it was an S&W Parabellum, a class weapon, in line with Harry's vision of himself.

'I could tell you to take your clothes off, Ralphy, but all right, we've been colleagues, the way Gerry says, and it would be out of order. My girl, Deloraine, thinks you're OK – well, as you know, you slavering sod – and I value her views, so no humbling you more than what absolutely has to be. Just sit down, Ralph, sit on your hands, and I'll be right opposite.'

Ember did what he was told.

'Gerry's tender, tender and fine, but Gerry hasn't thought it through,' Foster said.

'Perhaps he has, Harry.'

'Gerry's a good driver and, as for me, I can do the rough side. That's how you see us, Ralphy – labourers, dispensable. Not thinkers. No? Well, we decide now who's *really* dispensable.'

'Certainly not you two,' Ember said instantly.

'That leaves you,' Foster replied.

He said this plain, as a piece of basic logic, not as wit. But Ember went into a good laugh, to show he could still spot a dark joke, and also to say, but without making it too clear, that these two, Harry and Gerry Reid, could never run an outfit without him. Jesus – Foster and Mouth-Mouth! What sort of business operation could that be? Foster sat with his back against a tree facing Ember, the Parabellum in his lap.

Maybe Foster picked up that second message in the

laugh, though. He said: 'Barney can work with us. That's what he's always said. He was always worried you'd get knocked out of the scene. And it could happen. Yes, now it could happen.'

Gerry left the car and came and stood near Ember, smoothing down his quaint ginger hair, as if cool. He kept the sidelights on and they gave a decent little glow, like a campfire, so Ember was able to watch faces, try to read thoughts. Of course, you could not tell whether Foster and Gerry were doing this together, a joint show. They could have agreed that Gerry would give the friendly, temperate stuff. Boys like this learned from police questioning, the hard and soft touch. Ember had noticed when Gerry referred with such anger to the gun he still managed to call it loaded and big, maybe just in case Ember had doubts and should be told. The story was that Reid would never go armed, but, all the same, Ember tried to work out from the hang of his denim jacket whether he had something small and holstered, special for today. 'There was more to say about the meeting with Vine, yes, Ralph?' Reid asked. He spoke urgently. Perhaps he thought that if Ember said the right thing Foster might still be able to draw back. 'Tell Harry, Ralph. The great hazard in all these things, Harry, is over-simplification. You're good at that.'

Ember replied just as urgently. More. 'Vine came to me wanting merger and backing. I said fuck off. I knew what your feelings would be about linkage with that offal, Harry. But it didn't seem too clever to tell Barney – not when he was in that mood. Like the fucking Vine fan club.'

'Perhaps Barney knew,' Foster said. 'He knows a lot.'

'Perhaps he did,' Ember replied. 'I had to gamble. I've got to hang on to our supplier, or where's the business?'

Foster gazed at him. Harry had a long, undreamy face with blue eyes that tried to look like they had seen it all before, but came over as just harsh and edgy, maybe even more so in the half dark. This was someone low, low, low, yet fancying leadership. That kind of stupid yearning always got into the eyes. 'I can nearly believe you, Ralph,' he said. 'I don't say you're definitely lying.'

'Now, isn't he gracious, Ralph?' Gerry began to act relaxed, as though everything was over. 'Reckon you can put that banger away, Harry?'

Foster glanced down at the gun, and left it where it was. 'What do you see as next, then, Ralph?'

'Well, yes, maybe I do need to talk to Vine.'

'Of course you do,' Foster said. 'You're Panicking Ralphy, aren't you? You're shit-scared of Barney. You've just said – shit-scared he'll drop you, and scared he'll use his friends on you if you refuse to be dropped. You've waited too long on Eleri, so now you're scrambling.'

'Drop *us*,' Ember replied. 'We're an outfit, Harry. What Barney said makes some sense. We combine with Keithy to take on London.'

'Why didn't it make sense when Vine came to you first?' Foster asked.

Ember's triple vision was doing things to the Parabellum. 'It did, in a way.'

'But you said no.'

'At that point. In business you—'

Foster crouched forward, wagging the big shoulders: 'You're going to feed our fucking capital to this jerk – because you're so scared?'

'Capital?' Ember asked.

'You said Vine wanted backing. Not just merger, finance.'

'My name on papers would do, probably,' Ember replied.

'What name? Panicking Ralphy?'

Reid took a couple of paces. Perhaps he had realized it was wrong to be relaxed, after all. Reid was skinny and nimble. Ember saw Foster's hand tighten on the automatic. But Reid did not go close to him. He paused between Ember and Harry: 'This is so crazy,' he said. 'Ralph has answered every point.'

Now, Ember saw Foster's face break for a moment into regret or embarrassment, even terror. Probably he suddenly realized how idiotic he had been, yet was pinned in the situation. Slowly, Ember decided that most likely these two were not working a performance together. There had been that instinctive hard fondling of the gun, as if Foster feared Reid. And Harry looked troubled when Reid said Ember had covered all objections. From then on, Ember felt his panic shrink a little bit, and he watched for ways to get the Parabellum from Harry, maybe with Reid's help, but, anyway, to get it and use it.

Foster said: 'No, he hasn't answered every point. The sod hasn't answered any. Listen, Gerry, if he goes and talks to Vine, Vine's going to realize he's super-strong now, because here's Ralph W. Ember his very fucking self crawling back.

And Vine probably also knows Barney put the leverage on because Barney thinks Vine's a saint. Keith Vine can ask Ralphy for whatever he wants. Ralphy's overstayed the market. Ralphy puts the firm in hock, backs the bugger with money *we* earned. All right, guarantees only, but guarantees based on what? That's funds we've helped him to. And then you know Keith Vine, Gerry. OK, say a merger. Would Vine second string to Panicking Ralphy? Got to be top. Maybe he'll want to keep Ralphy, because Ralphy's done guarantor for him. Will Keith Vine want you and me, Gerry? He's got partners already. He works with Beau Derek. He's sucking out our money, but makes us discards. You going to accept that?' Foster seemed to have tired himself with the speech. In a while, though, he said: 'Look, instead . . . look Gerry, we adjust things here, now, and we control our future.'

'Adjust?' Reid asked.

'Adjust. I don't want to talk brutal, for God's sake,' Foster replied. 'Ralph used to be a mate. You know, *adjust* things.'

Ember spoke quietly to him, like a teacher with a thick child: 'Vine will need all the power – *we'll* need all the power we can get to counter London, Harry. You're vital to him – to the new company – both of you.'

'He's not going to split five or six ways. This boy thinks of one only, Keith Vine, Keith Vine. He's creating a dynasty. That costs. He won't share.'

Foster had begun yelling again and in his passion waved a hand, but not just a hand, his gun hand, a wide gesture at all the shadowy leaves to show the scope of Keith Vine's egomania. Reid moved another couple of steps very fast,

swung his foot and kicked Foster in the side of the head, no
token kick. Those two had been fine friends for years and
seen a lot together, so perhaps Foster could read him and was
expecting the onslaught. And he had been alerted when
Reid moved earlier. At any rate, Harry took some of the
weight out of that first blow by pulling his head back, almost
just in time. Gerry's lace-up still caught him hard on the
temple and, because Harry was already shifting his face
away, it drove his head into the tree trunk he was sitting
against. Ember saw Foster's face crease like a nut in a pair
of crackers and a wedge-shaped area of blood spread fast
down his left cheek, but his eyes kept their glint and sense.
He did not let go of the Parabellum. This boy had genuine
hardness. Ember would have loved to launch forward and
grapple for the gun but waited a moment in that way of his,
still sitting on his hands so as not to give offence, hoping
that another kick from Reid would make real changes.

Gerry screamed: 'Grab it. He'll kill you, Ralph, and we're
lost.' But Ember did not move. Suddenly, Reid seemed to
lose hope in Ember and bent for the automatic himself. But
Harry raised it full towards Reid this time, not just that little
finger twitch, and fired twice. Impossible to miss. Reid's body
was right over the weapon. He fell forward onto Foster,
crushing him for a moment, covering the gun. One of them
groaned, but only briefly. Now, Ember did force himself to
stand and forced himself to move. He thought of running.
Always he thought first of running. Maybe he could get to
the car and reverse out, if Gerry had left the keys. Firing at
a moving vehicle was not easy, especially if you had just

been hit half unconscious. Then Ember corrected, though. With him that could sometimes happen. If he ran or drove, Harry would have to try to kill him, and try hard. Ember had witnessed what was probably the death of Reid. Besides, Foster had brought him here to kill him, and nothing that had happened altered this. Ember made himself move but made himself move fast towards the two on the ground. There was no time to go for the gun. Reid had shown how tricky that could be. Panic and hesitancy had their positive side. Ember liked the way the shoe work had done such damage and, before Harry could pull the Parabellum out from under Reid, got two heavy kicks into Foster, one high on the head, like Reid's, the other in the face. Something broke – in Harry, not on Ember's shoe. It might be the jaw. There was a little twanging sound, like a cord going on a guitar. The noise upset Ember. It was not something you wanted to hear coming from a former working colleague, although he turned out evil. The jaw kick banged Harry into the tree again, and everything went out of his eyes. This was the point about not totally despising Nature: now and then trees helped. Foster nestled down half under Reid. Ember thought of Hansel and Gretel making the best of things in the forest.

It was easy to reach beneath Reid, unfix Foster's fingers and bring out the S&W. He shot Foster in the head once, wiped the butt of the gun and put it in Reid's right hand. Unavoidable. Was he going to drive back with Harry after what had gone on here? Was he going to leave Harry to come round and reappear wild again some day soon? Would

Harry ever agree to Vine? Would Vine agree to a lout like Foster? Harry's Deloraine would probably appreciate some real consoling after this.

Thank God Ember would not need to do any interment digging here, as with Caring at Cheltenham. He went through the pockets, out of habit really, nothing more. There was a bit of money and some identification. He took all that, then turned the car and drove out. They might stay unseen for a day or two, even a week. Identification would not take long. They both had form and prints. The police would probably work out there had been three people present, and might realize that Reid had not shot Harry, despite the gun in his hand. But it was worth a charade, would make some confusion. And the police might want to believe it.

Unless those two stayed undiscovered for a while, the car's marks on the track would say someone had exited. That was all right: no tracing through tyres. In any case, the car was Gerry's. Of course, Barney would speculate intelligently when he read of these messy deaths in the Press. That was all right, too. He would realize, wouldn't he, that this was an advance – the removal of all possible obstructions to an amalgamation with Vine? Barney would not be doing any talking. Also, Barney and his ladies might get to understand that Ralph W. Ember was hardly one to be pissed about or called Ralphy.

He picked up the side road and went on towards Winchester. Reid's words on the school had quite attracted Ember and he felt it would be a nice idea, now he was so near and unburdened, to slip along and admire these fine old buildings, even at night. He could dwell on the grand achievements they represented. As he understood it from Gerry, this college had always stressed the powerful significance of individual integrity, and Ember could respond to that. He was going to be very individual from now on. Possibly, he would be able to spot the school's motto on one of the gates. That would be in Latin, obviously. He always felt things sounded stronger, more global, in Latin. Generally, these days, he could make out meanings, following some swift sessions on the classics during his university foundation year. He had heard that comprehensive schools also gave their kids quick shots of Latin, to mock up a worthwhile education in these barbarian days.

17

Becky said he should not go to Eleri's funeral today. Keith Vine would have forecast this, of course, but did not blame her. Clearly, she could never see the many deep intricacies of the situation, its diplomatic points. There were matters that could be hinted at to her – and she was a bright kid, good at between the lines, normally – but some professional aspects must not be given right out, in full. For one thing, they would only trouble a woman. 'Drawing attention to yourself,' she said.

This might be true, but if you wanted to hand a full warning to street people you had to do some of that, the dim bitch. Those freelances could read plain signs only. The coffin was going to be one and Keith Vine the other. He would have on a good dark suit, dark tie and superior black shoes, telling of sadness and ferocity. He had advised Si Pilgrim to stay away – which delighted the yellow jerk – but most other pushers who took from Vine would be there from solidarity. Eleri had earned that kind of big rating.

It upset Vine to know he must ignore Becky's advice today. Above all, he believed in being reasonable and considerate with her. This girl, plus little Charles and any further babies were the next millennium – were the future. A bit of that fucking awkward recollection came to him suddenly then. It was Eleri flat, face down on the floor in the dirt, skinny legs together and speaking to him, bouncing the words up from the ground: *I'm free. I can go to whom I pick.* Well, so right, Eleri, so wrong.

Becky said: 'We've already had the police here, Keith.'

'A try-on. They fish. They don't know where to look.'

'They looked here.'

'They—'

'It doesn't matter you didn't do it, *couldn't* do such a thing. If they want you for her murder they'll arrange the evidence. You're on their books and every so often you come up for treatment. How police work.'

She had this habit of telling him what he knew a lot better than she did, from experience – but never mind, she was trying to be considerate, and the man should always make allowances for their hormones, and that kind of thing. 'Would I go to her funeral if I killed her, Beck?' he replied, giving a giggle. 'Not even the police would believe that.'

'They believe what suits them. Just lie low. Don't get associated with her, living or dead.'

'Oh, she was a good old friend, Beck. I feel a duty to Eleri.'

'Fuck duty. Send a donation to Victims of Violence. Anon.'

'I might do that as well.'

Charles started to cry in the other room and Becky went out. In a while she returned, carrying him, quiet now. This was that scene Vine hated so much. She and the baby looked wonderful – all holy motherhood and tenderness and the coming era, yet with this sodding last-legs sideboard behind her and the heartless wallpaper.

Of course, it was not the funeral at all that made Becky edgy and negative, but this place. What she was saying was they were losers. Their flat showed it. And police knew how to deal with losers – make them lose some more. If he was in sight of getting her The Pines she would not be thinking like this. She would know they were winning and would go on winning. Becky sat down now in a fairly steady armchair and stroked Charles's hair. Already he had quite a bit of this and was undoubtedly going to be handsome eventually. 'You're too damn blasé about the police,' she said. Becky had education and could come out with terms.

'I've studied how they work, that's all, Beck. Mostly it's a show.'

She bent over and studied Charles's scalp, or made out she was studying it, because she wanted to hide her face, being embarrassed by what she was going to say. 'I don't mean you to feel guilty, Keith, but— Look, you've never spoken a thing to give it away, not in so many words so don't imagine you've been slack, but I think you've got that cop Harpur aboard, and this makes you feel safe. Tiny hints, that's all.'

'Harpur? Detective Chief Superintendent Colin Harpur?' This is what he meant about her being so fucking intellectual and seeing beyond what she was supposed to see, like a gypsy. 'Aboard? What's "aboard" mean, Beck?'

'Oh, partnership, of course. He acts partnership, takes like partnership, advises like partnership. Then, one day, when he knows enough he turns. Police are police right through, no matter how they seem to act. I say *seem* to act. They're trained to fool. Perhaps he's begun dropping you in it already. Why that posse came? We should get out, Keith, if there's time. Forget the funeral, forget all of it, take your suit off. France, anywhere. You're going to be set up. You're prime.'

The worst aspect of it was, she spoke so quietly, so full of reason. Clearly, this was partly because she did not want to disturb Charles, but also it sounded thoughtful, her mind hard and stupidly set.

'Harpur?' he said. 'Harpur's Mr Integrity. It's known. Who'd be able to get Harpur "aboard", as you call it?'

'You. Up to a point,' she replied.

This could be the thing about Becky: because of the education she thought she saw more than he did – believed she could spot extras he was too backward to understand.

She said: 'He'll play along and then go righteous at his moment. It's what infiltration means.'

'Believe me, Keith Vine knows how to run a business, Beck,' he replied. Charles stirred a bit and Vine wondered whether he would turn out when grown up to be the kind of lad who could appreciate subtleties and act right. Of course he would. Genes.

Becky said: 'You think going to the funeral will proclaim you're not involved. But they could make it look like a brazen double-bluff – say you—'

Someone rang the front-door bell. Her face went empty. 'Oh, God, Keith, are they here again?' she said. 'You're a target?'

He wondered if she would make with the breast. 'I didn't hear anything on the stairs. Police like to thunder and scare.'

'Softly, softly,' she replied. 'They're going to take you?' Then suddenly she whispered: 'I love you, Keith.'

He stood and went to open up. 'Who is it?' he called.

'Keith, it's Ralph Ember. I've been mulling over the various matters. Can we talk?'

'Well, I—'

'It occurred to me after you left the club the other night that I might have given the wrong impression. The fact is, I see real promise in your ideas. Absolutely.'

'So, what's happened?'

'You caught me unprepared then. I'd be glad to discuss now.'

Vine did not want him in here, staring around, comparing it with his big country place, Low Pastures, and looking at Becky that way he had, as if every woman would grab a night with him and the chance to grope his scar and think she was having El Cid. Being a mother and holding the child would not make any difference to him, he'd still be sending out sex signs. Vine opened the door.

'Ah, grief gear! How much better than meeting in that damn, impersonal place of mine,' Ember cried. 'A lovely touch of home, instead. And Rebecca. So pleased. The babe – so bonny. He's you, Keith, absolutely. Happily, I've caught you before the funeral.' He did have a gawp around the room and at Becky. 'Here's a room that says relaxation,' Ember declared. 'There's a mind behind the layout of a room like this, or perhaps two minds, but in concert. And yet I can think a family might soon need a bit more space, say some grounds. Possibly a house with a gallery, Keith. That's how I see you, soon.'

'Gallery?' Becky said. 'The only house I know with a gallery is—'

'I just say a gallery as an example,' Ember replied. 'That sort of scale. And Keith deserves it.'

'You alone?' Vine asked. 'No associates with you?'

'I thought it ought to be one-to-one. This, after all, is follow-up to another private conversation.'

'Could you leave us alone, Beck?' Vine said.

She stood. 'I heard the message.'

'But I trust pretty soon we can all get together,' Ember said. 'There might be something to celebrate. A happy business matter.'

When she and Charles had gone, Vine gave Ember the good chair. 'Naturally enough, you ask about my associates, Keith. They've begun to war with each other, I fear. People of that class, it's always on the cards. I'm not sure how it will turn out, maybe tragically. Anyway, not something I want to be linked with. These are very gifted lads at their level, but liable to become unbalanced under tension.'

'Warring about what?'

'I watch them and feel sickened,' Ember replied, 'sickened by what appears be the decline of a long and good friendship between those two. I have to distance myself. I came to feel the truth of your parting words the other night – that I'm alone. It's not a good sensation, Keith. You asked me what had happened. This is what has happened. Hence, I'm here, looking for the kind of arrangement you proposed. And I'm very ready to help you in any way I can in acquiring the property you and yours deserve – no doubt of it – and which would, I hope, be a lasting inducement to stay and cooperate in business.'

'Where are they now?' Vine said. He had bottles in the flat, but Ember could do special Armagnac at the club and it seemed poor to offer supermarket rum. He said: 'Tea?'

'Lovely.'

'China or Indian?'

'Oh, pot luck,' Ember replied.

Vine called to Becky to make it.

'Harry? Reid?' Ember asked. 'As of a few days, I'm not in touch with them. I can't risk the future of my business through contact with people who are suddenly unpredictable and very dangerous. I know you'll understand that.'

Vine said: 'Those two—'

'Would be opposed to any arrangement with you, and especially Harry Foster. I know it. I've had to make my choice, Keith. I hope it still coincides with yours.'

Vine sat forward on his straight-backed chair. 'I'd have to consult.'

'Of course. Partnered with Beau Derek, aren't you – a lovely craftsman?'

'But as to the property—'

Ember smiled and waved a hand. 'Certainly. A personal matter between you and me – or, I should say, you and your fine family and me, Keith. No need for other involvement there.'

Vine wondered about it all, but did not want to seem sulky. 'This sounds pretty good, Ralph.'

'It's as you said originally, Keith, and I've been forced to admit it. We've got to get together to cope with the outside threat.'

'A fact.'

Becky came into the room with the tea and Ember did a good eye-tour of her body. Charles would be back in his cot. Becky put out the cups. 'We can talk in detail later, Keith,' Ember said.

'Ralph thinks he might be able to help us with a bigger house, Beck.'

'Only too delighted,' Ember replied. 'This is grand here and central, but I feel you need some style – all of you, that is.'

Becky said: 'Well, as a matter of fact, things have become a bit wearing and we were thinking of—'

'The Pines,' Vine said. 'I believe it's still on the market.'

'A true spot,' Ember replied.

*

Vine always thought that one of the things churches did well was a funeral. This was the kind of community occasion that went right back into history. It separated people – of course it did, because one of them was dead – and yet it also brought people together in a dignified and affectionate joint act. Some of the hymns they usually had thrilled Vine, and all were strong quality at Eleri's – 'Abide With Me', 'The Lord's My Shepherd' and 'Guide Me, Oh, Thou Great

Jehovah'. Funerals did what so many said – they gave a life shape and culmination. Some funerals excluded all the religious side and had readings from say a poet or a book on fishing. He despised heathenism. This funeral brought the dear memories of Eleri sweetly back into the reckoning for an hour or two. The vicar kept his talk short but said that Eleri had been a character who delighted many and who had faced the difficulties of life with admirable calm and bright humour. It was hard to guess if he ever met her. Perhaps he went to the *Eton* for snorts. A lot of these vicars had private money and only took on the church for spiritual reasons and to get a house, plus parish women with loneliness troubles.

Vine did not arrive too early, and chose a place up near the front, the best way to make sure he was seen. It would be crude to hog the occasion by glaring around at pushers who dealt with him – giving them the threat in a direct, heavy style. Christ, this was a *church*, for God's sake. But they would notice him come up the aisle, observe the grand suit and understand what happened to folk who betrayed Keith Vine, regardless of age or gender. Always he had liked being oblique – he would explain his methods to Becky like that, in just the single word, 'obliqueness'. In business, this was often the most telling method. You'd think with her intelligence and so on she would be able to understand that, but at times like today he wondered. As he took his place, he glimpsed Slow Victor a few rows back with one of his boyfriends. You could see in Victor's face that he knew this funeral was about more than a death – that it was a parable like 'The Good Samaritan'.

Seated in the front pew right behind the casket – a place that ought to say family – was a woman in her late twenties with red-brown hair done in spirals, no hat. Vine did not seem to know her. During the first hymn she turned and looked at him for almost half a verse – a stare, really – starting from 'I fear no foe' to 'Where is death's sting?' This was just the kind of attitude he considered so wrong for a funeral, blatant. Was this some relative of Eleri, come along not just for the funeral but for nosing? Did Eleri have relatives – a daughter? Vine disliked the idea. Where a death was concerned, he hated ramifications. In many ways he approved of family, a family could be the future, but a family definitely could bring ramifications.

She was with two young girls dressed in grey and with dark scarves over their heads. He recognized Harpur's children. So, what went on? How the hell were they connected? After the woman had gazed at Vine in 'Abide With Me', she turned and said something to Jill Harpur. The child glanced back at Vine, then nodded. Harpur sent his children to see off a pusher, like proxy? The hymn finished and they all sat down for a prayer. He did not mind that, it helped keep the pace nice and stately. Then, with his eyes half open, Vine was suddenly aware of someone, perhaps more than one, approaching from behind him quite fast up the aisle. Vine was carrying something, thank God, and eased his hand in under the serge lapel to his holster, unbuttoning. The way things were going these days, you could get terrible violence even at someone's obsequies. Becky pushed into the pew with him. She had Charles in her arms. 'I wanted to be with you, Keith,' she whispered. 'That's all.'

He pulled his hand back from the gun and patted her thigh. This was the kind of lovable, open girl Becky could be when she was not negative. Generally, she would manage to get to see that Vine's version of things was correct – why she was priceless. It would not be just the matter of probably landing The Pines now, though, plainly, she would love that. Her arrival here was about unity – about a bond – about family, really, but in the best way. When this congregation saw Becky and Charles with him they would realize what a glorious relationship he had, and understand why those who might shake his business and earnings, such as Eleri, had to be wiped out. They stood again, for 'The Lord's My Shepherd', and he took Charles from her. This lad was building to some weight. Vine and Becky gave the right subdued tone to 'death's dark vale' and then burst into those joyful, hopeful lines about the table set in the presence of foes, yes, and the overflowing cup. All their tomorrows would be like this.

18

Harpur was at home, listening to a description of Eleri's funeral by Hazel and Jill, when the telephone went again. For a while, nobody moved to answer. It was Sunday lunch.

'Another fink call?' Jill said. 'Don't they ever rest?'

Harpur liked to be present for this meal every week. It was blatantly familial and made him feel nearly up to scratch as a single parent. He cooked. Usually he did pasta with a strong sauce, but he could broaden out to a roast or chicken or turkey. He thought he was not bad on gravy.

Denise was with them today. He liked this, too. It seemed to bring her into a proper connection with his daughters, and showed his relationship with her was not all outings and sex. Although a great eater when she had the chance, Denise could not cook beyond egg on toast. And, judging by the state of her student room in Jonson Court, she did not know much about washing up, either. Harpur was pleased to think she had at least one prime meal a week. He did not want her any thinner at the behind or breasts. Occasionally he worried about his obsession with her behind. In the Judgement Day dream, God seemed to have noticed that.

Hazel said: 'Louise never dropped one tear, and yet you could feel a terrible grief there. Do you know what I mean, Dad, Denise?'

The phone gave up.

'Sorrow that lay too deep for tears,' Hazel continued.

'More poems,' Jill said.

'Plus rage,' Hazel said. 'Just touched the coffin once with her knuckles, like needing the feel of the wood. It was goodbye, it was a promise.'

'Imitation wood,' Jill said. 'And she wanted to know who everyone there was, such as that Keith Vine that you know, Dad. Like sorting out. A bit scary. I think she was hurt you didn't come.'

'Why not, Colin?' Denise asked.

'There are guidelines.'

'He's allowed to sympathize with certain deaths, not others,' Hazel said.

The phone resumed. 'This is how it is here, Denise,' Jill said. 'People flogging one another to our dad day in day out, Sundays included.'

Hazel left the table and went to answer. When she came back, she said, 'A woman.'

'Louise?' he asked.

'Don't think so. But no name offered and, as usual, none asked for. Chip shop accent. It's a bit much ringing when—' She glanced at Denise, and did not finish.

'What?' Denise said. 'What is this, Col?'

'It'll be work,' he replied, standing.

'Yes?' Denise said.

'Also often called duty,' Jill said, with a comic, left-handed salute.

When Harpur picked up the phone the woman said: 'Name of Deloraine?'

'Distinctive.'

'You know it? On someone's dossier?'

'Might be.'

'Could we meet? This is not for the phone. I asked around and people said if I had a problem you were the one to see. I mean, being more or less straightish. For police.'

'It depends where you ask.'

'I'm not going to walk in through the front door of head-quarters and search for you, am I – giving my name for the reception register, and so on?'

'I doubt it. Many don't.'

'Why you're in the phone book, regardless?'

'Of what?'

'Security.'

'Oh, that,' Harpur replied. 'Do you know the laundrette in Ladysmith Street? Open Sundays. Say five o'clock? It's comfortable and people chat constructively during the wash. I'll be wearing a red and black plaid Tall in the Saddle cowboy shirt.'

'Wow. I've seen you being terse on the media. I'll recognize you.'

'Have I seen *you* on the media?'

'Not yet. But you'll recognize me. I look like what you'd expect.'

'You're modest.' He went back to the spaghetti vongole.

'Who?' Denise said.

Hazel said: 'Denise, don't think I'm rude or anything, or telling you how to behave although I'm younger, but you don't ask him that.'

'No?'

'Work,' Harpur said.

'Yes?' Denise replied.

'Oh, most probably yes,' Jill said. 'Later, he'll have to go out, I expect – but work, yes, Denise. Duty?' She put her rolled hand to her mouth and did a battlefield trumpet call. 'We're left behind.'

'You have to go out, Col?' Denise asked.

'Later.'

His daughters disappeared after lunch. They said Sunday School, but he hoped not. As a boy he had been put through all that and still felt marked. Probably they knew he and Denise would like the house to themselves for a couple of hours. Leaving the dishes on the table the two of them went upstairs. Although careless about her surroundings, she believed fiercely in bodily cleanliness and showered now. Then she put all her clothes back on before coming to the bedroom. She liked to be undressed by him and he enjoyed this: it was one of their best compatibilities. In the months since they met, he had effortlessly turned himself into a bit of a fetishist about her knickers, and would take them off her slowly, usually with her legs in the air as she lay on top of the bed. She sometimes said she thought this particular section of the procedure rather schoolboy.

'Not when *I* was a schoolboy,' Harpur said.

'I'm right, then. You're making up for what you missed. I know you occasionally wonder what I see in you, Col.'

'Do I?' he said, gazing down at her.

'I mean, it's not just your age. But you're unpretty. Your hair and so on.'

He took his own clothes off and lay beside her. She turned towards him, pushed his cock flat and put her ear on it, like someone listening to a shell. This seemed reasonable. 'So, what's the answer?' he asked.

'To?'

'What you see in me?'

'I mean, I've got all this youth and intelligence around me at the university, some of it beautiful, male and female.'

'I've heard that,' he said.

'But the fact is, someone, some woman, rings you up and I'm suddenly ill with jealousy. It doesn't go away.'

'I noticed that. I thought to myself then, I'll give Denise an exceptionally loving time this afternoon, so she'll know she's the only one.'

'That will certainly go some way.'

'Yes, only some.'

'I know nobody else I could get upset about so badly,' she said. 'It's . . . well, damn degrading.'

'No. A very good sign,' Harpur replied.

'But how have you done this? I mean, despite your face and hair.'

'And age.'

'True.'

'By adoration, mainly, I should think,' Harpur replied.

'Well, yes, I *do* enjoy that. But, obviously, I've had it from others, and it wasn't the same.'

'I worship your long back,' Harpur said. 'There's an

esteemed porker with a long back, isn't there.' He gave two appreciative grunts.

'Yes, you've said so before.'

'Not worship,' Harpur replied. 'I said I loved your back before. I've moved on.'

'But this would mean that I love you merely because you think a lot of me. I'd still have to ask what I find in *you*, Col – *your* qualities, not just your regard for mine.'

'I believe you're very clever and intellectually rigorous and intuitive and can therefore appreciate the full quality of my soul. Its uniqueness. This, finally, was what worked in my favour and put me ahead of all the other bright stuff you mentioned – the varsity folk of various genders.'

As if impressed by this argument, she spoke slowly: 'Yes, I *am* very clever and intellectually rigorous and intuitive.' Relieved, she produced a huge smile and triumphantly struck the counterpane. 'Thank God we've got that settled at last.' She moved her ear off his cock and it was able to rise. 'Now I don't have to talk any more I can treat myself to a little mouthing.'

'Myself, I thrill to thoughtful conversation.'

'Can't do both.'

'Oh, very well, then.' This afternoon he could not take too much of her mouth and still stay capable of offering the jealousy antidote he'd promised. In a few minutes he pulled free from her lips and went in by those other lips. She put her mouth lips on his at the same time and he could taste what he thought must be himself. It did not seem too bad, though unrecognizable and unaddictive.

'I'm not exorbitant,' she muttered, 'no killing demands, but, please, just be there for a while yet.'

'A privilege.'

'Say it again.'

'No,' he replied.

'Why?'

'Tricky word. I need the breath.'

Later, when they were talking again, she said: 'There are times when I think marriage wouldn't kill it – the sex.'

'What kind of marriage? You and me, or you with someone else and me on the side, or me with someone else and you on the side?'

'You're so intellectually rigorous. It's a tangle. I suppose what I mean is, were you still fucking your wife with that kind of enterprise and run-up well into your marriage?'

'That's another of those questions you mustn't ask.'

'Like work, duty? Would it get like that – you and me if wed?'

'It's a tangle, Denise.'

'Col, what really bothers me is, if I can fancy you despite how you look and your age, then you must have something mysterious – or I'd be mad to want you. So, I need to recognize that other women might be pulled by this, too.'

'Or men.'

'A woman ringing up at Sunday lunchtime: this could be her deliberately smashing through one of the main, solid social routines because she senses it has nothing to do with the real you-ness of you.'

'Spaghetti vongole is very much the me-ness of me.'

'Always, I'm seeking the essence of you,' Denise replied.

'I don't think there's much there.'

'How old is she?'

'I'd have to look at some papers at headquarters for that.'

'But seventy? Twenty-two? Give me parameters.'

'She sounded mature.'

'I bet she bloody did. You see, Col, even post coitus the jealousy doesn't evaporate.'

'Of course not. It's an arrogant male legend.'

'*I* should be saying that.'

'Kindness would prevent you,' Harpur replied.

'Yes, I *am* too damn kind.'

Harpur left the bed. 'The kids will be back. It embarrasses them if we come downstairs looking satisfied.'

'*I'll* look satisfied. *You* I'm not so sure about.'

'*I* should be saying that.'

'Why do you have to go out, then?'

'This will be some minor crisis in a woman's life,' Harpur said.

'And you're supposed to plug it.'

'So young and intellectually rigorous and intuitive, and yet so vulgar,' Harpur replied.

'Where will you meet her?'

'I hope ten minutes' chat will put it all right,' Harpur replied.

'Not in headquarters?'

'No.'

'Why not?'

'Some people don't like going there.'

'Why?'

'Police stations are the enemy,' Harpur said.

'And you, you're a friend?' She rolled from the bed.

'God, that wondrous back.'

'Oh, fuck my back.'

'There'll be other days.' Harpur went downstairs, filled a plastic bag with washing and put it in the boot of the car. Then he returned to the sitting room. Denise joined him soon, and later Hazel and Jill came in. The four of them hung the sitting-room curtains. He felt it as a kind of betrayal of Megan, and saw his daughters did, too. The curtains were light in colour and made the room seem larger and brighter, but like a room in someone else's house. 'I must go,' Harpur said.

'You won't be invited to accompany him, Denise,' Hazel said, 'but you can stay with us if you like. Desmond Iles might look in later.'

'What?' Harpur snarled. 'Who said?'

'He did. He rang the other day. He said he might make a surprise Sunday visit to check what you'd done about security. A surprise to *you*.'

'What *have* you done, Dad?' Jill asked.

'That's next. I had to see to the curtains first.'

'They'll keep out an army,' Jill said.

'If Iles is coming here you'd better stay, Denise,' Harpur said.

'I want her to stay, but not for that reason,' Hazel said. 'He's often quite orderly.'

'I'd like you to stay with them, Denise.'

*

Deloraine was at the laundrette already when he arrived. He loaded a machine and sat with her. 'You run with Harry Foster?' he asked. 'Did I see you around the court once?'

'When he got off.'

'Of course. The drunken judge who closed the case down.'

'Harry's missing.'

'Dropped you?'

'Missing missing.'

'How long?'

'Three days.'

'Oh, well—'

'He keeps in touch, always,' she replied.

'Unless he's dropped you. It happens.'

'Why do you have to be cruel?' she asked.

Why did he? 'Do you want him Missing Personed?'

'Of course I don't. Would I have phoned you?'

She had not made up to come here and wore a long trench coat over what looked like a fairly old turquoise sweater and grey skirt. Harpur remembered her as polished and almost lovely at the court, a touch too much boniness in her features, but a neat body and very still, very dark blue eyes. She would be mid-twenties, like Foster, her fair hair expertly cropped close and her skin maybe at its best without cosmetics. It was a good haircut, but possibly a mistake, all the same: she needed the softness and sweep of a longer style to distract from the jut of her nose and jaw. Yet perhaps she did not want to distract from them. Harpur felt he could admire her. 'Where would I start to look?' he asked.

'He was on a business trip. You know he's in partnership with Ralph Ember and Reid? I'm not shouting any secrets, am I?'

She sounded so anxious he knew she would shout secrets just the same, if this might help find Foster. There was something good between these two, or something good from her side.

'Look, I flirt a bit with Ralph,' she said. 'He needs that. The Charlton Heston image. It's a kind of ritual.'

'Yes? You're telling me he'd view that seriously and get Harry out of the way? Ember? He takes what comes, what comes easily. Ember doesn't—'

He had been going to say 'kill', but a mechanic arrived and began to adjust something on one of the machines near them.

She said: 'Well, thanks, Harpur. You mean he'd never regard me seriously enough.'

'You said it yourself – a ritual. Tending his ego only.'

'All right. In any case, Gerry Reid's missing as well, so it doesn't look like a love/lust thing, no. That was the first check I made.'

'Ember?'

'At the club. Fine.'

'You've been there to ask him about Harry?'

'I didn't think that would be sane.'

'What business trip?' Harpur replied.

'Southampton way. That's as much as I was told.'

'Was Harry carrying anything?'

She put out a hand and let it rest for a moment on his shoulder, the way a parent might. 'Look, Harpur, there are all kinds of new mysteries and hazards. You've heard of the London Pathfinder? Of course you have. Is Harry's disappearance part of large changes?'

'Was he carrying anything, expecting trouble?' Harpur replied.

Deloraine left at once then. Apparently she had brought no washing. Harpur waited for his. When he went out he saw Denise standing at the corner. 'I tailed you,' she said. 'But you knew, didn't you? That's why she left early, as if not with you. Why did she feel your bloody collarbone like that? That supposed to be erogenous, too, for God's sake? Does she know such things because she's *mature*?'

'Iles is alone with the girls?' Harpur asked.

'Who is she? That outfit she had on!'

'Work.'

He went to his car and drove home. She did not follow. When he reached there, the Assistant Chief, Hazel and Jill were playing basic poker for pence on the kitchen table, using only the nines, tens and pictures. Iles was winning.

'He washed up *and* dried,' Hazel said.

'Someone has to,' Iles replied. 'I hear an emergency, Col.'

'Minor key.'

'Should I be put in the picture?'

'Ongoing,' Harpur replied.

'That's the kind I do like to know about, Harpur.'

'One element in a patchwork.'

'Try me. I might understand,' Iles said.

'I'm doing new locks and an alarm very next thing, sir,' Harpur replied.

Jill said: 'He's been perfectly decent, Dad. Not once alone with Haze. I noticed that.'

19

In The Monty you knew at once when someone strange or unsuitable entered the club. This was probably true of most clubs, such as The Cavalry and Guards or The East India in London, but Ember thought it especially true of The Monty, and quite useful. The flavour of The Monty was distinctive. In his little office behind the bar, he felt a sudden tensing-up now: that abrupt suspension of noise among members, and then its ragged resumption as people went normal again, so as not to seem frightened or guilty. This would be the kind of effect Harpur and Iles had when they called, and at first he thought it was them. One of their swaggering invasions to pick up free drinks was about due. Ember could deal with them. He had good local status now, following several letters to the Press on environmental matters and signed Ralph W. Ember. These two officers would know it was unwise to fuck him about, or, at any rate, to fuck him about too much. They were not the law. Their boss, Chief Lane, believed things should be handled properly, even if these two did not.

But when Ember came out of the office he saw that the visitors were Barney and his two fifty-plus, flotsam women, Maud and Camilla. They were approaching the bar, all beaming at him, Barney waving like the sailor home from the sea. He even managed to get what could be regarded as genuine bonhomie in his face, if you spoke loosely. Did they know somehow about Harry and Reid? Nausea took a grip on Ember's upper stomach, and even higher, so he feared he would spew at their feet. Waving back cheerily, he covered his mouth with the other hand, wondering if he would be able to hold it all without visible seepage through the fingers. What did you do with it afterwards? But then the spasm eased. Although he still felt dazed and could chart the first symptoms of a panic – sweat and that deadly shoulder ache – his yearning to vomit declined. Christ, Ember had never wanted Barney here, even alone. Quickly, Ember surveyed the members present, dreading that some of the most obviously pathetic small-timers might be in.

'Here's an august den, Ralph,' Barney cried. 'Calibre fitments – polished mahogany, buffed brass. This is a credit to you, Ralph, wouldn't you say, girls?'

'I can stretch a point and allow you in as my guests. The Monty is strictly members only,' Ember replied.

'I knew you would, Ralph,' Barney said.

'We talked things over exhaustively, Ralph,' Maud said, 'and voted three-nil that it was probably time you relinquished leadership of your syndicate to Gerry Reid.'

She spoke this at pretty near full volume, a real upper-middle-class cow bellow, brought up to scratch over half a century, and Ember stared about to see who was in earshot.

'Yes,' Barney said. 'I was going to take it more slowly, Maud, but yes, Ralph.'

'True. Can't gainsay it, can't gainsay it at all, Ralph, that three-nil,' Camilla said. 'A caveat, though. One was pressurized – not too strong a word. One was indeed *pressurized* because they wanted a solid vote to thump you with, Ralph. Unanimity, like in the old Iron Curtain countries. Myself . . . myself, I don't see you as necessarily clapped out or indecisive, not at all, kid. Clapped-outness is hardly in your face and bearing. No, I was overruled, see it that way, do, Ralph.'

'Perhaps we might talk at a table over there,' Ember said.

'Near that big fucking picture of reprobates on a trip?' Maud replied.

'This was the very successful club outing a few years ago to the Louvre, et cetera,' Ember said.

'The French deserve all they get,' Maud replied.

The four of them moved over to the table and sat down. Ember brought the Kressmann and glasses. 'I'm afraid you can't pay, as non-members,' he said.

'Oh, dear, dear, dear,' Barney hooted, the jolly sod.

Camilla said: 'I can pride myself, Ralph, yes, I think pride myself, on at least getting them, in fact us, to come and see you. They would have done it by phone. I pleaded, yes, pleaded, pleaded for some decorum. And, to their credit, they finally consented. I always say, if you're going to cut someone's throat, do it face to face.'

Barney gazed at the photograph. 'Some beguiling heads.'

'Self-educated, yes, many of them, yet with fine, all-round cultural interests,' Ember replied. He hated to be seen sitting with women dressed like this and as old as they were, plus the legs.

Barney leaned across the table chuckling and gently took Ember's wrist in a comradeship grip. 'We want you to remain in the syndicate, naturally, Ralph,' he said. 'But we think leadership responsibilities might be interfering with your more basic role in the team. It's the way some cricketers play better when freed from captaincy duties. See it as a way of maximizing your unique skills, Ralph.'

Camilla sucked in some Armagnac through the teeth. 'Compromise. I did manage to enforce a compromise, Ralph. I have to tell you they wanted Harry Foster to take over. This view was based on their reading of him from, what is it, two visits to Barney? Two visits! Maud clairvoying something stout in the jockey shorts, probably. Large nose. I keep quoting that line from *Macbeth* to her, you know, Ralph, "There's no art to read the cock's construction in the face", but she won't listen. They'd have picked Foster and trampled your susceptibilities, Ralph. I don't think I'm overstating: *trampled*. Clearly, they were entirely aware that it would be a monstrous snub for you to have to work under Foster.'

'I love vim,' Maud replied. 'Foster's got éclat.'

'But Camilla convinced us,' Barney said.

Ember thought the whole thing might be a scenario. They come to notify him he's dead as number one in his own firm and then make it sound like an Ember triumph, because they pick Reid not Foster. He could not tell them why he didn't give a shit which they picked. Equality had set in.

'Binding-up qualities,' Camilla remarked. 'Conciliation. This is how I'd see Gerry Reid's supreme attributes. Oh, there's an appearance of Celtic mist and drift, but also a hearty impulse towards bringing folk together. An organizing brain lurks behind the bullshit. I say "lurks" with no sinister tinge. Subtlety. Can anyone tell me that subtlety and conciliation will not be crucial in this era of mergers?' She gazed about invitingly, maybe expecting the lads playing pool to reply.

Ember thought, if Barney's fucking both these despite everything, at least he needn't wear himself out doing much of the talk. Maud was probably not too bad a long while ago, but she had one of those faces that seem in some women to turn rectangular in middle age, the way a sweater will hang straight when life goes from the wool. She recognized this problem and wore big, round, pink spectacles in an attempt to get some noticeable curvatures into the show. But the effect was only like looking at two gaudy cups at one end of an oblong tray.

Barney gripped Ember's wrist again and chortled guiltily. 'We talk as if we can give you orders, Ralph. Sheer lese-majesty when we're in your own burnished palace. You're not our employee. Simply, though, we would be happier dealing with a firm run by Reid, in the state of things as they are at present.'

Maud said, still broadcasting: 'We stop supply if you don't step down soonest, Ralph. One ought to alert Reid to the change. Does he come in here? We hoped to surprise him.'

'Off and on,' Ember replied. 'My feeling, though, is they're both away at present. They took what they call some "leave", like in the Civil Service.'

'Revitalizing,' Camilla said. 'This is good. This is someone who will return refreshed and ready. It's almost as if he had an instinct that leadership would call. Quite often those with the gift of command reveal a kind of mysterious sense of destiny. I wouldn't say I'm putting this too romantically. De Gaulle?' She was smaller, a face that had real delicacy, especially her mouth and chin, which could have been those of a pretty child. Her nose was oddly forceful in this setting, built to a different, bigger scale, almost to Foster's standard, yet with very small nostrils which somehow suggested she was stingy. Her voice was small-scale, too, and it worried away at whatever she was talking about, like unravelling tangled string. Barney would stare at her with veneration when she talked. Perhaps she was his favoured girl. Tough choice.

Maud said: 'So, can we reach him? We travel this bloody distance to tell him he's our nominee and the sod's on his hols.'

'It's possible Harry or Gerry will ring in. They don't take a mobile with them on leave. I can understand it. They want full peace after some trying months.'

'At the worst, then, Ralph, *you* could, perhaps, inform Reid,' Barney said.

'Intolerable,' Camilla replied. 'Inhuman. Certainly that. Both. One cannot ask you, Ralphy, to be the one to notify somebody he's replacing you. Like asking someone in the electric chair to pull the switch. We must do it.'

They spoke all the time as if it was settled. For credibility, Ember thought he should make a show of resistance. 'As to conciliation and a flair for building up new combines, I've acted as suggested on our visit to you, Barney. First moves towards an understanding with Vine have been made. I mean by me, personally and alone. And there will be some backing of him financially. That's personal, me to him, concerning a property. Don't tell me Gerry could manage that.'

Barney beamed again: 'Grand, Ralph.'

'We knew you could handle these initial stages, Ralphy,' Maud said. She poured herself another plump Armagnac. 'What you do is open the path for Gerry – or for Foster, if Camilla hadn't vetoed that.'

'Vine knows me, appreciates my background, is comfortable dealing with me,' Ember said.

'These are certainly points, Ralph, but not substantive,' Barney said. 'There has to be a change. Maud sees disaster in you. I must say it is the kind of rumour I've heard about Ralphy Ember for a long time. I ignored that, but now there is Maud's independently built view, too.'

Fuck Maud. Yes, *you* fuck her, thanks. 'So, this is just a feeling,' Ember said, with a small yelp of contempt. 'No evidence or logic.' In a way, he felt pretty pleased. His voice was fine. His brain seemed steady. He could give them the required offended, hurt act. All this steam and argument about two bosky corpses!

Barney said: 'Camilla is spot on, as ever. It's unthinkable that you should have to inform Reid, Ralph.' He stood. Barney had dressed down to come here, no question, the arrogant, boating shit, and had on a grey-brown, Eventide Home loose-weave cardigan and commissionaire's black trousers. His tan was top-class, though, ingrained and muted, constructed without intent while at sea. There were definitely times when Ember thought Barney might be genuinely upper class, not just rich yesterday on the brilliant spread of snorting. For example, he was presumably shagging these two loud, ungainly slabs, which would hint at taste foully stunted by years in an authentic public school, before they admitted girls. Barney had a small, congested face, not often bright with good humour. They were the kind of features you could imagine at their best receiving news from a top-level solicitor about the nice will of a loaded baronet father, or even higher. Barney said now: 'May we ask you to put Gerry in touch with us as soon as he arrives? This would settle things very decently, I feel.'

'Certainly,' Ember replied.

Camilla put her head back and gave a small whistle up towards the ceiling. Still looking in that direction, she said: 'As if . . . as if you don't really expect him to reappear. Am I absurdly turning a sudden, microscopic inkling into something more?'

'Not reappear?' Barney said. 'These are business people, Camilla. Do people walk out on a beautiful livelihood?'

The two women also stood now. Maud was looking at the trip picture again. 'Ralphy, the Louvre? What did they come away with?'

When they had gone, Ember sat on at the table for a while, not drinking, in pain. Christ, Reid and Foster had better not be found. Barney nominates a new leader one day and he's discovered dead the next, or the next, as well as the runner-up. Whatever the police believed and said, Barney would never accept they killed each other. If the police statement was vague about how long they had been dead, Barney might even think Ember had done both of them since the proposal for change was announced. It would look like an outright and effective strike to bugger his plans. And if he felt thwarted, Barney could call up a network of rough people to retaliate, rougher even than Maud. Of course, the location near Winchester might say to Barney that the deaths had happened on their way back from The Wharf. He would think then that Ember had sensed at that last meeting in Barney's house how things were going, and had decided to act first. No matter how he interpreted things when the deaths were announced, Barney would have a good idea that Ember was with those two when they were finished. And he would note that Ember had behaved throughout The Monty encounter tonight as if he believed Reid and Foster were alive, and merely on a day or two's jaunt. Deception. These were dangerous thoughts in someone like Barney.

He must get to that wood at once, tonight, before they were found and the story made the media. He had to pick up the bodies for dumping, or bury them. Jesus, all that digging again? He did not make up his mind about the disposal method but went to The Monty storeroom and loaded a pickaxe and two spades into the boot of his Rover, plus five flashlights. He also put in four paving stones from The Monty yard and some lengths of rope, in case he decided on water and needed sinkers. He called home and told Margaret he might sleep on his camp bed at the club because the barman had spotted prowlers. She was anxious. He promised that if he saw or heard anything he would not risk himself but dial 999. 'Will the police come, Ralph?' she asked. 'Things being as they are.'

'As they are? This will be Ralph W. Ember calling. I'll tell them to get here fast, or there will be repercussions.'

'Will they come, Ralph?' she replied. She could enrage him like that, questioning his civic worth.

*

He had loved that spot where Foster and Reid died because it was so nicely hidden. Now, he worried about whether he could find it in the dark again. He must not drive fast: somewhere not far ahead of him on the motorway would be Barney and his women, and Ember did not want to overtake them, because his damn profile might be unmistakable, even in the night and at speed. It would be a drawback to have Maud turn up in that wood. Sad, really, to visualize it: in their car they would be discussing Mouth-Mouth Reid and his charming, warm gifts and leadership potential, and Ember might hearse past them on his way to fill Mouth-Mouth's cold mouth with clay. Or possibly water. The memory of the terrible labour burying Caring Oliver was still strong and discouraging. He might get the two bodies into the boot and find some decent stretch of pool or sea for them. Possibly the stones would hold them under long enough to become unidentifiable.

He located the right Winchester exit and then had a sweat-laden hour getting wrong minor roads, wrong woods, wrong earth tracks. At this time of night, jumpy folk in a big country house might pick up the phone to report a vehicle

casing the district. He did not want police brought into the
area at all, and definitely not when he was here with a load
of committal-to-the-deep gear aboard and the night digging
kit. At around 2 a.m. he found them. There had been a
couple of likely-looking spots earlier when he feared they
were already discovered and removed. The sweat ran down
both his shins then in a wide rush and his socks came to
feel like soaked paper. But here they were, in the headlights,
still cuddling each other, Reid holding the gun, and not
looking a bit like a placator or binder-up. Ember switched
off the headlights. There was a fraction of moon, which
would help. He left the car and tested the ground with a
spade. It was fairly yielding, not hard with roots. The idea
of a grave here seemed now more attractive than water
burial. The main point was, a grave seemed to work. Caring
remained undiscovered. After so long, there would be ferns
and tendrils all over that Cheltenham spot, possibly the start
of a housing estate. Caring had returned to Nature, and
Nature knew what to do with him. To secure paving stones
to a corpse sounded easy enough, but it was not. In the sea,
especially, the motion of water could loosen bindings and
bodies came back far too soon, bobbing about pushily for
attention. Getting them to water deep enough was not
simple, either.

In any case, although Ember knew the digging would be
a trial, there seemed something decent and respectful about
placing them in country soil. He had felt the same when
putting Caring under. After all, the three of them – Reid,
Foster and Caring – had been his friends, in a sense. Dis-

posing of them in dark water would be offhand. He liked the idea of doing his best by these two now, although Foster had been such a bullying jerk and Reid would have slimed his way to dominance. Ember put on wellingtons, stripped to the waist and began to dig. Mainly he relied on the moonlight, but occasionally used one of the torches for a while. He calculated on four hours with breaks, by which time it would be dawn. He needed to be home before Margaret awoke and began wondering whether he had been hurt at the club. She would telephone. 'Mouth-Mouth,' he said, 'I don't think you could ever have done it – I mean, run the outfit – so, in a way, what's happened is a bit of a let-off for you. You died with a reputation, a reputation good enough to reach Barney, the opulent dolt, and those chirpy guardians. You died at the high moment of promise, Gerry, your abilities and brain still prized. How about the poem that used to come up in school during Remembrance Week: "They shall not grow odd as we who are left grow odd"?'

Ember liked the feel of this soil – the gluey weight and friendly, fertile texture. It was worthy of Harry and Reid. He would lower the bastards in carefully, not simply drop them, and especially not the second one, whichever, or he would smash down on the other with unnecessary violence. So far, Ember had not decided who should be at the bottom. He used to hate Foster far more than Reid, and that would have meant Foster first. But now he knew Gerry might have taken over, he could not prefer him all that much, the oily, spieling sod. Maybe it did not matter about order.

At the end, when he would have them at a proper depth

and filled in, Ember intended to scatter the surplus soil elsewhere, so he could get a neat, flat surface, which would tell of a conscientious job, neatly done, yet tell him only. It would have been neat to give them to the water, too, perhaps: the murky surface would instantly close again after two welcoming splashes and lie there looking back at you as if it had never been disturbed. Always, though, the chance of untimely re-emergence existed: a bloated and possibly gnawed face would not be neat at all. Foster and Reid would have appreciated this site much better and might have recognized the care and effort Ember was putting into things. Probably Reid would feel a rightness about being so close to Winchester College.

20

Vine invited Ralph Ember to come with him and Becky to meet the estate agent at The Pines. It seemed right. Ember was not going to put any actual money into Vine's offer, but he would be guaranteeing a couple of very fat, short-term bank loans – from banks Vine never heard of before this. Ralphy deserved to see and get a feel of what he was financing. Of course, this was supposing Vine made an offer at all – likely but not a cert at the price they were still asking. The agent reckoned the recession had ended, and the house market was picking up ... some tale. Oh, no, not a cert purchase at all.

Vine disliked bringing Ember close to Becky – would have disliked bringing him close to any woman he valued. There was the Charlton Heston stuff and Ralphy's big-time charm – when he wasn't twisted up from fear, that is. But Becky had the baby with her and would have her attention on the property, so creepy approaches from Ember should get nowhere.

Vine and she had looked around the place before and really loved it – not just a gallery but paddocks, stables and such space inside. On that earlier visit, though, they had had no hope of buying – like trippers in a stately home. Now, with the agent here, this visit might signify. Another reason for bringing Ralphy was people such as estate agents knew him – he had this glint of civic glory, somehow. Well, probably those letters to the Press and his own properties. Reputation. An agent would see that if Ralph Ember was somehow in the deal the deal must be solid – and that could mean the price might sink a bit because the money would be for sure, no delays or maybes trying to raise it.

'This room,' Becky cried, 'so beautifully proportioned. So large. Big enough for a ball. When we move in, yes, a celebratory ball, Keith.'

All the shit about quitting and moving to France was gone now. This was the thing – you had to know how women thought, and Keith Vine did, none better. They had ideas, but not ideas that stuck, and as long as you gave a little kindly attention and suggested something else they would usually agree. Of course, her screams of joy would blot out the advantage of having Ember present, and this fucking agent would think if the lady of the family longed for the place he could stick at the asking price. Vine did not want to spoil Becky's fun, though, so he let her burble. It was more useful than that stuff about the red tiles and slow, wide rivers of Provence.

Ember said the wiring looked a bit amateur to him, as if Oliphant Kenward Knapp's cash started to falter before he had the house quite right. Brill, this sort of comment from Ralph! He was not some soft girl who would talk crap about proportions and shapes. He was a businessman. He saw what was what, and, even if it was not really like he said, it was worth saying – to get the deal Vine's way, not the agent's. Christ, it must be a bit fretting for this agent to know the sort of backgrounds he was in the middle of. This had been the home of Oliphant Kenward Knapp, one of the biggest dealers in Western Europe, including Holland. God knew what kind of associates might be interested in the sale, plus his lady, Constance, and the people *she* would know in her own right. Then came Ralphy Ember – of Low Pastures and The Monty, yes, but with another sort of reputation rumoured, too. And lastly, Keith Vine himself, someone very ready to be polite and reasonable if things went nicely but also, Keith knew, someone who gave a very big don't-mess-with-me-or-else aura.

'And no alarm system, naturally,' Ember blared, 'because this property belonged to someone who could not risk rousing neighbours or the police, in case they got inside and saw the kind of materials he stashed here.'

'Mr Knapp had many business interests, I believe,' the agent said.

'He was gunned down just outside, you know, Keith, Becky. The blood marks might still be there. This would put off a lot of buyers. We'll have a look at the spot, shall we?'

A prince, Ralph – a thinker, a chum, despite those difficult earlier times he and Keith had. The agent looked half beaten already. And this bargaining flair was possibly only one of Ralphy's strengths. Vine had come to recognize lately that Ember might have true grandeur in him – if something on the jungle drums turned out true. This tale said Harry Foster's girl, Deloraine, had been touring the streets and calling at Reid's dump off the Valencia looking for both of them – but especially Harry, of course. According to the information she seemed frantic. Vine treated himself to some joy – not full out yet, in case it was balls. But if these reports had it right, they would prove top-class sincerity in Ralph Ember. Those two, Foster and Reid, were against an alliance with Vine – so if Ralph had had them taken out it proved a really nice zappiness. Probably Panicking could not handle that sort of tidy-up himself, but never mind. He must have commissioned some gifted people, and the impulse would be all his. Vine felt obligation. He must stop calling him Panicking – there was a fine decisiveness here, and true, long-term strategic thought.

Briefly, he heard himself speaking to Eleri: 'Don't open it. Just pick it up and hand it to me.'

The agent took Becky and Charles to look at possible nursery accommodation. That was all right – he was old and full of wheeze and dandruff. 'How are the lads then, Ralph – Foster and Reid?' Vine asked, when they were alone.

Ember gave a perky laugh, stuffed with contempt, and it echoed around the empty drawing room, like a bagatelle ball. 'Those two – they go their own way, you know, Keith. Well, as I told you, they *can* go, as far as I'm concerned. That partnership is over. I tried to instil the need for business discipline, regularity and so on, but they're not made for it. If they wanted some trip, some treat, some excitement, they'd just take off, leave everything.'

'Now?'

'Exactly. Do I care?'

'Honestly, Ralph? I couldn't believe it when you said you three were through.'

'Oh, they'll be back in touch, naturally – when they get fed up or the money's gone. And they'll expect to move in to the places they had before. Not fucking likely, Keith.'

'Maybe you're tough on them, Ralph.'

'It's happened too often. And at this particular time it's so damn irresponsible. Terminally irresponsible.'

'This particular time? The London thing?'

'What would they care, supposing they were still part of the team? They'd do whatever they felt like doing, go wherever they wanted, regardless. Tell them about crisis and they think, "Ralph can deal with that, Ralph will deal with that. See you in a while, Ralph, when it's all been sorted." It's good they've gone, Keith. No question, they would stand between you and me.' Ember was walking around the room, admiring cornice work. 'We'll land you a true bargain here.'

The obligations to Ember piled up. They confused Vine. In one way what Ralphy seemed to have done was great. But Vine loathed to be in this kind of debt to someone – especially to Panicking, this quaking old piece of rich shit. Vine did not mind a money liability to him, such as guarantees, but part of him hated the idea that Ember had done high exploits for Keith's advantage, such as wiping out Harry and Reid. He did not want to think of Ember as like a knight in history, full of style and action, bringing what was called succour. To be left behind in achievements damaged Vine's sense of himself. He had to equalize – at least equalize. He would need to do something in return – maybe something even bigger than the slaughter of two non-quality operators like Foster and Gerry.

That conviction built in him slowly. But the way of doing it arrived in a beautiful rush. Suddenly he saw what the obvious ploy to match Panicking or beat him was. Vine would eliminate the London pathfinder – that lovely mover. Of course. Ideal. It would be such a practical move – and, brought on by the sod's own behaviour and role. Plus it had scale and glory. Task for a gifted leader. This would be a true Keith Vine mission, and at once he began to plan how to manage it. Three possible venues. That lad would probably return to *The Eton Boating Song* to see how the new arrangement was working. If Si looked as good as Eleri he would make him the supplies offer he had been sent with for her. Or, if he failed to appear there, Vine had an address for him, and he might still be using it. Otherwise, get to him when he went looking for pussy again at the Valencia. Plenty of very quiet streets around all those areas – quiet meaning nobody in them ever talked or ever even saw anything. Vine loved the idea of Keith Vine as sly, deadly huntsman, and he blamed himself for having waited so long. Even if Reid and Foster did show again, it would still be the time to remove this invader. The future was available, ready and glorious, but you had to take it. He had always known this, yet it was as if he had forgotten.

Ember began jumping up and down now, testing for rot in the joists. 'The Pines is the sort of property that you'll fit into so well, Keith. It's a thrill to me, watching the way you've galloped ahead. Foster, Reid, they lack that central requirement for our game – dedication.'

'I heard Harry's girl is worried about his disappearance.'

'That's just like the idiot – not to mention to her he was off on a break somewhere. As I say, irresponsible. This is a lovely, hearty girl, Keith – much too good for him.' Ember put his face against a wall and squinted along it, testing plumbness. He said, just like a by-the-way statement: 'Sometimes I wonder, do we share a supplier?'

'Mine's London-based. Holborn way.'

'Not the coast?'

'Which?' Vine replied.

'Isle of Wight direction.'

'No. That would be Barney and the noisy women, yes? He thinks well of my business, I've heard that.'

'Yes,' Ember said.

'But I don't deal through him. Wouldn't.'

'Oh, why not?'

'Never,' Vine replied.

Becky and the agent came back and Ember said: 'Yes, Keith, I'd say your offer shouldn't move far above two forty grand or you're making them a gift.'

The agent coughed and winced and giggled. 'We're looking for *three* forty, as you know, Mr Ember. Much sought after type of dwelling, now we're into recovery. Executive standard. We're a long way apart if Mr Vine is at that figure, I fear.'

'Oh, Keith,' Becky cried, 'such views from upstairs!'

Ember stuck his scar out towards the agent and said: 'Get on to the executors today. I'd hate to think you were standing in the way of a happy deal. Really hate to see you in that light. I mean you, personally. Two four. This is a tidy figure.'

Ember was in the back of the car on the return to town. Vine drove, with Becky and Charles beside him. Ember leaned forward behind Becky and, from the side of his eye, Vine saw him place his hand on the bare skin of her neck and the start of her shoulder. 'We'll get it for two six or seven, Beck. Don't be troubled,' he said.

'Honestly, Ralph?' she said, excited.

'We've planted some fruitful ideas today.'

Ember left his hand there for quite a time after this statement, one bent finger moving gently up and down. Vine could not watch it non-stop because of the road, but whenever he did glance it was still working away at her, like a . . . well, like intimacy. 'The baby looks so happy,' Ember said. 'He knows something good is on the way. They have such instincts.'

She did not seem to mind that hand and finger. Naturally, she bloody didn't. That's how they were with a man who could sound as if he had it all in his grip, and especially a man who could talk big cash quantities, like he did it every damn day. People saw other people in different ways. Whenever Vine looked at Ember he saw Panicking Ralphy – someone full of money and good on deals, but still just Panicking. When Becky looked at him she saw and heard Mr Masterful, and probably her blood was doing something tumultuous from that busy finger. This hurt him – a nursing mother, and such casualness with his feelings.

Then, something really hellish happened. Charles on

Becky's lap was watching that finger and suddenly stretched up and took a hold on it. Vine had to slow to see this better. Ember let him keep the tiny grip and Becky smiled at the sight, all so comfortable and placid, like a fucking family group, for Christ's sake. Keith Vine knew something so strongly then. Even if he had been uncertain before, he was sure – so sure now – sure he had to knock over this London lad and prove that even if he did not look like Charlton Heston when young he could still stay ahead of bloody Panicking. If Keith Vine did not do this, Panicking would be among everything Keith Vine loved. Keith Vine had to prove it to Keith Vine, and then to everyone else.

He dropped Ember a few streets from Shield Terrace and The Monty. Ember bent down by Becky's open window to say goodbye all round, but there was no kissing of Becky's cheek, nothing like that – Ember could see Keith Vine was watching. Anyway, Ember would know he had left a little message on her body skin. 'Rest assured, Keith, that if and when those two reappear, they'll get nowhere with me. They're out, dead.'

'I love the sound of it, Ralph.' Vine did not even mention the neck grope as he drove Becky and Charles home. He needed to stay superbly calm to go after that London creature later today. There were three things you could do if a girl behaved like that – you could beat up the man, or you could beat up the girl or you could get the girl somewhere and make love to her, long-drawn-out love at all points, so she would realize where she belonged. He thought this third would be best. But, then, when they reached home she put

Charles in his cot at once, although he was yelling for a feed, and walked to the bedroom, taking her clothes off on the way. Christ, she had been really brisked up by Ember's finger and wanted the full thing now, the full thing from whoever was on tap, which meant Keith.

'I've got to go out,' he said. 'Immediately. This is important.' Did she think he would come on as substitute for Panicking Ralphy? For Panicking?

It was still only eight in the evening, much too early for the *Eton*, and he went out to Dobecross woods and did some shooting practice with the Russian job he liked these days – lucky he had a good stock of ammo in the car. He used some more time to make a tour of the street pushers – checking they were getting enough stuff and generally helping them with morale. You had to now and then, and they appreciated it. At just before 11 p.m. he went to the *Eton* and stood not far from Si Pilgrim, waiting – trying to look small-town harmless.

This was not just about reaching equality with Ember – better than equality. This was about looking after Harpur, too. Col talked about getting security and armament, but he never would. He had this cop ego – this belief he would always be all right, eventually. Another aspect of how Keith Vine had to take care of people who depended on him. The duty came with leadership, and he would accept. It was to protect Harpur that he had still not mentioned Col's recruitment to Ember. One day he might have to, obviously. You tried to play open with a partner, even someone like Panicking. He had decided, though, that Ember was not ready for the Harpur information yet. This was another leadership quality – timing ... a skill that could not be learned, but which was given by the good God as a flair. It was because his timing instinct pushed him so hard that he had come here tonight to see to the friend from London.

21

A lot of calls used to come to The Monty on the public payphone in a booth at the corner of the bar. Members reckoned it would not be tapped. Ember wondered. If anyone tapped The Monty's business phones it would be sloppy to leave the booth untouched. He never said anything, though. Now and then, everyone had need of confidential communication from outside, and this was about the most secure method. The alternative was to hang about noticeably in the street waiting for a box call, if it wasn't occupied or smashed to buggery for the coins.

Barney rang the booth early one evening. Naturally, Ember was expecting some word from him, them. It was a couple of days since their visit. Also naturally, Ember was expecting the call would go on for a while. There was a chair by the phone as standard equipment: complicated deals and detailed threats would come and go here. Ember took a lager with him. He wanted his brain in good form and could not risk Armagnac. Closing the door, he sat at ease, his legs stretched out, the glass of lager reachable by his free hand on the floor. These sods were beaten before they began, but he meant to be pretty gracious.

'Ralph, we're so surprised not to have heard from . . . let's call him G.R.,' Barney said.

This was part of the bonny farce of these calls: people

would use Ember's name and even their own, but went codified for the subject matter.

'We feel there's some urgency to the matter, Ralph.'

'I do see that,' Ember replied.

'Are you sure you do?' Barney said.

'Organizational restructuring is bound to be urgent,' Ember said.

There was a silence. Ember guessed something shitty was on the way. Barney said: 'Frankly, Ralph, in view of its nature, we wonder whether you've passed on the invitation to be in touch. Feet dragging. But I have to warn you, delays like that will be useless. We are set.'

Ember took a couple of lager sips. 'He's not been in contact with me yet. They're an ungovernable, playful pair, Harry and Gerry. Bright, but, yes, ungovernable. And playful. I try to think of it as playfulness, nothing worse.'

'But this could be worrying, surely, in someone destined for . . . Maud's on the extension.'

'When did you last see them, Ralph?' she asked.

'It's days ago.'

'I suppose what I mean is, have you seen them since you made the visit here, the three of you?' Maud asked.

Ember had another consoling swig: 'Oh, yes, since then, clearly.'

Maud said: 'Camilla wants a word.'

'Obvious, Ralph. Just wished to ask what I'm afraid is the very apparent. Yet perhaps sometimes it is the seemingly obvious, the heart of the matter question, that goes furthest. I think I'd enquire whether you are worried about them, you, personally, Ralph, their as it were state. None of us knows them as well as you. I think I'm right on that.'

'Not *worried*,' Ember replied. 'Possibly a little irritated at the thoughtlessness. But one is accustomed.'

'They've done this kind of thing before?' Barney asked.

'I wouldn't want to prejudice things for G.R.—'

'Please, say whatever you wish, Ralph,' Barney said. 'Better at this juncture than too late.'

'Well, yes, once or twice they've hopped off.'

'Drinking jags? Snort jags?'

'Possibly,' Ember said.

'I really don't think I like this,' Barney replied. 'A prospective leader.'

'Camilla wants a word,' Maud said.

'Spirited, hedonistic, apparently casual: this combination can be promising, nonetheless. These are folk who will take their fun wholeheartedly, yes, even selfishly, but who return in due course and apply the same wholeheartedness to the business. One could see that wholeheartedness in G.R.'s face, and it's why I insisted on him in preference.'

'Ralph, what we have to consider is that they might have been taken out by someone as a business ploy,' Barney said.

'Taken out?' Ember replied.

'Don't think because there are no bodies this is impossible,' Barney said. 'Well, I don't have to tell you, Ralph. Disposal methods. This *is* your secure phone, isn't it?'

We trust. 'Oh, yes, Barney,' Ember replied.

Maud asked: 'No untowardness between the three of you on the way back from here, Ember?'

What made Ralph almost depressed was you had two ragged old pieces like Maud and Camilla, women who ought to be trawling hard for any sexual responses, yet they obviously did not get the smallest tremor from himself, even though he had taken the trouble once or twice to mock up decent lust looks at each. 'Why would there be untowardness, Maud?' he replied. This bitch, calling him Ember, like the handyman.

'Ah, there was, was there?' Maud said. 'Camilla wants a word.'

'Internal strifes are always the worst. We've all heard of the special agonies of civil war, and look at the Conservatives. But then one has to ask whether you, Ralphy, would have the flair to see off two folk such as G.R. and H.F. Without disrespect, would we be intent on displacing you, Ralph, if you were capable of such strokes?'

'I don't know that I'd like to qualify as leader through a talent for snuffing out excellent friends,' Ember declared.

Barney said: 'Clever and with fine information, these London operatives. How would they know we had G.R. marked for eminence? Yet they *did* know, and have probably removed him and his number two, thinking this will destroy the syndicate. It's not unreasonable, not at all.'

Putting Ember at fucking three, or less. 'We should try to see the positive side, Barney,' he said. 'There were times when Harry especially did not really seem a team entity.'

'Best we don't use names, Ralph,' Barney snapped. 'The practicalities are that I have to worry about how your business continues to run with two of its principals dead.'

'But you don't know that as fact, Barney,' Ember cried in protest, and took more lager.

'My level of the trade, one gets to sense things, Ralph. In a way, it's admirable of you to retain hope for your colleagues, and to believe they will return, but I fear this is also the kind of sentimental woolliness which makes me sure you are not made for main manning. You blatantly refuse to accept the possibility of their deaths. By all means indulge your tender side, your comradely side – not, though, in a command role, where sharper qualities are called for.'

'But how sharp exactly *are* you, Ralphy?' Maud asked. 'You always seem to come out all right, somehow.'

Occasionally, Ember would try to think of a motto, in case he were ennobled for civic activities and required to provide words for the College of Heralds. How would 'Always come out all right, somehow', go in Latin?

'What's apparent is that the conflict on your patch is now fiercely under way, Ralph,' Barney said. 'We must, I fear, yes, *must* take the worst scenario and assume that G.R. and H.F. will never return. The—'

With despair and defiant hope fighting in his voice, Ember said: 'Barney, I simply cannot assume that, regardless of what implications this has about officer qualities. These are my mates as well as colleagues.'

'Were,' Barney replied. 'We must progress, plan as for the worst. This means the protective alliance with K.V. is now even more vital. You see that? Suddenly your firm is disastrously weak.'

'The K.V. thing – very much in hand,' Ember said.

'Of course, those merger talks will stress that he, not you, controls the new-formed syndicate,' Maud stated. 'We do not want him put off.'

'He's just a bloody kid,' Ember replied.

'This kid's the future,' Barney said. 'He takes his supplies from elsewhere. From elsewhere at present. This will need attention. That's for me to settle with him, personally. No need for you to get your oar in. Your task is to create the alliance.'

'With K.V. as unquestioned chieftain,' Maud said. 'Camilla wants a word.'

'Achievements, triumphs, I mean yours, Ralph, can never be cancelled or gainsaid. But time, Ralphy. Time is at once the aspic which preserves our memory of those achievements and triumphs, yet is also the torrent that rushes on, leaving those very achievements and triumphs behind, demanding the new.'

'So do it, Ralph,' Maud remarked. 'Keep saying to yourself "K is king."'

Ember's uneasiness continued after the call ended. He still found it baffling to be addressed in that utterly non-hormonal style by those two wrecks, and to hear them order him to crawl to Vine. Baffling? Damn shaming. Ember's pride in self needed to be restored urgently, and he decided to drive over to see Foster's Deloraine. This was the kind of bereft girl who could quickly reaffirm his still current pull. Jesus, that batty tart, Camilla, must think it kind to call him a revered slab of antiquity. Maybe something serious should be done about Vine.

It was only early evening, and there would be nothing off-colour about calling on Deloraine. In fact, he thought that at this stage he would definitely not try anything beyond commiseration. This was a girl sure to be into anxiety. Although it seemed almost unbelievable that any woman could fret about Foster, they were like this – they committed themselves to some freak and, in their fine, female way remained committed. There was a perfect reason for visiting her. In fact, he had a duty to call. To act with responsibility and consideration was a patent obligation on a syndicate head, and he *was* the fucking head, regardless of Barney and those two unkempt main board members.

22

Harpur decided he had to get out of the mock partnership with Vine. It was as abrupt and definite as that. This did not mean turn him over for prosecution. Yet. Harpur wanted to get clear, that was all. The make-believe had worn thin. He drove across to see if he could catch Keith at the flat. It was early evening and he might be there.

Fear had taken a half hold on Harpur, and maybe more than half: part plain, physical fear, and then something else. Although he had had the alarms fixed at his house now, and he might still find an unofficial handgun somewhere, he had no idea what kind of numbers might be looking for him, and how safe the children would be. Iles had failed to come up with a gun. Well, of fucking course. He still wanted Hazel and Jill at his house – or, he wanted Hazel there and would take Jill as unavoidable – so why help Harpur feel more able to guard them at home? There probably were not many police forces where the head of CID had to devote non-stop thought to preventing an Assistant Chief Constable (Operations) from getting close to his, the head of CID's, underage daughter.

But it was the escalation of war in the town that unnerved Harpur most. What Deloraine had said convinced him things were moving towards chaos. Or not just moving now, tumbling. If two old hands like Foster and Reid could be taken out so neatly, some exceptionally weighty people must be about, perhaps in crowds. And then, according to Jack Lamb, Eleri's daughter would bring in her own accomplished syndicate to fight for a share, or more than a share: for everything. This made at least two formidable outside teams at work, plus local firms like Ember's, Vine's, perhaps Shale's, and, on top of that, the freelances. Very soon, Lane would see enough of what was happening in his realm and insist on prosecutions where prosecutions had a chance, no further waiting. That would be completely reasonable: what police were for. But in the turmoil sure to result, Harpur thought his hope of emerging clean, as an undercover cop, not a bought cop, would be flimsy.

Harpur climbed the stairs and knocked on the door of Vine's flat. Normally, they would rendezvous at those secret, remote spots, but Harpur wanted to speed things. For a while, nobody answered. He felt lonely and exposed on this landing – the way he had begun to feel generally, in fact. These days, juries offered no friendship. If it came to a case, they were bound to deduce a slide into general evil on the patch, and would fling blame. Some of it they might fling at people who brought the evil, if they were caught and charged. Some of it they would fling at any officer who seemed to have tolerated the decline, and possibly taken a profit from it. Juries were bribed or intimidated or lawyer-conned to interpret things like that. Or at least to get the real offenders off.

Now, suddenly, Harpur wanted the break from Vine before all that hazard could begin. He would hand over the Avantage watch tonight, bought with his first pay from the syndicate. He would have handed back the cash, if there were any left, but he had needed to spend with some show. You had to prove you were fully purchased. This was exactly the kind of point judges and juries found impossible to swallow. They had heard of undercover work, of course, but stayed primly ignorant of the way it worked. How could they know? How could they, if they would not try? True, Iles might testify for him, but what would a court make of Desmond Iles, radiating flagrant contempt for everyone present, including and especially the judge? Some folk on juries were damn perceptive, and two or three judges. Two. In any case, Iles would possibly refuse to help, if that suited one of his purposes at the time. He had a lot of purposes. Hazel was a purpose, the further destruction of Lane another, and retaining the love of his wife, Sarah, and Fanny, their daughter, another – and supreme. Harpur would figure only low in the list.

Eventually, Becky opened the door. She had been putting the baby down in his cot. Keith was out. She did not know where. 'What's so urgent?'

'Yes, urgent. Out where?'

'I think he was angry – stormed off early.'

'But where? Angry about what?'

'Oh, just sexual. No business implications. Jealousy. You know what he's like. Ownership. Someone touched my bare neck, no less.' She took him into the small living room. 'We're still here, you see.' She gazed around, taking in the dim furniture and shattered decor. 'You came once to tell me to get out of the area, out of the country.'

Harpur remembered it. 'You didn't.'

'Things have changed.'

Harpur now also stared around the room. 'Yes?'

She smiled. 'We're buying Kenward's pad.'

He made himself stay unastonished. 'Nice. That much cash about?'

'Some *arrangement*? Keith's suddenly what's called bankable, I believe, like Anthony Hopkins. He rates a guarantee.'

'And now you're happy to stay?'

She smiled again and shrugged. 'Not really. But I'm his, aren't I?'

'Ownership.'

'Like that,' she replied. 'His soul's into this deal, The Pines. It's the babe's future. I can't wet-blanket. Keith needs praise and backing. He's got wonderful tenacity and drive, but he's feeble, too. A woman needs that in a man, or she's never going to get close.' She put Harpur in an armchair and sat on the floor herself. When she spoke next she kept her head down, staring at her midriff. People did look away when due to talk rough, but he was surprised at it from Becky – not one for tact. 'Have you come to tell him something bad?' she asked.

'In a way.'

'Something that could hit the business, hit our chance of The Pines?'

Harpur said: 'I don't know. If he's bankable he's bankable.'

'Maybe not so bankable if you pulled out.'

'Pulled out of what?'

'Come on, Harpur. Or not bankable if you've decided it's time to turn him in.'

'No, not that.'

'But you'll pull out now?' She looked up and gazed at him for a while, eyes contemptuous. Then she said: 'Perhaps it won't make that much difference. I mean, who knows you're in Keith's firm, anyway? His credit standing might hold up even without you.'

'Of course. He's got his own status. I need to see him.'

'Oh, you feel exposed suddenly – the pace of things?'

The child had been crooning in another room but now began to bawl and she went and brought him back in her arms. Harpur thought she looked magnificent: this fair-haired, lovely mother-figure standing among all the background tat, and seeming so unassailably apart from it, like the eternal future. Perhaps she saw how he was moved and kept the attitude for almost a minute. Vine had done well to land a girl like this. Keith knew it, of course, and all his struggles were aimed at holding on to her, her and the child. When she said 'ownership', she was really talking about *his* non-stop fear of losing *her*. Harpur could sympathize. But Becky was probably not a girl to be forever won by Oliphant Kenward Knapp's big house. She looked more deeply, and a lot more deeply than Vine ever would or could.

'Usually for police I pop out a breast and feed Charles. It makes them feel loutish. I'm comfortable with you, though, Harpur, so I won't.'

'I'm flattered. Can I hang on a while to see if Keith arrives?'

'No date with the young girlfriend?'

'Bit of a rift.' Becky had met Denise once or twice.

'Oh? She's playing about with lads of her own age? Bound to happen. Or you're playing about? Bound to happen?'

'No, not ownership, Beck. Stupid, really. About care of my children.'

She put the baby on the old carpet and went out to the kitchen to make tea. When she came back she said: 'So, don't your children like her?'

'Yes. It wouldn't matter if not, though.'

'Oh? But children *are* important, up to a point.'

'Yes. So is she, but more than up to a point.'

'I liked her. She's a strength to you, Harpur.'

'Yes.'

'I mean, at your age. And with your education. Lack of.'

'Yes.'

'She's clever, isn't she? At university?' Becky asked.

'Yes.'

'And pretty. A body.'

'Yes.'

'Well, then,' she said.

'Yes.' Harpur finished his tea and stood. He had begun to grow restless. It seemed wrong to be talking about Denise to this woman, though he was not clear why.

'Keith might show. I don't know,' she said. 'He's busy. Well, I don't need to tell you.'

'I'll have a drift about, see if I can spot him.'

'Around the pushers? He won't like that.'

Harpur said: 'I can be discreet.'

'With that haircut and build? Do I give him a message if you miss him?'

'I expect you will.'

She sat down in the chair Harpur had left. 'Let yourself out, will you? That's what you came to do, isn't it?' He was on to the landing when she called: 'Harpur, have I got it right? I forget The Pines?'

'Ask him to get in touch.'

'You're going to ditch him . . . us?'

Oh, yes. He did not say it, though.

Harpur drove to *The Eton Boating Song*, but it was much too early for real activity there. Then he toured a couple of pushing streets off the Valencia. He did not see Vine and after half an hour gave up looking. From a card telephone box he rang Denise at the university flats. It was a long, worrying procedure: the calls went to a general phone, and anyone might answer, or nobody. Someone did, eventually, and said he would see if Denise was in. After six or seven minutes, she answered. 'That took a hell of a time,' Harpur said. 'Entertaining yourself with someone your own age?'

'What are you on about, Col? I'm two floors up. Remember?'

'I was talking about you to someone, so I thought I'd give a ring,' he replied.

'Great.'

'It seems idiotic not seeing you.'

'Yes? Since when?'

'All the time.'

Her voice fell. 'Yes, idiotic. I thought you must be busy with the mature laundrette lady and your children.'

'Can I come round there now?' he replied.

'I hate that "mature". That was so bloody unfair, Col. What's it mean – she doesn't get emotional or too dependent, just needs sex?'

Somebody else seemed to want the telephone at her end, and Harpur heard her tell whoever it was to piss off. 'Should I come around there now, Denise, love?'

'Who were you talking to about me? Her?'

'Of course not. Keith Vine's Becky.'

'I liked her.'

'She likes you. She made me feel so stupid. I'll come round?'

For a time she did not answer. Then she said: 'No. Your house. If you come here you won't stay the night, because you'll worry about the kids. I'm not criticizing. You're a dad as well as a lover. I think it should be an all-night occasion for us. It seems so much more . . . well, *mature* when there's breakfast together afterwards.'

'The kids like it, too.'

There was a bit of silence. 'You can annihilate me, Col, when you shut off the way you did,' she replied after a while.

'Don't want it, that sort of power.'

'You've got it,' she replied.

*

There had been those occasional times when Harpur and Denise's lovemaking at the house was interrupted by furtive

visits from Keith Vine. Harpur almost wished that would
happen tonight. For his own sake, Harpur needed to see
him, but he also worried when Vine was unaccounted for.
Keith was a target. And he had his weaknesses, as Becky
said. You could develop a closeness to a villain like Vine, so
that when enemies encircled him, or even when the law
eventually took him, it was like watching someone dear to
you dragged under by the current and beyond your ability
to save. Jesus, 'dragged under by the current'! Now and then,
Harpur wondered if he were turning gay.

There was no undressing rigmarole tonight, not time for
Harpur's knickers fetish. This was joyous flesh reunion after
a bad couple of weeks. Slowness in the build-up would have
been absurd and an obsession with garments seedy. He
recognized that they were both acting up a bit, constructing
the passion and spontaneity, but never mind: it showed they
were in harmony and eager to make the most of this chance
of renewal. At his age, that would be natural, because
renewals were scarce. It thrilled him, though, to see her
doing the same. She was shouting, 'Yes, yes, Col' – as if
there were doubt – in that throaty, cheerleader style she had
sometimes, maybe not quite as loud as a cheerleader, but
loud enough, and liable to wake up the children in their
rooms. Well, they knew how these things worked and probably realized excitement was important. They would think
no less of Denise for that, and everything would be fine at
breakfast.

Also, Denise had that trick of gripping two handfuls of
hair at the back of his head and pulling his face down hard

against hers, like clutching a trapeze. On its own, this would
have made him feel wanted, but, of course, it was not on its
own, because he was moving slowly up and down in her, or
as slowly as he could manage after the lay-off. Usually, she
smelled of cigarettes. He did not mind this. Harpur liked
women with enthusiasms, and smoking was one of hers. He
was not happy about being held with his face so close to
hers, though, because it meant he could not look at her
properly and wonder how a girl with such neat, mild features
could bang up at him so ferociously from the hips and speak
the sort of graphic coarsenesses she had progressed to now,
and which he tried to be worthy of. He forgot Vine.

In a while, she released her grip on his hair and simply
pressed her hands flat on his shoulder blades. She had done
this to him before, too. He could draw back a little now and
look at her face. Her hands on his back put him in mind of
a priest's hand doing a blessing on someone's head, gentle
and presumptuous, as if she were relaying some virtue
to him. That was all right, too. He would take from her
anything he could get. To be patronized or comforted or
congratulated by Denise were all treats. Whenever his
children talked to him about her, they were approving, in
their plodding, sensible style, but he could read beyond their
dull words and see they thought him brilliant to have landed
her. It scared Harpur when she said he could annihilate her,
and it gave him a sweet buzz.

In a spell of calm later, Harpur said: 'When we break up
after a spat like that, what do you think, Denise? Good
riddance to the bloody has-been?'

'Some of that. Sour grapes.'

'Now and then I believe you'd like to drop me but haven't got the will – are too tender. So, you're glad when *I* do it.'

'If I was glad would I be back with you now, in full bed-and-breakfast situation?' Denise replied.

'Because you can't be cruel to me.'

'Don't make yourself sound so fucking pathetic and passive. You're not. Didn't I tell you, I'm wiped out when you walk away.'

'What's it mean, wiped out, annihilated?'

'It means I'm a bright pretty nineteen-year-old girl and none of it counts if you stop telling me I'm a bright pretty nineteen-year-old girl.'

'Don't make yourself sound so fucking pathetic and passive. You're not. And I don't believe you'd ever think none of it counts.'

She took her cigarette from her mouth and gazed at him for a while. 'It's about half true, honestly, Col.'

'That's not bad. Not much in life is more than half true.'

'I still beautify myself when you're not seeing me, yes. I don't huddle in a corner and wait to decay.'

'I've told you, sometimes I think we should be together, properly,' he replied.

'Sometimes I do, obviously.'

'How often?' Harpur asked.

'What?'

'How often do you think it?'

'Twice a week?'

'If you're into talking half the truth that means once a week.'

'Yes, probably about right.'

'I could beat that.'

'It's nice, isn't it?' she said.

'What?'

'Thinking it, but not too often, and without having to do anything about it.'

Harpur sat up in the bed. 'This conversation is too mature and cold for me. I meant it – I meant we should be together.'

'I'm going to think more about this.'

'Really twice a week?'

'I'm nineteen, Col. But, yes, all right, twice a week. You're definitely worth that, regardless,' she said. 'Every screen fuck now, the woman's on top.'

'Political.'

'Well, yes. There's a book called *Women On Top*. Should a shag be a sociological statement?'

'It's also so the camera can show more of the woman's body. She's not hidden under.'

'Whereas, I like your weight on me, Col. It rounds off the day.'

As he moved on to her again, her face seemed to glint unnaturally white, and then again and again. 'Jesus,' she gasped, 'what's that?'

'The alarm.'

Harpur had stipulated no bells or sirens. Like rich crooks, he did not want a din that might bring police on to the premises. His intruders had to stay private. Instead, this super-bright bulb in the special table lamp flashed and flashed.

'Is it that bloody Vine again?' she asked.

'It's great,' Harpur replied. 'I love the way it lights you up. Like a mystical glow. It makes fucking seem sacrilegious and brilliant.'

'Yes?'

'Oh, yes.'

'Oh, yes. Give it to me, heathen.'

'Yes, it'll be Vine,' he said. 'He's out and about tonight. He can wait.'

'I don't want any hurry.'

'No, it's not that kind of night.'

'I have to be reached, Col. Love's an enduring thing.'

'I'm fond of that word,' he said.

'Which?'

'Love. You don't say it very often.'

'Don't I? It's exactly what I meant, Col. I'm a linguist, you know.'

'The least that can be said.'

He thought he picked up some sound, possibly a breakage downstairs. He would place it in the kitchen. Denise did not seem to have heard. He ought to do something. More than something – he ought to make sure the children were safe. Tonight, though, he felt it would be wrong to show more concern for them than he did for Denise. He must not offend her again. He stayed in the bed. Love was an enduring thing, and he endured her jealousies and possessiveness. You alarmed your house, and then ignored the warnings for the sake of rebuilding love. Life was choices.

'Talk to me, Col.'

'Well, I told you: I've decided I need you here, permanently. And the kids do.'

'I need you *there.*'

'Always so damn fleshly and of the moment. How did you get like this so young?'

'Come nearer,' she replied, grabbing his hair again and pulling his head down. Close up, her ear became almost transparent off-and-on in the harsh flashes of the alarm light. It was like looking right into her: not quite her soul, but her nice, busy, sealed-off and scholarly system.

Afterwards, he put on a dressing gown, switched off the alarm and went downstairs. A kitchen window had been broken. If Vine visited in the middle of the night, he would generally tap this pane. He must have overdone it from impatience. He had some big news? Well, Harpur had some for him, too. But when he opened the kitchen door, he found Becky in the rain, leaning against the house and carrying Charles Louis in a waterproof plastic sheet. He brought her inside, and saw at once she had been weeping and still seemed distraught. She talked in a sort of long gasp as he closed the door. 'Harpur, Keith phoned but couldn't finish the call. Something happened.' Her face knotted and her voice went to a grieving whisper. 'He, lost the phone, or . . . I don't know.'

'Sit down, Beck,' he said, offering a kitchen chair, but she did not take it. From not so far back he remembered urgently trying to sort out another fractured, distressed telephone message. That one had come from a terrified, kidnapped girl and was answered by Hazel. It could be an agonizing drill: trying to help whoever took the call out of their shock, and into remembering detail, fast enough for it to be of use. Becky stayed stiff in the middle of the room. Even full of tears, she still looked good – too good for Vine – but she was hitting no mother-and-child poses tonight. Her fair hair lay soaked and tame. She had on a grey short-sleeved pullover and a cream shirt or blouse. The rain had stuck her long fawn and grey cotton skirt to her legs and thighs. At least the heavy boots she wore would keep out the weather. Harpur had seen brighter gear on hitchhikers, but she was still a beauty. She glanced at the broken window. 'He said to tap there. But I couldn't make you hear. On the job? I'd have smashed some more if you hadn't turned up.'

'His voice?'

'Oh, yes, definitely Keith.'

'No, I mean, how did he sound?'

'Sound?' Suddenly, she was snarl-shouting. 'How do you expect him to sound, Harpur, for Christ's sake? He had peril. Has. He was afraid, obviously, and that's how he sounded. Out of his depth and no swimmer. You know that way he can suddenly fall into a little boy squeak? *Save me, save me*, directed to all the world. His shell all gone. Keith never made it to a public school – doesn't know about the stiff upper lip. He was going to say where he was, what was happening, but he let the phone go and then lost it.' The child was awake in her arms, and gazed up as she spoke, fascinated by the mouth movements. Some spit flew now and then in her frightened excitement, spraying Charles but he did not flinch.

'I heard,' she said.

'What?'

'Like a blow. A moan or grunt. Then the phone put back.'

'A house, a public booth?'

'How do I know? I did 1471 for a trace. Number unavailable.'

'Probably a payphone. Traffic sounds?'

'I don't think so.'

'Any other sounds – voices, TV, kettle, radio?'

'Oh, Christ, I don't know.' She began to weep again.

'Come on,' he said, 'take this,' and pushed the chair under her. He went into the sitting room and brought whisky. He poured two and gave one to her, but she would not drink. After a minute, he picked up the glass and held it against her lips. He kept it there until she took a little.

'As if you'd know something,' she said. 'That's how he talked. As if you were sure to know something. "Get to Harpur. Knock the kitchen window." Like *Fetch a priest*. Of course, you're in with him. Or seem to be. I spotted that an age ago.'

'I don't know anything. I never found him tonight.'

'But can we look again?'

'Of course.' He would certainly search but would have preferred to go alone, or with a team. He couldn't tell her that, though.

'You've got the girl upstairs? I mean, the time you took.

It's all right again? That why you didn't bother to look for him properly? I shouldn't have mentioned her to you. You might have gone on trawling.'

Yes, he could not argue. 'She won't mind,' Harpur replied. 'She knows the work I do.' But, of course, Denise *would* mind. It wasn't just the ruin of their all-night reconciliation. She might not like the notion of him driving around at night with Becky, even with Becky carrying a watchful child. 'Can you tell me the exact words, as you recall them?' Harpur said.

For a couple of seconds, she seemed to be thinking about this, but then she stared across the kitchen table at him and said: 'Oh, look, listen, Harpur, you think he's dead? He's all bluster and tiny clevernesses. So many enemies. So much bloody envy and greed and strong-arm about.'

'It's called business competition,' he said. 'Keith's used to that.'

'He's not up to it. And I love him for that. Please. Let's just drive and search.' She stood up.

'I've no idea where to start, Becky. I covered most of the ground.'

After a minute she seemed to feel the sense of this. She sat again, took a sip of the whisky and tried to force her mind back to the broken phone message. '"Becky, Becky,"' she said, '"this has got to be quick."' Now, she gazed across the kitchen at nothing. The child reached up and touched her lips with his fingers, as if to tell her to go on. 'I think he . . . well, yes, I think he sobbed then, maybe swore – "Oh, Christ", "Oh, God", something like that. "Get to Harpur."'

'I might need help on this.'

'What help? You mean that Iles? He's in it, too?'

'No. A posse. A search needs numbers.'

'No,' she said. 'That would be a proper police operation. Nobody knows where it would go. It's not what he . . . "Get to Harpur." That's you, on your own. The window-tapping – everything unofficial, private.'

People did seem to recommend one-to-one with him and off the record.

She said: 'I mean, Keith's got other colleagues. There's Beau Derek. But he didn't even mention him. He thought you could do it. Wanted you to. Listen, Harpur, you might have been stringing him along – well, obviously, *were* stringing him along – but you've got a responsibility, all the same. You know him from close. There *is* something to Keith, isn't there? He's not rubbish through and through, is he? Not like most of the people you deal with. I mean your colleagues.'

The delay worried Harpur. 'Becky, when he told you to come here, he could have been saying that I'd know what to do. And what to do is get a crew of people to look at every likely spot. No delays.'

She turned her eyes on him again. 'I know that, don't I?' It was almost a scream. Then she said, quietly: 'All right. We search together first. The obvious places again. If no good, you can call your people out.' She had another think. 'But do you *want* to call your people out? Can you? I mean, they'll wonder how you know he's missing. How? Because he asked for you. Why would he ask for you?'

Yes. She had not moved. Harpur said: 'What else did he say – exact words, if you can?'

'He's trying, trying, but he's crying too much, weeping. Contemptible, really. Lovable.'

'But some words coming through all the same?'

She thought. '"Christ, he's seen me." Or no, maybe, "they've seen me." Yes, "*they've* seen me."' That's when he hit maximum terror – those words.'

Again Harpur had the notion of someone drowning – Keith Vine about to be dragged to destruction, squeaking for help, to use her word. You witnessed it, or listened to it through another voice, and could do nothing. Maybe didn't want to do all that much. Wasn't this a full-scale villain? But the responsibility she spoke of did exist, and even the closeness. If Vine went under now Harpur would feel it as a loss, a little loss. And feel some guilt, a little guilt. 'It sounds like a public box, then. As if there was distance – they seeing him across it, him seeing them.'

'Does it bloody matter?' she asked.

No, not much. Not unless she heard a train shunting or a circus organ or a ship's hooter behind, when they might have a location. 'Then?' he asked.

'The gun,' she said. 'He spoke about the gun. "I've got to get the gun out." That was the last I heard. The last I heard from Keith. I think he dropped the receiver, let it hang, as if he needed two hands.'

'Is there a button on the holster? Undo it with the left, draw with the right in a rush.'

'I'm shouting, screaming, telling him not to go off the

line. I was going to lose him, Harpur. I knew it. I'm talking to nothing. I can hear him breathing, wheezing, sobbing still, and maybe fumbling with the holster, but it's all away from the receiver.' She readjusted her hold on the child. 'Harpur . . . Harpur, was I listening to someone in the run-up to death?' she whispered. 'He sounded too broken even to draw the damn gun. He's dropping to extinction and I just have to listen to it. This is a man I've stuck to, regardless. He played fair about the baby, and more than played fair.'

'And no other sounds, background?' Keep on and on at her, but Christ, as if she would notice them, those other sounds, when she was yelling herself, and itemizing his sobs and groans, waiting only for the words to say where help should come if she could get it.

'Yes, other sounds very soon. Terrible sounds.'

'Voices? Accent? All men? A woman with them?'

'No voices.'

'Are you sure, are you sure? Think. Push Keith out of your head for a couple of seconds. Forget *his* sounds. Try to isolate anything else.' He worked to keep it all moderate, but was nearly barking at her himself. It had been the same with that call to Hazel. The brutality sneaked in, because of urgency and dread.

'"Forget his sounds".' Disbelievingly she shook her head.

'It's the others that could lead us somewhere.'

'The other sounds are some sort of impact, heavy impact, maybe a blow,' she replied. 'Maybe more than one. He's just an incident to you, isn't he? A grunt, and what could be a fall, a fall not at once or direct, but a sliding fall, like someone half propped, but going down all the same. I'm holding this fucking phone, blaring and blubbing into it, and in my head I'm watching him fall.'

'What did you see?'

'What?'

'What did you see in your head?' Harpur replied.

'I saw a silly kid axed.'

'What was the place? When you imagined it, Beck, what did you imagine?'

'Why?'

'You might have heard some background stuff you haven't told me about, stuff you're not conscious of. It would come out in how you saw this fall.'

'I told you – gradual.'

'Yes, but where, Beck? What do you see?'

'I see the realization on his big, brash face that he should have got out months ago. We could have been living by a river in France.'

'*Sliding fall*. Half propped against the side of the phone booth.'

'A rustling, faintly crackling sound.'

'Cloth or buttons against glass.'

'Then the receiver handled, I think. Maybe even put to someone's ear for a moment. There was a silence – a silence from that end.'

Harpur said: 'Think now – *total* silence? Nobody's talking, but what's behind?'

'One-way silence only. I'm yelling pleas, yes, pleas, prayers – pleas for Keith, pleas to be told what's happening, prayers to God to stop it. This is a would-be man I've tried to run from, but I'm still there. He's got worthwhile bits. He shouldn't be out alone.'

'No noise of a shot?'

'How did I get into this kind of life, Harpur? But some of it I've loved. Oh, of course. No, no shots. Then the receiver's put down.'

'Banged down?'

'Put down.'

'What, gently?'

'Gently enough.'

'How a woman might put a phone down?'

'Do women do it differently from men? What woman? Christ, now there's a woman in it?'

'If this was a payphone, there could have been witnesses. It would be a hell of a scene. I'll ask the Control Room if we've had reports of a disturbance.'

'A late-night fight in a phone box. Who's going to report that? It's just Britain.'

'With a handgun on show, possibly. Or more than one.'

'Just Britain.'

She was right, and the Control Room knew of no phone-box incident. He had left Becky in the kitchen while he made the call on the sitting-room telephone. 'Anything else I need to know about?' he asked the Control Room Inspector. Like had a male body of around twenty-five been found. But, of course, they would have already told him. The Inspector had nothing major. Harpur was still talking to the Control Room when Denise appeared wearing one of his jackets as a dressing gown. 'I worried, Col. You were a long time. Who's here? The shouting. A woman. Not Keith Vine?'

'I've got to pop out. Vine might have trouble.'

'Ah.'

'What's that mean?'

'"Ah" means you have some special obligation to him. Becky's here?' She went into the kitchen. When Harpur joined them, Denise said: 'She's given me the outline. I'll come.'

'Well, I—'

'You're concerned about leaving the kids? Ring up Iles to babysit,' she said.

'OK, come.' If they did find Keith Vine dead, Harpur might be glad of help with Becky.

'What woman?' Becky asked, as they were going to his car.

'Woman?' Denise said.

'He thinks possibly a woman involved. He spoke about her twice.'

'I'm looking for any kind of indicator,' Harpur said.

'Is there a woman he should have been scared of?' Becky asked. 'In business?'

'Col sees hazard everywhere.'

Harpur was still thinking payphones. People like Keith did not use mobiles, because of security fears. Becky had said she thought Vine let the receiver hang, while he fumbled for the gun. Yes, a booth: in a room the phone was usually on a table, and he would have put the receiver down on it. First object was to find a public box on Vine's likely route where there was no noticeable background noise – not enough to stick in Becky's conscious memory. Exclude most of the pushing streets: traffic roar from dealers and pimps in their rich engined cars could drown out a phone voice. So, one of his other business spots, possibly. Harpur thought he remembered a dockside booth far enough from *The Eton Boating Song* not to get its bar and restaurant sounds. Standing there Keith might have seen any pursuit coming from the *Eton*. Harpur drove towards the docks now. Perhaps he should have hung about longer at the clipper in his earlier search for Vine. He'd been preoccupied with getting to see Denise again and making repairs. Becky might be right, and Keith was not fit to be out on his own. Harpur should have known it and done more. Well, he *had* known it, but had not done more.

He parked near the *Eton*. Becky looked at it: 'Yes, I've heard Keith talk of this place. Some star businesswoman here. Is she the one – the one Keith should have . . . the one Keith has to worry about?'

'Not now.'

He walked to the booth. It looked all right. The receiver was in the cradle. But then it would be. She had said it was replaced, and others might have used the phone since. He checked and found it worked. The booth was lit and he had brought a torch with him from the car. He examined the floor for bloodstains and then the glass walls, in case her description of the fall was accurate, and Keith had rubbed against one of them and made smears. He found nothing, though. Denise, Becky and the child joined him while he was inspecting the walls, and Becky began to weep. Seeing and hearing her, the child cried, too. A bell sounded four times from the *Eton*. They did that – marked the hours with a maritime touch by ringing the sea clock.

Becky stopped weeping. 'Yes,' she said. 'I do remember. I heard that behind him. But only one chime.'

Harpur looked back towards the *Eton*. 'If people came for him from there, he'd see them. And *they* could spot *him*. He'd be lit up. *They've seen me.*' He'd be on toast.

Gazing towards the *Eton*, Harpur thought he saw a man at the rail watching him, someone youngish, not tall, in a big-shouldered, modish jacket that could hide a broadside. Perhaps realizing Harpur had spotted him, he turned and went towards the bar, moving with an ease and grace visible even at this distance and in the dark. Harpur came out of the box and searched the ground around it with his flashlight, but again found nothing.

'Well, I think he'll be all right,' Denise said, looking around the phone booth. 'Tidy here, and, if there'd been trouble, someone on the *Eton* would have been sure to see it and call the police.'

'Not that kind of place,' Becky said.

'Which kind?'

'Very few who go to the *Eton* call the police, never mind what they see.'

Denise said: 'But this would be ... we're talking about something, well, serious.'

'I know he's dead,' Becky replied. She was looking at Harpur, wanting his answer, but it was Denise who replied.

'That's ridiculous, alarmist,' she said. 'We've found nothing.'

'Is it ridiculous, alarmist, Harpur?'

He watched the lad in the wide jacket come down the gangplank and walk in that brilliant style he had up towards the Valencia. Lincoln W. Lincoln, if Lamb had it right, and Lamb always did.

'Him, for instance,' Denise said.

'What?' Harpur asked.

'He was looking over the rail, just now. Perhaps he stood there earlier, too. We should ask him.' Before Harpur could stop her, she began to run, calling in her nice, educated voice that presumed ready cooperation from all, 'Excuse me, sir, excuse me.'

This time of night and in this area he would probably think she was a Gold Card tart. Harpur walked quickly after her.

The man turned and waited for Denise. Harpur was not near enough to hear what she said first. But when he reached them she was asking, 'So, we wondered whether you'd seen any, well, bother around the phone box an hour or so ago.'

'Bother?' He gave her a good, patient smile.

'Violence. We're looking for someone called Keith Vine.'

'I'm not local. Well, you've gathered. The accent.'

'This is his wife, his partner,' Denise said. Becky had arrived now. 'We're all so anxious.'

'A quiet night out,' he replied. 'I'm a stranger in this town. I need some company in the evening, that's all.'

'Keith Vine,' Becky said, staring at him. 'You know him? Do you?'

'I told you, I'm from away.'

'So?' Becky replied.

'Keith what?' he asked.

'Just stop pissing about,' Becky yelled at him. 'Of course you know him. You're in business. You look it through and through. You're part of this fucking London invasion? Where is he?'

Denise said: 'Oh, Becky, you shouldn't—'

'These two with you?' he asked Harpur. 'You're police, yes? From the haircut. You ought to get her in order.'

'You can't have been trading in the *Eton*,' Harpur replied. 'They wouldn't let you, don't know you. What are you here for, Lincoln, to buy up Si Pilgrim, now Eleri's gone? Keith's in the way? What are you here for, besides to get rid of me?'

'These names,' he said.

'You know him, Col?' Denise asked, startled.

Becky yelled: 'Keith in the way of what, Harpur? Eleri? That crazy moniker. This is the woman dead in the die-works, isn't it? On TV. Was she the star, then?' Disturbed by her shouting, the baby cried briefly then was quiet again, though not asleep.

'It's a dangerous area,' Lincoln said. 'Why you ought to watch your mouth, lady.'

'Has Keith been making things tough for you?' Harpur asked.

'Who's Keith?'

'Oh, you sodding, sodding liar,' Becky shrieked. She

lunged forward, steady in her boots, one hand a fist, the other holding the baby to her. Charles began to scream.

The man grabbed her wrist and held her arm aloft. 'Do you always travel with this crazy crew, Harpur?'

'He's got your name, Col,' Denise said. 'Why don't I know any of this – like you and Becky?'

'Well, of course I know him,' Lincoln said. 'A famous loser. Payrolled.' He released Becky and turned away, was going to continue walking.

'Don't let him go, Harpur. How can you?' she said.

'No, Col, don't.'

'I can't hold him.'

'Oh, Christ.' Abruptly Becky shelved her anger and called after him in a wheedling, beaten voice, making pleas again: 'Wait. Forget everything that's been said. Just tell us if you saw anything.' He walked on and did not look back.

'Would he tell?' Denise asked. 'You both think he might have been part of it? Might he, Col?'

'Would he stay on the *Eton* if he was?' Harpur replied.

'Wouldn't he?' Denise replied. 'Act normal. Alibi. General contempt for out-of-town police.'

'Yes, he might,' Harpur said. Easy enough to clean up a phone box.

They watched Lincoln go out of sight. 'I want to see where that woman was found dead,' Becky told them.

'Oh, but why?' Denise said.

'I've a feeling – that's all. Some sort of terrible circle here, some vengeance thing, tit-for-tat.'

Denise said: 'But Keith wasn't involved in that, was he?'

'I want to go there, Harpur.'

'I ought to talk to someone aboard,' Harpur said.

'Useless,' Becky replied. 'They're all like him – liars, hard, able to hold you off. I know Keith will be where I said.'

'But you can't know it, Beck,' Denise said. 'You absolutely can't. That's just stress: imagination.' She said it with all the clipped certainty of a bright kid, university trained. Harpur thought she might have it wrong. 'Let Col do it the way he wants,' she went on. 'He always knows so much more than the rest of us. Or so much more than me, anyway, the sod. Keith could even be back at the flat now, wondering where on earth you and Charles are.'

The pair of bouncers at the head of the gangplank tensed when they saw a woman dressed for a Greenpeace march and carrying a wide-awake baby. Then they tensed some more, recognizing Harpur. One of them spoke into a handset, alerting the management. Trade would be suspended. It did not bother Harpur. He was not here to do the Drug Squad's work. By the time the women and Harpur reached the bar, Simon Pilgrim was away from his special table and buying himself a drink, not rum and black. 'Si, you're looking jaunty, a real sea dog already,' Harpur called.

'That child should be in bed, Mr Harpur – if I may say.'

'Do you know whose child this *is*, Si?'

'Well, Mr Harpur, I—'

'This is Keith's child, Si. See the strong jaw and the love-me-do eyes? This child's looking for his daddy.'

'He knows Keith?' Becky asked.

Pilgrim gave a solid, very comfortable laugh. 'Well,

everyone knows Keith Vine. I don't mean he's attention-seeking or ostentatious, not in the least, but a great regular here. Keeps himself very much to himself, yet not aloof.'

'That's Keith,' Harpur replied.

'Have you seen him tonight?' Becky asked.

'Tonight?' Pilgrim replied.

'Oh, Jesus, Harpur, let's go, please let's go,' Becky said.

'Well, *do* we have to play around like this, Col?' Denise said. 'Yes, I suppose we do. It's a game with rules.'

'Perhaps much earlier,' Pilgrim said. 'Yes, I think much earlier. But you feel he's missing?'

'Feel?' Becky replied. '*Feel.*'

'Did he actually bring you stuff tonight, Si?' Harpur asked.

'Often he'll come in early for a quiet drink, on his way home after a busy day,' Pilgrim replied at once.

'Was he with anyone?' Becky asked. 'Talk to anyone?'

'Or was this one of those nights where he kept very much to himself, yet not aloof?' Denise said.

'Did you see any trouble, hear any trouble?' Becky asked. 'You realize your fucking supplies could be up the spout, do you?' She turned to Harpur. 'Is he the new Eleri ap Vaughan?'

Charles stared at Pilgrim, unblinking. 'The child really should be in bed, Mr Harpur. 'I'll be away myself very soon. At my age, these late nights can be a killer.'

'No, it's not the late nights,' Becky replied.

*

They drove to the die-cast works. Keith Vine lay not quite where Eleri had been, but it was a good try. There was no hut constructed over the body this time. Harpur did the formalities – hopelessly felt for a pulse and went through his pockets. They were empty. He decided he would not strip the corpse. Denise stood with an arm around Becky's shoulders. Becky did not weep again, not here, anyway, as if her mourning had been pre-done. She said: 'He's got parents, you know, Wales way. I don't fancy telling them.'

'Col will handle that. He can be all tact.'

23

Harpur broke into Keith Vine's flat. Denise had taken Becky and the child home to Harpur's house for at least the rest of the night. Becky seemed grateful for the offer. She could not face the flat. Her sorrow had begun to surface again, and she needed company. He dropped them off in Arthur Street. 'But shouldn't you report finding him?' she asked.

'I will. Of course. But I want another look around the die-works before the police mob arrives,' he said.

'That's detection,' Denise said. 'You see it all first and steal everything that counts, so nobody else can get level.'

So right. 'The alarm is still off,' he replied.

He drove immediately to their flat and used his credit card on the lock, then closed the door behind him. He had brought a torch again and did without the flat's lights. Harpur needed a thorough look through. He must make sure no notes or accounts here linked him to Vine's business. Those could be misunderstood. Vine, the budding tycoon, was just the kind to keep records. He was also the kind who might have a safe, and a smart one. If so, Harpur's visit would be useless. Plastic on a simple lock was the top of his burgling skills. He had hoped to find keys when he searched the body, and it had dismayed him all round that the pockets were empty. Obviously, someone else had lifted the lot. Perhaps Vine carried business details with him in a note-

book. In that case, Harpur's name might already be up in
lights somewhere. Now, though, he had to do what he could
here, and quickly. Someone else might find Keith and set
things moving.

He began to go through drawers and cupboards, masking
the flashlight as much as he could. He felt foully anxious.
Normally, this was the kind of police work he adored. It
would delight him to penetrate someone's den and gaze at
the apparatus of their life, the routine as much as the intimate. He knew of no better way of learning a target's profile.
But tonight it was not like that. He himself was the target.
The private material he wanted was not about Keith Vine,
but Colin Harpur. He already knew enough about Colin
Harpur. It was a matter of keeping the information close,
though. He must get it out of the flat and destroyed before
the body was found and a troupe of his colleagues arrived,
eager to turn Vine's place over. To excuse some of their
raid failures, Drugs Squad people were always looking for
evidence that traders had been forewarned by a bought
police voice. If they found something here, Harpur would
qualify, and Harpur was finished.

His hands shook a bit and, when he came to anything
written down that might be a giveaway, his eyes galloped
over it at stupid, panicked pace, looking for his name, coded
or in clear. Aware he might easily miss crucial material, he
paused and fought to get himself back into a state of
conquering intruder, natural to him when doing someone's
premises illegally. That mood of dominance should have
been so easy to hit in this sad dump, but he still could not

get it. Instead, his brain kept telling him at top volume that he was dangerously linked to someone who lived in this place, and all evidence of it had to be found and taken. Stolen, to use Denise's cruel, linguist's term. Both these women, she and Becky, could be ruthlessly blunt. The papers he found had nothing to do with the business, as far as he could tell – not unless the coding was brilliant. They dealt with what letters and documents dealt with in most houses: rent, car, hire purchase.

He resumed, and went very carefully through the baby's bedroom. To hide sensitive stuff here would be the kind of trick Keith might fancy. Harpur found nothing, though, except woolly toys, nursery rhyme clothes, napkins and the baby's christening certificate. They had had him done in the cathedral, for a proper start to life: Charles Louis Vine, a grand run of royal first names. Somehow, Becky must have convinced them she was Keith's wife. They probably would not have done the service otherwise. He forced a locked jewellery box in Vine's and Becky's bedroom and found half a dozen of his love letters to her, dated three or four years ago and sent from Saudi, where he must have had a job. This kind of thing above all was what Harpur thrilled to pry into, and he did take a little time reading now. They were as full of third-hand phrases as everybody's love letters, and yet Harpur was captured by the intensity of them and by the sudden sparks of a real voice among old-hat declarations like, 'My life is nothing without you, Beck', and 'I shall love you until the very end of my days.' Even these words had a terrible, personal aptness to them now. And then at the end of one letter was the original shrewd, weak Keith Vine: 'I love you for your brain as much as for your face and body, because your brain tells me where I should aim, Becky, and shows me how to do it.' In another: 'I have never known such full harmony with another person, Beck, nor ever felt so content with and dependent on somebody else.' This had been a lovely relationship – enduring, to pick another of the linguist's words. Harpur put the letters back and tried to relock the box, but had done too much damage.

In the living room the telephone rang and went on ringing for three or four minutes, then died. Harpur did not go to it. Perhaps he would have learned something about Vine if he had answered. But that's not what he was here for. He knew everything necessary to know about him. The phone rang again, for not so long this time. He still ignored it.

So where was the fucking safe? There must be one. He had still found nothing to do with the trade. He went through all the rooms, looking for signs that a carpet or mat might have been regularly lifted to expose a floor safe. Then, back in the baby's room while easing a Habitat rug out from under the cot he thought he heard someone on the stairs outside. He switched off the torch and tried to freeze. The flat was in a block, and other residents might use the stairs, even at 3 a.m. Whoever was moving was moving quietly, so it would probably not be a police party. He waited for the footsteps to pass Vine's door, up or down. He had the impression it was someone coming up from the street, though he could be wrong. And then the movement seemed to end. He listened for the door of another flat opening and closing: a stop-out back from a club and not wanting to rouse the neighbours or the wife or parents. Then, though, Harpur thought he caught the sound of someone working quietly on Vine's door. He was crouched by the side of the cot. Standing, he brought himself to readiness. He still carried no arms, of course, but the torch was a decent size and might do some damage. For a second, he wondered if Becky had changed her mind and wanted to be at home, after all. But Becky would have a door key. This was not that sort of sound.

Did it have to be someone who knew of Vine's death? Was Lincoln W. Lincoln here for business loot, or for Vine's list of pushers, or both? Or was it Eleri's daughter or some of her outfit here for the same? Any of them could have been in on Vine's killing. Or even some of the local competition: Panicking Ralph, Shale, if he was still active, or the fat free-lance, Les Tranter. There was an inheritance in this flat. At least, there ought to be, though he had failed to find it. Most of the likelies would come hunting that inheritance with a gun, and especially Lincoln in his big jacket. If Harpur had been in a room with a phone, he might have dialled 999 now. Yes, he might have.

He thought he heard the outside door of the flat open and then softly close. Someone delicate – the kind of touch he had wondered about when Becky spoke of the booth receiver being unviolently replaced. Might this searcher ignore a baby's room? Harpur had not ignored it, but Harpur was trained to thoroughness, and trained to treat the unlikely as likely. He moved silently to a spot behind the cot and crouched low again. From there, he watched the door through the cot bars. It always troubled him to look through bars, made him think about a long future. There might not be a future, long or short.

He had left the door to the nursery part open, but saw no light. Someone familiar with the flat, who could move about in the dark? Once before he had watched an unlit bedroom like this, shielded by furniture. Last time, it had been in a small-time crook's house, where Iles brought a woman reporter and made brisk love to her in Harpur's view. Jesus, could it be Iles now? How could Iles know of Vine's death? But 'how could Iles know' was a naive question to ask about the ACC.

The nursery door was pushed full open and Harpur saw an enormous frame in the doorspace. 'That you down there, Col, cowering?' Jack Lamb asked.

Harpur said: 'I'm looking for a safe.' He stood up.

'Of course,' Lamb replied. 'This would be the room. You're damn quick getting here, Col. I mean, for police.' Lamb finished what Harpur had begun and pulled the bright rug clear. There was enough light from the window to show that five floorboards had been sawn through. Lamb produced a bunch of keys and used one of them like a lever to prise a board up enough for him to take a hold. But it was not just one board. The five moved together, battened into a unit on the hidden side and hinged as a trapdoor. Under it, they could make out a small but formidable-looking Chubb floor safe. Lamb went to the window and pulled the curtains over, then switched on the room light. He glanced at the safe's keyholes and quickly selected two keys from his bunch. With them he opened up. Harpur saw a wad of money and some cheap, red-covered account books.

'I didn't know you were a cracksmith, Jack. That's some bunch of keys.'

'Vine's.'

'You vacuumed the body?'

'Someone had to, Col. Clearly, first thought I had when I heard Vine's corpse lay there was, Col Harpur could be at bad risk with this one.'

'Heard how?'

Again, the sort of question you did not ask Jack Lamb, or any informant of stature. Maybe someone on Jack's paid newsgathering network had accidentally spotted Vine. For several on Jack's network the old die-cast works would be a natural, quiet meeting ground or loot-sharing venue. Or maybe someone on the network had actually seen what happened to Keith Vine and had decided to cash in.

'Heard how, Jack?' Harpur said.

Lamb was turning over pages in one of the account books. 'Do the initials C.H. mean much to you, Col? At a quick viewing, I'd say C.H. was on the plus side to around £27,000. And that's this book only.'

'Shall I have them, Jack?' Harpur said.

'Oh, look, Col, you wouldn't want to be surprised with things like this on you. This is tampering with evidence.'

Lamb put the books into his pocket. That was how it worked, this fine and vital rapport between a detective and his grass. The detective could lean on the informant by threatening to abandon him and/or to point hard colleagues towards his dark businesses. And the informant could lean on the detective by putting a couple of lid-off books like those away somewhere passably secure for a rainy day. To protect the detective, there were elaborate and careful rules for dealing with informants, but Harpur broke most of these, too. So did every other successful detective he knew. The rule saying an informant belonged to the police force, not to an individual officer, meant an informant should never be in a position to put the squeeze on a detective because the grass would have nothing secret about the detective to disclose. But Lamb belonged to Harpur, and to Harpur only. Another rule said that all informants should be registered in their proper name on an official list, this list to be held by the head of the CID, as registrar. The knowledge that there was a written record of him somewhere would keep an informant well-behaved. No written record of Jack Lamb existed. Harpur was head of the CID and in his head and only his head he registered Jack Lamb.

'Does C.H. want any more?' Lamb asked, picking up the cash wad.

'No.' He took off the Avantage watch and put that into the safe.

'You're sure nobody's seen you wearing that? Say, Iles.'

'No. I put it on only when . . . only when I needed to look as if I'd genuinely gone over.'

Lamb wiped the money against his coat and replaced it. 'Think this will still be intact after your drugs boys have been through? What I mean – I see need, Col. There's his girl and the baby, after all. Would authority let her keep it, supposing it's still here after your lads have visited?'

'Might. Nothing's proved against him. That was you phoning to check they weren't here, was it?'

'But how did *you* know they weren't, Col? They're at your place, tucked up? Sanctuary? I rather thought you were looking priestly.' The second time tonight Harpur had been accused of being in orders. Jack wiped the safe with a handkerchief, relocked it and put the rug and cot back in place. 'You made a hell of a mess of that jewellery box.'

'I think I forgot to wipe it.'

'I wiped it, Col. That's my eternal, pleasurable role – to take care of you.'

They put out the light and left, Lamb first, and then Harpur three minutes later.

24

Taking a breakfast of raisins at his desk, Iles was about to read Harpur a poem he had written. 'Occasionally you reveal a kind of uneasiness about myself and Hazel, Col. I don't think I'm exaggerating this, am I?'

'Not at all. More than occasionally, I hope. You've got pederasty all over your face, sir, the way others have intelligence or beards.'

The light on Iles's intercom box flickered red, indicating a priority call from the Control Room. The ACC ignored it. 'I feel this poem might help set things right. Harpur, there are admittedly youngish girls, but there are also girls that are *too* young. And you may assume I know the difference. Sometimes I'm bewildered by my probity.'

'Should you answer that, sir?'

'You really must let them come and stay with me – us – for a while, for safety,' the ACC replied. 'That's exactly what it would be. I deplore the sexual exploitation of child-girls. Look, Col, I know you've heard of a novel called *Lolita*, not just because it's famous enough to have reached even you, but, of course, we had a child rapist and killer here we dubbed The Lolita Man.'

'Yes.' It was the case when Hazel had taken the broken, desperate telephone call.

'In *Lolita* an ageing lech called Humbert Humbert

seduces what he calls a nymphet. One adores the novel, yet at the same time deplores, absolutely deplores, his behaviour. Here's a sonnet, Col, called, as it happens, "Humbert Humbert".'

Harpur leaned across and pushed the reception button on the intercom. The Control Room said a body had been spotted by a member of the public at what sounded like the identical place in the old die-cast works where Eleri ap Vaughan was found. This one was male, in his twenties. A patrol was on its way but there had been no identification yet. The Control Inspector thought Iles and Harpur would want immediate notification because of the place.

'Thank you, yes,' Iles said, switching off.

'I'd better go,' Harpur replied. He stood.

'You know about this one already, Col?'

'A lad so young. My God, what's happening, sir?' Harpur replied.

'Yes. I'll come. And I'd better tell the Chief. He's very keen on cyclic, symbolic incidents. Likes to view for himself.'

'Is that what this is, sir?'

Iles finished the raisins, then folded up his poem and put it in his breast pocket. The Chief was not in his room when Iles phoned, and the ACC left a message. Harpur drove. He said: 'This grows . . . grows almost terrifying, sir. The scale. The repetition. Some message in this death?'

'Why I notified the Chief. He's not tuned into much, but he does hear certain cosmic drumbeats. This will be Keithy Vine laid out for us, won't it, Harpur? There must be a queue to kill him. Oh, yes. For instance, he wasn't threatening to claim you'd sold out, was he? Pressurizing you? Had you come to see him as a disposable menace? Suddenly you're decisive enough to do something like that? Perhaps you're maturing at last, Harpur.' The ACC shifted in the passenger seat and for a moment Harpur thought he wanted to shake hands in congratulations. But Iles was reaching for his poem. 'Here's the sonnet then, Col,' he said.

'No, thanks, sir.'

'A poem deploring in fourteen devastating lines the whole notion of so-called nymphets.'

'No thanks, sir. Your poem won't deplore it *enough*. Can't.'

'This is a kind of censorship, Harpur.'

'You bet.'

They parked at the edge of the works and walked. Iles wanted a good look at the surrounding ground. 'So, you see, Col, it's harsh of you to grow tetchy about Hazel and me – and cruel of you to blame your little student friend for leaving them unchaperoned.'

'And keep your questing eyes off her, too,' Harpur replied.

There were a couple of uniformed constables with the body. Iles hoisted his fine grey worsted trousers a couple of inches and crouched very close. 'Small-calibre pistol. I call them ladies' guns. Is this getting to be the mode for traders? Understatement? I'd heard the bigger you thought yourself the bigger the piece you carried.' He pondered. 'This is almost one of those display crimes, as if the Chief's been giving someone lessons on the thematic overtones of violent death. A nicely neat revenge, Col? Would Eleri have relations, friends?'

'There might be some, somewhere, sir.'

'Ah, you know of one?'

'But this assumes Vine did Eleri in the first place.'

'No, it assumes one of the relatives or friends assumes it. Vengeance can get things wrong, like courts.'

Lane arrived, looking ill. He had on one of his beigeish suits with a newscaster's tie in vivid red and silver cubes. Somebody must have bought it for him as a tonic or savage joke, possibly one of his children. Harpur feared Lane might relapse into breakdown any day. 'Keith Vine, sir,' Iles said. 'You'll have heard of him. A would-be baron long close to being snuffed.'

'My God, Desmond, this is appalling. A boy. The whole thing is so damn—'

'Cyclic,' Iles said.

'Patterned.' Harpur had noticed before how Lane's tortured voice echoed exceptionally in here, as though custom-made for the place. The Chief, too, crouched, but very briefly. 'Desmond, you're going to tell me, tell me again – yes, the repetition of your statement itself becomes part of the pattern, the cycle – you're going to say we have no hope of finding who did it. This terrible silence of the trade.'

'How it looks, sir. Is it vengeance for Eleri? Is it someone wanting to make it *look* like vengeance for Eleri through the locale, but actually, say, a London team or their pathfinder removing competition? Or a local team, or a local freelance?

Or then again, someone who feared Vine could damage him in other ways?'

'I don't understand that.'

'Someone who feared Vine might betray him.'

'Betray him how?' Lane asked.

'If we discover that, we might discover who did him.'

'Killed here?' Lane asked.

'Hit on the head first,' Iles replied, 'then shot close up elsewhere, possibly while still unconscious. Afterwards, eloquently dumped.'

The Chief said: 'I feel it almost as an insult to myself, personally, Desmond. To the Force, obviously – the effrontery of repetition. But a mockery of my known personal wishes for this realm. An insulting, flagrant declaration that things are as they are, and as they were.'

'This mocks the whole structure of law and order, sir,' the ACC replied. 'I don't imply this is a larger concept than you personally, but perhaps more general.'

'I shall round on them,' Lane replied, 'be sure of that.'

'We *are* sure, aren't we, Harpur?'

'I'd agree with Mr Iles, sir – a heavy blow to the head and the killing at some spot away from where the blow was given, but not here.' More likely at the place where Vine had done his doomed stalking. More than more than likely.

Lane paced frantically though carefully, keeping out of the oil patches. 'On and on and on. Can we counter? We must, *must*, or what are we for?'

Speaking across the body to him, Iles said: 'We had a

nice, balanced situation here, sir, in known, local hands. We should have fought to preserve it.'

'Fought to preserve a drugs trade – local or otherwise?' Lane cried. 'My God, Desmond, we—'

'Then suddenly things are askew,' Iles said. 'It's outside influences. People see their chance.'

Scene of Crime officers and others were arriving. Lane drew Harpur and Iles away from the body and spoke secretively: 'Yet we shall never surrender.'

'Churchill, sir?' Iles asked.

In his despair, Lane grew incisive, but only according to that cyclic style they had spoken of. 'I have proposed in the past and I propose again that we must try to infiltrate one of these syndicates. It's something I still hate to contemplate – the risk. I know we have lost at least one good man like that. But what else?'

Iles said: 'Infiltrate, Col. How does it strike you? Is it on?'

The Chief spoke hurriedly: 'Not Colin himself, of course. Not at his rank. And he's known. Someone younger, someone very credible in the role.'

'No, certainly not Harpur, Chief,' Iles said. 'He's been well past anything like that for years. And naturally clumsy, anyway.'

*

Lane returned to headquarters and Iles and Harpur drove over to Vine's flat. It was already crowded with the drugs crew.

'Where are his girl and the child?' Iles asked. 'She'll have to be told.'

'I'll look after that, sir,' Harpur replied, 'whenever they turn up.'

'She's at your place, is she?' Iles said. 'Knows already?'

'They had a remarkably powerful relationship, Becky and Vine,' Harpur replied.

'Why remarkably, Harpur?'

'In the circumstances.'

'He being a villain, you mean?' Iles asked. 'You're so fucking narrow, Harpur.'

Wayne Timberlake said: 'We think someone has been into the flat and done some removals, sir.'

'Really?' Iles replied.

'A box of love letters broken open,' Timberlake said.

'Do they show a remarkably powerful relationship, Wayne?' Iles asked. 'There'll probably be a safe somewhere. But nothing in it of any worth, except possibly cash. Try the nursery. That's Vine's kind of thinking, I'd guess.'

In the car on the way back to headquarters, Iles said: 'So, you're let out very nicely, aren't you, Harpur? What you wanted. It's bound to make one wonder. You managed to get armament after all? Damn clever, the ladylike calibre. I mean, clever when I hear, in fact, that Eleri has a daughter about the town, you opaque bastard. You do it and point us towards her via the little gun? Well, I don't always regard murder as an unspeakable offence, in the larger context. But would I? You're not moving on to Becky, are you? Fine forearms and grit. But you'd take over that child?'

'Sir, the Chief's idea about infiltration—'

'Is piss, Col. We've nobody who could handle that properly, except conceivably yourself, and you want out. Vine's body had been vacuumed, of course. You'd been there early again, Harpur.'

This was not a question, and Harpur kept quiet. In any case, he would not have been able to say that Jack Lamb did the vacuuming.

'Things are bound to get worse, Col. Another gap in the business scene. More violence from people trying to fill it.'

'I think so.'

'You're out, but you'll still be at appalling hazard. Obviously. You're marked, Col. I do feel you should let your daughters come to me. That is, us.'

'No thanks, sir.'

Iles said: 'Perhaps you can read my poem at another time.'

'I'll look for it among your posthumous papers, sir.'

25

At lunchtime, Ralph Ember was in The Monty, doing some paperwork, when another call came from Barney on the payphone.

'Ralph, we're amazed still not to have had anything from you about G.R.'

Maud, on the extension, said: 'Go over your exact movements after you left here last time.'

Ember rarely drank brandy at lunchtime, but today he did up things from lager and brought a heavy gin and French into the booth with him. This he regarded as an energising drink. He arranged himself comfortably on the booth chair again. 'It's become a little beside the point,' he replied.

'Oh?' Barney said. 'Oh? I can assure you, Ralph, that we rarely raise matters that have no relevance.'

Ember drank and felt very sound. 'You won't have heard yet, nothing released so far by the police, but we have a likely death here. I fear this would make all preparations for a merger, including the elevation of G.R., obsolete.'

'What the fuck's this about, Ralph?' Maud replied. 'What death?'

'This is K.V.'

'My God,' Barney muttered.

'When?' Maud asked.

'Overnight,' Ember replied. Through the glass door of the

booth Ember saw Margaret and Fay in school uniform come into the club. It was prize-giving at Fay's school this afternoon, and the three of them would have a quick lunch at The Monty and then go on to the ceremony together. Fay was to receive prizes for Classical Studies, Domestic Science and Chemistry. Ember felt proud. It was the Classical Studies he esteemed most. The classics meant so much, even when taught in English. The school had capitulated on that, feeble fucking bitch Head. He waved to Margaret and Fay and signalled that he would not be long.

'Camilla wants a word,' Maud said.

'Status, Ralph. I.e., status of the information is surely crucial in this kind of report. Not to be foolishly sceptical, I hope, but – I think I recall the phrasing right – you said, did you not, Ralph, a *likely* death? Loopholes would appear to be left. Authenticity, kid. Can you satisfy us on that, or, really we could be barking at shadows.'

Ember took another helpful sip. 'Someone in the club told me not long ago. He'd picked it up, the way these things *are* picked up, you know.'

'No, I don't know,' Barney replied.

'Jesus, I'll tell you my feeling, shall I?' Maud asked. 'Shall I?'

Probably.

Maud said: 'You did them all yourself. K.V., the other two, G.R., H.F. You've been warrioring? Camilla wants a word.'

Fay came and pressed her nose hard against the glass of the door and pointed to her watch. Ember leaned forward on the chair, bent his own nose against the glass and crossed his eyes.

Camilla said: 'Status. I say status again, but – bear with me, do – this is in a quite different sense now. I refer to your personal status, not that of the info. The kind of activity which is being mooted for you here by Maud, Ralph – what she just said about how the deaths happened, I mean – well this would imply remarkable application in you and signal very hearty status indeed.'

'But who did it, Ralph?' Barney asked.

'There's the London interest, obviously,' Ember replied. 'K.V. might have been stalking someone – someone from outside – who turned it around and stalked him. Significant setting.'

'What setting?' Maud asked.

'Where he was found. Reminiscent. Then again – apparently a daughter of E. ap V. was in town. Motive there, plainly. Motives, rather – revenge, succession – I gather she's in the business. Or alternatively we have the possibility of a worried cop, inside the syndicate undercover and wanting escape. This might have looked like the only way.'

'I'd heard a cop rumour,' Barney said.

'But it's all speculation,' Maud said. 'And so might the report of the death be.'

'The death's a fact,' Ember replied, finishing the drink.

'Which death?' Maud asked.

'K.V.'

'And G.R? H.F?' she said.

'Absolutely no news on those, one regrets to say,' Ember

replied. 'Still possibly on a protracted jolly somewhere. It wouldn't be the first for those two, believe me.'

'Where does your certainty come from – on K.V?' Barney asked.

'My informant. Categorical.'

Maud said: 'Listen, Ralph, have you been clearing a fucking career path for yourself regardless of our wishes, just moving awkward people out of the way? Camilla wants a word.'

'Grief. Certain to be a problem. It seems tragically probable – I see no other word but "tragically" as apropos here – tragically probable that K.V. as well as G.R. and H.F. would have wives-stroke-partners almost frantic with grief or uncertainty. It's a fair supposition about young, youngish, men, I'd say.'

'Two of them, yes,' Ember replied.

'Such need they'll have. For consolation. Comfort, Ralph,' Camilla said.

'Oh, yes indeed,' Ember replied.

'Have you been lining up these two pussies already, Ember?' Maud asked. 'Do you always come out of things with a profit?'

Fay had moved away from the booth door, but now Margaret came and frowned at him. She did a throat-cut gesture on herself, telling him he should end the call.

'But, my Lord, Ralph, that realm is going to need someone truly strong, creative and talented now.'

'Thank you, Barney,' Ember replied, putting the phone down.